PRAISE FOR OTHER WORK

"What a fun, witchy little read! *The Horned Women* takes a creepy old Irish fairy tale and spins it into something fresh, smart, and totally charming. I loved Maura — she's got that "holding it together with duct tape and coffee" energy I can seriously relate to — and seeing her face off against twelve different horned witches with nothing but folklore, stitching skills, and pure mom grit was just so satisfying.

Christy Matheson writes with a cozy, heartfelt vibe that makes even the spookiest moments feel grounded and real. It's a quick read, but it really sticks with you. If you like your fairy tales with a bit of chaos, a little magic, and a lot of heart, you'll love this one."

—Gina Rae Mitchell Reviews

"Christy Matheson takes ancient folklore and breathes wild, bloody life into it, conjuring up a story of grief, anger, magic, and survival.

The atmosphere is thick with shadow and myth: dark woods, whispered warnings, the gleam of horns; I was spellbound. The characters are raw, fierce, and painfully real. Maura is a woman who refuses to be quiet and refuses to be broken. She may not be unscathed but she has more than enough tenderness for her children to balance the rage she feels when anyone threatens them."

—Claire's Reviews

"Matheson deftly illustrates the love of a mother for her children and the relationship between a mother and her stepchildren..."

—Karla "Bookish Life

"Matheson skillfully intertwines traditional Irish folklore with contemporary themes, creating a narrative that's both enchanting and relatable."

—Erik McManus, Breakeven Books

"Matheson did a wonderful job incorporating unique elements into this story while still staying true to the source material! ... You're going to find this story extremely riveting until the very last page!"

—Shawn, Mr Geek Book Reviews

CHRISTY MATHESON

THE CASTLE IN KILKENNY: FAIRY TALES BOOKS 4 & 5

ALSO BY CHRISTY MATHESON

The Castle in Kilkenny Fairy Tales
Book 1: *The Horned Women, A contemporary
retelling of an Irish fairy tale*
Book 2: *The White Deer of Kildare*
Book 3: *The Knight of the Terrible Valley
and Aiden of Florida*
Book 4: *The Squire and His Magical Library*
Book 5: *The Knight & His Magical Armlet*
Book 6: *The Boat on the Lake of Regret*
Book 7: *Oona and the Swan*

*The Horned Women and Other Stories: Castle of Kilkenny Fairy Tales
Books 1, 2, and 3*

Book 0.5: *The Leprechaun and the Castle* (only available through author's
newsletter)
Magical Libraries (only available through author's newsletter)

In *Feisty Deeds: Historical Fictions of Daring Women,* "The Inner Good"
In *Where Kindness Lives: A Women's Fiction Anthology,* "The Irish Library
in Kilkenny"

CONTENTS

THE SQUIRE AND HIS MAGICAL LIBRARY

DEDICATION

This book is for all of you who are fighting to make the world a better place
and defend what is right...
even when you don't know how.

Series Compass

Where am I in the series, what am I reading, and does this book stand alone?

The Squire & His Magical Library comes 4th in this series of interconnected fairy tales. However, time-wise it is the first and earliest book. Therefore, the characters have no knowledge of anything that happens in any of the other books, so you don't need to know either.

Rian returns as an adult in *The White Deer of Kildare*, "The Knight & His Magical Armlet," and a yet-to-be-released novel about making a princess smile three times. Therefore, this is the first of Rian's books.

Reading Notes

Rian = Ryan

The Milesians (like Nessa) are the people we now call the Celts.

The Fir Bolg (like Rian) are an earlier race, who came from the Middle East to Ireland.

I know that some readers will look for romantic storylines everywhere...but you might be more satisfied with this book if you note that this was never meant to be Rian's love story.

CONTENT WARNING

I try to write uplifting stories about hope and love, but this one is set among the warriors of a society that was engaged in constant warfare. There are no battles on the page, but characters do mention injury and killing without any graphic detail. The only fight scene involves a wild boar.

The mythological story of Nessa involves some ugly moments around her sexuality. Again, this is not on the page, but it is implied.

There is, on the page, a non-detailed description of childbirth. It goes smoothly and everyone is fine.

Also, in this society it was normal to foster out children, including babies. In this time, this was not abandonment but a practical way to care for children, who were considered very precious.

11 YEARS OLD

CHAPTER ONE

My face is squashed into the mud and there's a rock jutting into my hip, but at least it's quiet now. I stretch out my fingers, relieved to feel the hilt of my sword. Ache. Cold. Will just stay right here.

Today worked just the way I planned, but it hurts worse than I expected.

It's awfully cold down here in the mud.

Someone shoves me with their foot, and I bite back a groan. Maybe if I stay still, they'll just go away and leave me alone.

They kick me. Just lightly, against my leather backplate. If I weren't so bruised, it wouldn't hurt.

Another kick. "Get up, you worm. Come on!"

The voice surprises me enough that I half-roll so I can look at her directly. I expected the training master, or one of the servants come to take pity on me, but certainly not one of the other students—let alone one in the upper division, training to be a knight. Nessa mac Eochaid is a tall shadow, glowering down at me, her blond hair glowing against the sunset.

"Up!" She swings back her foot, enough for a proper kick, so I scramble—

Well, not anywhere, really. I'm stuck in the mud, and my too-large armor has slid around uncomfortably, and my left shoulder won't do what I tell it to. But I wriggle and struggle towards being upright, and apparently that's enough for Nessa, because she doesn't kick me again.

I don't know why she came all the way out here, or why she would care about me. She's high-born enough to dine with the Family, and practically an adult at fourteen.

I manage to get to my knees before I have to stop, panting. I think I need to get the breastplates off, so I yank at the cords.

"Up," Nessa snaps again, but this time she reaches both hands for me. I hesitate.

"C'mon, what, you afraid to get a girl dirty?" she mocks. "Grab on."

Of course I know Nessa doesn't mind getting dirty, or bloody either, but normally I'd no more grab her with my muddy hands than I'd bother Prince Ardgal. He's also one of us, technically. Almost a full warrior. But he's royalty and I'm... me.

Knowing there's no help for it, I put out my hands and let Nessa haul me out of the mud. She's none too gentle about it.

"You're bleeding." She twists my elbow to look at my shoulder.

I yelp. I don't care if someone thinks I'm a coward, and that hurt!

"You're stupid! You know what can happen with an open wound? There's no point to it, bleeding on a Trial day. You idiot. Come on." She heads back towards the castle, picking her way to the edge of the field, which is churned to muck.

"Where are we going?" I yank my wooden sword out of the mud and follow.

"Well, do you want to get that cleaned up and live to fight another day? Or are you going to get a fever and die, right now, at only eleven years old."

I slog after her, not answering. I don't like either of those options. I sure don't want to die, but I don't want to be a fighter, either. I never did, I never chose this life, and it's really no good. I want to go home. Lacking that, I want the other boys to stop bothering me.

Once we reach the back courtyard, Nessa works off my breastplate, then dumps buckets of water over me. Six months of training have done their job, I guess, because it hurts real bad but I stand tall and don't make a squeak.

Nessa points to the bin. "Leave your clothes there. The blood in them will go sour and make you sick."

In my village, men didn't take off their léines around women, but here we are all supposed to treat each other like warriors, not men and women. I strip down, feeling like a bug under Nessa's unblinking glare. She's elegant and important and the best fighter in our entire training program, and I wish she would leave me alone. I don't know what I did wrong. I don't know why she cares.

She grabs my good elbow and hauls me into the castle, naked and leaving wet footprints, down a few stairs and around a corner and a corner again. Before I came here, I'd never even seen a building with more than one room. It would make a fine story for my brothers and sisters around the evening fire; trying to tell them all the rooms in this place, and what each one is for.

Several turns later, Nessa leads me through a door. Mother would like this room. I inch towards the fire, trying to remember every detail for her, while Nessa bangs jars and bowls onto the counter.

She swings to me, hands full of bandages and a strong-smelling bowl. "Well? What's it going to be?"

"What is what going to be?" Is it me being muddle-headed, or does her conversation jump more than a pond frog?

"Your choice."

"What? I don't understand!!"

I didn't mean to snap, but a grin spreads across her face.

"There, that's a bit of spunk. Do you want to live or die, Rian of Kilkirk?"

"Live, of course!" I can't get home if I die.

Nessa dips the wooden spatula in the bowl, coming up with a glistening glob. "Then you have to promise to never do that again."

"But—"

"No conditions. You must promise."

I drop my head, discouraged. That's what it's like, here—I was just going to say I didn't understand what she's saying, but no one cares. They all want me to jump and swing and promise, no explanations. "I promise," I tell her.

"Do you vow it on the graves of your ancestors?"

"I vow it on the faerie meadow where my youngest sister was born." My people don't bury their dead.

"Fine then."

Without warning, I'm hit with a splash of cool ointment, and Nessa's fingers press against my shoulder. I grit my teeth, refusing to wince or cry out again.

Well, I try not to. From the way she's working it, I can tell this is messier than my usual wounds. We were using wooden weapons today.

I know the weapons wasn't the biggest part. I know—

"They took advantage of you, didn't they?" Nessa demands.

"Harrr." It's all I can manage.

"Four against one?"

I squeeze my eyes closed. So she was watching.

She glares at my wound. "This is a mess! I'm putting in extra moss, the kind that keeps away the fever. But it will soak through. Come and find me again tomorrow so I can do it again. Don't go to the training master! He won't be careful enough. Come to me." She gives the bandage a final tug.

Nessa probably won't remember me tomorrow. I'll just go to the master; he does just fine—

"Don't disobey me now!" Nessa puts fists on her hips, blocking my way to the door. "You've sworn loyalty to me now."

I don't recall doing any such thing. She really does jump about. "I'm too young," I answer, instead of arguing.

"Not fealty. Just…" She furrows her brow. "Well, I guess you didn't. So. Rian of Kilkirk, swear loyalty to me!"

I'm about to say I won't, but she puts out her hand, two fingers tucked in. It's the symbol of fighting together.

Of equals.

She's offering something too.

I tuck my two fingers and clasp her hand. "Nessa mac Eochaid, I swear loyalty to you." I don't know what happens now, but I don't understand anything around here, so what's one more thing.

Nessa nods, sharp. "And I swear loyalty to you, Rian of Kilkirk—as long as you never do anything stupid like that again."

I shiver. "What did I do?" How can I fix it if I don't know why she's mad?

Nessa sighs, a gust of winter wind. She unpins her own cloak, wraps it around me, and shoves me onto a stool by the fire.

"I didn't even know this room was here." What I mean is that I'm not sure I can find it again.

Nessa goes to tidy the counter. "It was just another storeroom. I moved everything in, and I barter for the herbs and oils. We're allowed to take all the firewood we want. So now…" She shrugs, smiling like she's pleased with herself.

She's made it cozy. It's a little space, earth on one side and the rough palisade logs for the other wall, with an actual door that opens and closes. The fireplace is only knee-high, but the stone hearth radiates warmth. She's even decorated it—there's a worn cowhide underfoot, a faded tapestry on the wall across from her workbench, and a cheerful red earthenware vase with only a few chips out of it.

"It's really nice here."

Nessa must hear the admiration in my voice, because she turns and grins at me. Something flashes between us, and I feel a little bit…good.

Nessa starts humming, and I join in. I prop my feet on the warm stones while she ladles water into a dented kettle, props it in the fire, and settles herself on the other stool.

Sensation tingles into my muscles along with the warmth, and that hurts. But I'm a little giddy, since I've been dreading today. And I might be injured, but I did what I planned. Lugaid and his buddies won't care about me any more. Maybe I can make it through the training program after all, and then I'll be able to go back home and lead our village defenses. I'll fulfill what the druids predicted, and my mother will be pleased.

The kettle boils, and Nessa pours water into two mugs. The tangy smell of herbs fills the room.

"What did I do wrong?" I finally work up the courage to ask.

Nessa stirs the teas and narrows her eyes at me. "Today? On the battlefield? You tell me."

"It wasn't a real battle."

Nessa snorts.

"Fine, I know we're supposed to act like it is. But it's just the other boys. Our swords weren't even real."

"It's establishing your order for the entire year! Even among the youngest cohort, the best warrior must be the leader. That's the way it works!"

Despite her anger, I flush with pleasure. That's right; Lugaid is our new captain, and he's the biggest and has the highest rank from home. The other boys are happy to follow Lugaid, and I can stay quiet in the back, out of their way.

"You should have been awarded the Squire's Trumpet today." Nessa speaks with so much venom that I hunch away from her, pulling her cloak tight across my chest.

"But I'm from a village! And a Fir Bolg! And—just a no one." And all the other boys hate me enough already.

"But you're smarter and quicker than any of them."

"They ganged up on me."

"You could have defeated them all four at once!"

"But they're bigger!"

"They're clumsy louts!"

"I tried but—"

"You did not!" Nessa half-screams. "This is what I mean! You did not fight with honor!"

"You know what?" I rub my eyes with a fist, like a stupid child. I'm so tired and angry, not to mention naked and sore and bleeding, and it's worse to be yelled at when it's the one person who has been friendly to me. In months. "I'm tired of hearing about honor! I'm tired of bravery and valor! Do you know what really matters?"

I'm braced for Nessa to yell again, or punch me onto the ground—I've hit it plenty today.

She cocks her head. "What? What matters to you, Rian? And drink your tea."

Startled by her change in mood, I slurp the brew. It soothes my throat, and I drink again, breathing in the bright and woodsy smell.

"This." I lift the mug, thanking her. "The blessings of the earth. Being together. Do you know what spring means?" I start to cry for real now. "My father and all my uncles are plowing the fields. My mother is sorting the seeds from the storeroom, and my brothers and sisters are gathering the fresh new sprouts in the woods."

"And fish in the streams," Nessa says.

"Yes." I put aside my empty mug and wipe my nose. "Honor and bravery are just words. Just a reason to hit someone. What really matters is sitting together. And family. And telling stories. And"—I hiccup a bigger sob than I meant—"Mother is having a new baby this spring, and it's the first one I won't get to hold. My brother Euchu is old enough to set snares, and I could be teaching him. Everything is green, except the Fair Valley is full of yellow blossoms, and the Shy Mountain glows purple with all the heather. And it's beautiful and the farms and the people and that is what matters, not who gets the silly Squire's Trumpet!" I gulp a breath and sit back, waiting for her to scold. Here in the lowlands, warriors are more important than new babies or spring planting or beautiful sunsets. They've been trying to beat that into my head all these months.

"Oh, Rian." Nessa just shakes her head. She takes a breath, and it shudders a little. "How many brothers and sisters do you have?"

"Eight, with the new one. I am the eldest." Of course, there is no way to send word unless a traveler passes through Kilkirk and here, and the back of my mind prickles with fear that something could have gone wrong this time. But Mother has always birthed a healthy baby. I have to trust that they're all there, and I will go back some day.

"You must be very proud."

It's not the lecture I expected, but Nessa sounds sad, even though that doesn't match the words she is saying.

So I wait.

"But Rian..." Finally, she looks up, and her eyes are haunted. "Don't you see, that's why all this matters? And that's why you must never hide your true strength and be any less than you are."

"I don't see." I bury my mouth in the cloak, and finally burst out with the truth. "And I don't want to be a warrior at all!"

"But you are one. And everything you said—don't you love it? Don't you want your father to have his fields and your mother to rock her babies?"

"Of course!"

"Then it takes warriors. Good warriors. The *best* warriors to protect them!"

"The raiding bands don't come up so far into the hills. The kings don't care about where we are." But even as I say it, I remember that my aunt's village was burned when I was little. It's in one of our story-songs, and sometimes when I was hunting I came across the ruins, charred beams sinking into the vivid green woods.

"Then do you not care about anyone else's farms and families?" Nessa asks.

That blow strikes my heart. I turn away, pressing my mouth together. Already, I care about people in the Theastír village, the vast sprawling castle with all its maids and guards and lords and laughter. It's beautiful here, too. I don't want this land to be lost to blood and fire.

"Rian, sooner or later the raiders come. The clans start another feud, or the war-boats come from across the sea. That, or there are simply...bad men."

I turn back, curious. Nessa has her own story here. "What bad men?"

"Evil men. Who want evil, nasty, bad"—Nessa gasps, tangled in her own words—"evil things. Like...Cathbad the Evil."

I suspect this is not his real name, but I'm intrigued. "What did he do?"

Nessa shakes her head, coming back to herself. "Never you mind. It's a story for another day. But the point is, if you can be a warrior, you have to be a warrior. That's the only way to keep the rest of it! The farms and the babies and the tapestries and the harps and the flowers and...all of it."

I really want the story, especially since now it's got harps in it. I definitely didn't mention harps.

"No—stop looking at me like that!" Nessa laughs. "I'll tell you more later."

She's a little confusing, the way she is so caught up in one thing but then a moment later she's totally different. But it's fine. Talking with her is kind of fun, especially compared to all the boys who just want to bash people with swords. And I bet she's got lots of good stories, being a high-born woman enrolled in warrior training and all. That's probably even trickier than being a Fir Bolg boy in the lowlands.

"But listen. Here's the point. And then we've got to get supper and get to bed. But the thing you've got to remember is that the evil men might come for us at any moment. And they'll come for your baby sister and your mother and Euchu and his snares, don't think they won't! And you never know when the moment is going to come, and what if Lugaid is the leader of the squires and he makes a mistake and does something wrong that you would have done better?"

"The invaders aren't going to worry about the squires—we're not warriors yet!"

"Don't you know the tales?" Nessa shakes her head, and her shoulders crumple. "You never know when one person could have saved everything. If only he knew what to do. If only he were doing his best."

I don't think I'm that important. I don't think the adult warriors would falter and let the castle's defense rest on the squires, but...

My mind leaps through a thousand possible stories.

But if it happened, Lugaid would make a mistake. He's far too predictable, which I proved in the trials today. Nessa is right; I could have beat all of them and not gotten hurt, either. I could lead them better.

If they listened to me.

If I dared.

Chapter Two

Nessa goes to the feast, but I just eat in the kitchen and creep up the stairs. All of us squires are assigned to sleep in a big room on the top level, fifteen or twenty of us. I don't like being so far from the heartbeat of the earth, the way my mother taught me to listen and love it with my breath and my feet. People are not squirrels. We are not meant to sleep up in the treetops.

Tonight, everything is aching, so I pause at the top of the stairs to catch my breath. Around the corner, I hear the boys teasing and laughing, and I don't want to go in there.

Aw, drat. They're talking through the girls at the castle. I hate listening to this even more than when they tease me directly. They say I'm too young to understand, but I know what it feels like to be attracted to a woman, I just don't think it's very nice to want to grab a girl and take what you want. In my village, any man who forces a woman has a worse punishment than an adulterer, and that's painful. Once I finally get a wife, I'm not going to do anything that would mean she's allowed to choose a new man.

"The king had his little daughter right next to him at the high table. Did you see her, Lugaid?"

The words catch my attention. I'd forgotten that she made her first appearance at the feast tonight and I was curious about her.

"Yeah, she's going to be quite the catch," Lugaid answers. "The king thinks the sun rises and sets on her."

"Is she pretty?" asks one of the other boys.

"Not yet," Lugaid answers. "But she's been sick for months."

I'm suspicious that he's not making fun of her, like he does everyone else.

"Is it weird? Now that she's blind?"

"Yeah. She just sat there. Barely ate."

My heart goes out to the little girl, trying to eat in front of everyone when you can't see your food.

"Did you know her before?" asks a lower voice, eager.

"My uncle is one of Cuaodh's lords," Lugaid brags. "I practically grew up in the castle."

There's a flurry of questions, and Lugaid starts in his usual stuff about how important his uncle is. This time it's about what a great marriage prospects he's going to be. I figure that will distract him from thinking about me, and start to sneak towards my bed, when Nessa's name catches my ear.

"I'd want a woman with bigger tits," Lugaid says.

I freeze and my blood pounds in my ears, so I can't hear the boys' replies.

"Well, fine." Lugaid laughs. "I'd take her for a wife, but I'd need someone else to warm my bed."

"She can warm me up," says one of the older boys, and goes into detail.

I should go in there and fight. Nessa and I swore loyalty, so I should defend her. I should remind them of our training rules, and how we are to treat the women warriors as our comrades. I should challenge anyone who speaks of my friend's body parts to a fist-fight in the training yard, all properly witnessed, so no one would ever do it again.

But my shoulder hurts, and my ribs, and my knee.

And if I did beat him, everyone would know I was faking it at the Trials.

Besides, I'm not high born. My uncles aren't anyone important.

I guess I'm not a good friend or a good warrior either, because I creep back down the stairs and away. I'll find somewhere else to sleep tonight.

The servants and guards are settled in various big rooms on the main floor. Sometimes when the boys are teasing me, I've pulled out an extra palette and joined them. No one minds, but I don't really belong. But tonight, I feel guilty and shameful. Leaving the squires' room because the boys are teasing my partner is much worse than because they are teasing me.

I pass one of the stairs down to the cellars and pause. I went this way with Nessa, and of course I would not dare go into her private space without permission, but now I know the chimney system goes all the way down here. She said her room was just a storeroom at first. Maybe I can find another storeroom and curl up there.

I turn through one narrow corridor and another, letting myself get a little lost. It's completely dark, but my fingertips trail the walls, wattle in some places, thick bases of logs in others.

Wait.

Here's a door, fashioned from scraps of wood, like Nessa's. Firelight glimmers between the cracks between the unfinished boards.

"Hello? Excuse me?"

No one answers.

For some reason, it just *feels* like the room ahead of me is empty. It's so quiet and otherwise dark, I think I would know if there is another human here.

Perhaps someone was working here and they finished before the fire went out. I don't have my blanket or palette, and my injuries will heal better if I can stay warm.

What if I get in trouble?

I shiver, and my shoulder throbs.

I guess I can't get much more lonely and shameful than I already am.

The door swings smoothly at my touch, and warmth hits me as the light makes me blink.

No one's here. And it still feels welcoming.

I hobble to the fire and sink onto the soft chair. Whoever owns it isn't using it, and I'll leave soon. After a long moment, I open my eyes. At my fingertips is a steaming cup and a jar of salve.

I sniff them both. The castle policy is that anyone is allowed appropriate supplies. I'm a warrior, even a junior one. I am definitely allowed to take medicine.

I rub the salve on the worst of my injuries. It works even faster than usual, the pain fading right away.

So by the time I drink the tea, I'm feeling well enough to look around. Carefully.

My first impression was of luxury and beauty, so naturally I thought this room belonged to one of the women of the Family. Perhaps King Cuaodh created a room for his wife, and keeps returning to remember her? But I know the deceased queen's family crest, and it is not anywhere here.

It doesn't have the king's crest either, and he is always busy with the warriors, not worrying about magic and the dead. So he wouldn't keep a room down here.

Prince Ardgal has a room upstairs just like the other knight trainees, and he has no taste for beauty. The three younger princes are all fostered out. The only princess is Barrdhubh—the one who was very ill, lost her sight, and only went from her private rooms to the dining hall for the first time tonight. This wouldn't be hers.

Besides, this elegance is...different. I warm my hands against my tea, feeling more alert with each sip. The patterns on the rugs seem familiar, but the construction is softer and denser than anything else in the castle. I understand what the furniture is for, but the shapes and materials are like nothing I've ever seen. The mantle is constructed of absolutely smooth stone, gray and red veins swirling against the white, and the ironwork for the fireplace is more delicate and complicated than anything the king's smithy could produce. On top there is a line of colorful decorations, all soothing to the eye. The light is coming from tall vases with colored glass hats, and the hats are glowing. I examine one closely, and find a little toggle that makes the flame go on and off. Definitely magic. Besides, even a king couldn't afford that much glass, and he wouldn't put it in the basement if he did.

I'm not sure if that's better or worse. Are there fae living underneath the castle?

Well, I'm here now, and I've already drank and used their medicine—so if it's a magical trap, I'm already caught. I finish my tea, letting my gaze wander up the walls, which are covered with some sort of thin cloth with a pattern of dark red diamonds. I like it. Instead of tapestries, the art is flat and trapped within swirly gold rectangles. I think it's painted, but again, it is more delicate than anything I've ever seen. I savor each view of beautiful flowers and streams and—

It can't be.

It is. The longer I look, the more I am sure that is not just any mountain. That is Shy Mountain, the exact view I could see from my favorite meadow. Where I meant to build my house.

Not caring about the pain, I hobble closer to the painting, and then another one. It's true! It's not just any meadow or any stream! That is the particular twist of Grandfather Oak! These are all around my home! Mine, mine—and I am the only person in the entire palace who knows these places. Even the druids who brought me here were travelers, passing through and telling fates, and I have never seen them again.

If this is my home...

...if every detail appeals to my heart...

...then this magic is for me. This is *my* room.

I don't know why, but the Fae give rewards and punishments where they will. Maybe I've been chosen for tonight. I prostrate myself and give thanks to all four directions.

Then I explore in earnest.

On one wall is a bed with a real wood frame, so the person can sleep up off the floor and behind curtains too. The curtains are my favorite colors, more red and gold with vibrant blue. I squash the bed, which feels soft and comfortable. And there, a close-stool in the corner.

There's a cabinet and a table on the wall by the door. I recognize the things on the cabinet: basin and jug, basket with—little breads, I think, but unfamiliar shapes. I test—one is sweet with dried fruits in it. I open each jar sitting in a row, sniffing. Tea for every mood. Salve for cuts. Here's honey. And something white, but not salt. Tentative, I dip in a finger.

Oh my! It's like....powdered honey! The sweetest thing I've ever tasted!

Skipping past the little table, I lean back to study the stuff that covers the entire last wall. It's like a cupboard with no doors, the shelves made of gleaming dark wood going from the floor to the ceiling. And on the shelves are...little boxes? Lots of narrow tall boxes—hundreds. I run my finger across them, and lean close to smell. There's leather, and something else.

In the middle of the wall, the cupboards stop for the big painting of Shy Mountain. Under that, there is a flat shelf with a basket of shells, one of the magical light-makers, and one colorful box sitting on a pretty cloth.

It's a very nice box.

I lean closer, still not touching. It's quite flat, with a little painting on top. Unlike the realistic pictures on the wall, this is just a few strokes. A boy. His hair is yellow and his skin is light, so he is not me, but the expression on his face...it is something like how I feel inside. Waiting. Lonely. Quiet. He is looking at stars, like I look at the stars and miss my family.

Finally, I touch it.

Nothing bad happens, so I might as well open the box. Perhaps there is an answer from one lonely boy to another.

In my hands, it does not feel like a box at all. It falls open on one side, but instead of a cavity, there are...many things. Like crisp silk. Or big square leaves from a white tree. I slide my finger across one, and it slides and crinkles through my hands, until the lid of the box is laying flat against my left hand and one leaf is on top of all the others on my right hand.

If it's a painting, it's a very boring one. Just wiggles of black.

I turn the leaf to the left side, hoping the next painting might be my home, or perhaps the boy again. It is not, but this is better. There's more of the black marks but also a snake, wrapped around some sort of creature with its mouth wide open. That's interesting! I bring it closer to my face.

And the black dots—*do* something. My eyes move down to them, and it is like there are words inside my head. "When I was six years old..." It is like I am hearing a story, but it is *all inside my head and makes no noise*.

Horrified, I drop the box.

But...are the other boxes the same?

I pull out a blue one, tucked next to a big shell. This one is heavier and the edges are pretty gold. I am not surprised when it opens to one side, and this time—aha! It *is* a painting! This is a little girl, pale skin and dark hair, going into a house which is the same size as a mushroom. Now that looks like a good story. Intrigued, I move the box closer to the light and study all the details.

What happens to the girl? Are there paintings with more of her story? I flip it over.

This one has a little drawing of the girl running, and lots of black marks all around. I look carefully at the girl and—

The story goes *into my head again*. But this time, I hear the word "petticoat" and I know exactly what it means! It's the white thing under the girl's skirt, and in their world, only girls wear skirts and petticoats—I know all that!

This is very strange. Glowing vases are one thing, but I'm not sure I like magic that goes into my head.

I go back to tend the fire and make a cup of tea, showing the fae that I appreciate their gifts. All except the boxes.

I sip my tea and hum a song of praise.

But what happens to the little girl? Does she want to be the size of a mushroom?

My little sister would like that story, but she is not here. I have no one to share stories with.

I scowl at the fire. *When I was six years old...* That is the boy in the box talking to me, Rian. One thoughtful boy to another. Am I supposed to talk back to the box?

My sister would like the story about the girl and the mushroom, and what about the little princess who can no longer see? Maybe she'd like it too. If I told the story to the sad princess, then I would be doing some good in the world, right?

So I go back to the shiny smooth counter and I fetch the blue and gold box to the squashy chair. I look at it all ways, and touch it and smell it and admire the shiny gold edges. When I open it, the girl and the mushroom are gone, but I figure out how to turn the—the pages. The word comes to me.

I brace my teeth, scared of the magic. But I want the story.

I find her again. I study the painting, then the black marks. After careful consideration, I figure out how to turn pages back to big black marks, where the story begins, although they do not use the traditional words. The girl and the mushroom only take a few pages, and then I recognize the ending words.

I look at all the black dots, and I can hear the whole story in my head. A story! If I don't think about how weird this is, it's pretty amazing. I look-listen to the story all the way through twice, and then I put everything away carefully. I glance back at the boy, and this time I look-hear the words at the top of the painting.

"I will come back to you, Little Prince," I say out loud—then realize what I have done.

I have made a promise to the fae.

I look around, startled, but I'm alone. Right? I just explored everything and—

That's definitely a noise! I'm already on my feet, my eating knife in my hand.

It's over by the cupboard with the bread and tea. I slink closer. If this room belongs to someone else, I will beg forgiveness, but this sounds more like an animal. Or a burglar! This is really rich stuff down here.

The door is still closed. Here's the food cupboard, and a little table next to it, lit by a covered torch—aha!

There's a tiny being sitting on the edge of the sconce. She is as green as a leaf with bird wings instead of arms, and the only thing she is wearing is clouds of her own green hair. She doesn't look very dangerous, but it's always best to respect the fae, so I sweep into a low bow, tucking my knife away as I move. What's the proper form of address for the fae? Should I—

"Don't you want to see what's inside?" she chirps.

What? I'm startled out of my bow.

"I thought you were the curious type." She flutters her wings, rising slightly above the sconce and settling back down. She looks...excited? Eager? Why would she care?

"I—I am always curious," I say, partly because I don't want to disappoint her and partly because it's true.

She claps her hands in delight. "Well, then open the table, young Rian!"

Her smile is adorable, and also filled with needle-like teeth. I don't want those teeth on me, nor a spell either—how does she know my name?—so I stumble around with the front of the table. It lift smoothly, revealing an inner compartment lined with dark blue velvet, more fine and delicate than any I have seen. Resting in the center is a gold armlet.

I glance at the wren-faerie, nervous.

She twitters in excitement, leaning forward to watch me. "What do you think?

As I study it, I realize it is not quite finished. The layers of gold twist together, cleverly making the eye believe they are silken threads. The ends of the spiral flatten, and when I lean close I can see intricate etching of leaves. But there are rough open places where jewels would be inlaid, and the tips are just tiny screws, as though they are waiting for the terminal to be put on.

I don't think I am a greedy person. I admit I've gotten jealous of the other boys' friendships, or when it felt like my mother loved a different sibling best, but I've never been tempted to steal a thing that someone has. So I don't understand this craving inside myself, the need to pick up the armlet, to hold it and wear it. It's like I am starving and only this one thing can fill me.

Before I can even blink, the armlet is in my hands. I slide it up and over my left wrist, twisting the spiral slightly so it goes over my upper arm. It's far too big for me, but—there! I hold out my arm to admire and show the fae.

It falls off, clattering to the velvet.

"I'm sorry, I shouldn't have…" I retrieve it, mortified. Good, it isn't hurt. I check for a clasp I missed or something.

"Of course you should! It's yours, and no one else's."

"Mine?" I touch my chest, amazed. I've never had anything that is mine alone.

"Yours, Rian of Kilkirk." She smiles, her needle-like teeth glimmering. "But be careful, for once you put it on you are bound into it forever."

"But it fell off." So it must not be mine after all. Not that I want to be bound forever, but something about it—

But the fae just laughs. "Of course it did. That is a man's fate, and you are just a little chick."

"Fate?" I turn it around in my hands, thinking hard. "But the druids already rolled my fate."

"The druids make a prediction," the fae says sharply. "It is we who make the fate."

"Of course. I'm terribly sorry." One thing I've learned lately is just to agree with anything.

"So what do *you* want?" She sings a little wren song.

Hard little lumps fall tapping into the velvet. Amber, lapis, little gold terminals—yes, they even have the screw hole, all waiting to be put onto the armlet. I lean closer, seeing lions and birds and snake heads.

But more importantly, she said that I'm not stuck in the druids' fate. I don't *have* to be a warrior!

But that this fate will be binding forever. I don't want to be stuck into something even worse.

I set the armlet down carefully and look up at her. "What do you mean, my lady?"

"Call me Dreoilín." It means wren, the bird who is honored in our stories but also caught and killed for ceremony. "Put the jewels away if you are not ready to choose."

I brush the jewels to a little box at the side, thinking carefully. What do I want? "I want to do the best thing, Honored Dreoilín. I want to help the world and do something good and worthwhile!"

There, I have said it! I feel victorious, as though I have won a race. I have been thinking about this since we heard that the druids would come to Kilkirk—thinking about what I really want in life. I have said it out loud now!

Dreoilín sings again. Now, carved knucklebones and small stone figurines scatter across the velvet.

"May I touch them?"

She waves a wing graciously.

They are the tools of the fortune teller. The astragali—sheep's knucklebones—are etched, two of them dyed red and blue. I pick up the figures one after another. These are smooth and goldish-white, possibly ivory.

"Each of them are a fate for you," Dreoilín tells me.

So many choices! I like that. I lay them out in a row, glancing up at Dreoilín to confirm each guess.

A boat the size of my palm. "The explorer."

A tiny jar, and the lid even works. "The healer."

A miniature scale, with tiny gold chain holding up the ivory plates. "The magistrate." Now, that would be interesting. I like the idea of making things fair.

A sword; that's easy. That was what the druids gave me too. "The warrior."

A circlet. "The king—that's not me."

Dreoilín twitters. "It simply means the leader. It could indeed be your future."

I still don't think so. The next one has several indistinct human figures. "The artist?"

She shakes her head. "The teacher."

I cup my hand comfortably around the plow. "The farmer. But I don't know these." I push the last two out so she can see.

The first is a heart within a circlet. "The lover," she explains, "but this fate is about power—like all of them. You create a social standing for the woman you love, who uses her wits or wiles to rule. Or perhaps you don't love her. It doesn't matter."

I can't decide if that sounds like partnership or manipulation. Perhaps both. "And this one?" The ivory is carved into something like a scroll of fabric, rolled up on both sides, with a feather resting on top.

"That is the scholar." She bares her teeth in that eerie smile, spreading her wings to indicate the room we are in. "All of this—books. Knowledge. Stories. In this fate, you will retreat from the world of men and create something meaningful in the world of books."

All of that sounds like gobbledygook right now, but the word "stories" caught my attention. And retreating from the world of men sounds better than killing them.

"Very well." I adjust the boat, then the circlet, neatening them up. "So any of these could be me?"

Dreoilín nods. "You will notice that not all the fates are before us, because they are no longer possible. You have not been selected to study with the bards or the druids, for instance. Those are already gone, as is working as a smith or a tanner, or some artisan where the apprentices have long since begun."

"But these are all possible?" Nine is so much better than one!

"Don't choose too fast, little chick. You have a long time before your man's age of eighteen. Each year, you will learn more about the fates, and more about yourself."

"So I choose one each year?" I am so eager to be anything besides a warrior.

She flutters. "You make choices. The world around you changes. Every year, you roll the astragali and see which options are left."

If I were a leader, I could encourage people to be nice to each other. If I were a healer, I could fix things after a battle. That all sounds good!

Dreoilín flutters again, half-lifting from the sconce. "Roll the bones, Rian!"

I scoop up the astragali, enjoying the sensation in my palm. Eight months ago, when my family walked into the roundhouse where the druids were telling fates, all of my choices went up in their perfumed smoke. This time the dice are in my hands.

I roll them onto the velvet.

Dreoilín tips forward, peering at my ivory figurines. And as I watch, amazed and horrified, the little hoe disintegrates into dust.

"The farmer!" I touch the white pile. "I'd be a good farmer!"

Dreoilín swings back to her perch, chittering. "But you left. Your brothers are doing the work, and the callouses on your hands are fading. You see how it goes? That choice got weaker and weaker. Now it's gone."

Tears prickle the back of my eyes, and I squeeze my lips together. I'm not sure I like this.

"You still have eight choices left," the faerie reminds me. "And seven years to learn."

Eight choices. And some of them still have a nice home and family, like a magistrate or healer. Does a scholar live in a room like this?

"And look around, Rian." Dreoilín spreads her wings wide. "All of this is your gift. To learn. To understand yourself. Enjoy!" And she springs forward, dropping off the sconce, fluttering through the room, and—gone.

CHAPTER THREE

The next day is a rest day, and my main goal is to avoid Lugaid and his friends. I search out Nessa, and when I see her wearing a dress among the other young women I realize that I was hoping that maybe we could take a walk together or something. Maybe we could talk more about springtime, and fishing in streams. I'd ask about her family, and suddenly the yearning to talk about mine hurts worse than all my bruises from the failure yesterday.

Nessa changes my bandage and goes back to her womanly things.

I walk into the town by myself, pausing to look at pretty rocks and singing back to the birds, but even so I only use up a couple of hours. When I come back, the squires are playing games on the lawn, so I walk around the fortress walls, acting like I've been sent with an errand, so they won't invite me to join them. Squires get sent on errands all the time, so that's normal.

Maybe I could look for my special room! I wonder if it is still here, and I could read about the Little Prince. That word—*read*—it just popped into my mind. Today, with the sunlight and the smell of roasting meat, it feels more exciting than ominous. After all, Dreoilín was a very cute little fae.

I walk through the side yard, through women busy with tubs and lye, into the palace. I never come in from this side, so I'm a little nervous. Someone comes towards me, carrying something big, and I jump out of the way.

It's a staircase. My room is down, not up, but I can go up find the ramparts and find stairs on the correct side of the castle.

It's quiet, so I let my footsteps slow. It's pretty up here, with bright tapestries and the horn windows glowing in the sunlight. We don't have those in my side of the palace, and since no one's around, I dare to reach out my finger and trace the—

"Who's heee-eeere? Who is it?"

I leap back in shock, but then my breathing steadies. That's just a girl's voice.

"It's just me," I call back, accustomed to obedience. "Rian of Kilkirk."

I come around the corner, and in little nook is a small girl with dark hair.

"I can't find the bowl! Where is it! Where!" she is demanding before I can even bow. "I was helping with the peas and now it's all gone!" She slaps the table in front of her, back and forth, tiny hands like desperate fishes.

This must be the little princess. Since she's Milesian, she's probably supposed to be paler than me, but no one is supposed to have that gray tinge. Her dark eyes are sunken and her black hair is lank. She looks only to be the size of my five-year-old sister, but let's see…I know she's born near Lughnasadh, the summer festival, and mine is near the following Beltane. So if I'm eleven, she must be nine. My heart skitters right past being intimated by her rank and fine clothes, and straight to pity.

"It's all right." I'm talking easily as I move things around. "Your bowl just got away from you. You need them both, right?" I arrange them in front of her.

"Where?" She raises a splayed hand, ready to swing wildly, which would knock all the peas onto the floor.

So even though it's not appropriate, I grab her hand, and she relaxes, her little fingers curling around mine. I guide her hand gently to each bowl, then show her how to find the peas inside.

"I'm shelling them," she tells me, defensive. "I can do that. I'm still useful—look!" She breaks a pod open, her thumb sliding down the joint.

Little green balls fly everywhere, escaping down the hallway and rolling across the table. "See? I'm still a good helper even though I can't see. Is my bowl half-full yet? Tell me!"

The second bowl has two lonely peas sitting at the bottom, but now that I look, there are dozens around the alcove. My heart goes out to her, so I dance past the truth and focus on soothing her.

"You are a good helper," I say. "Everyone does their part, and you are doing yours, even though you were sick."

"I'm all better now," she tells me.

"And that's why you're so helpful."

A smile breaks across her sallow face.

"But look here. Do you think you can get your hands lower? Put the pod in the bowl as you do it?" I'm guiding her as I speak.

"I'm too little! I can't reach!"

It's true; she's just too low on the bench to reach over and into the bowl. I think for a second. "Wait. I know something that can help."

"Are you leaving? Don't leave me alone!"

"I'll be right back. I promise. You can listen to my footsteps."

She pouts, but I see the determination on her face. This is hard for her. "All right."

I make a point of letting my shoes flap against the stones as I run down the hall. It's down and around but I know I saw some bags stuffed with straw. Ah, here they are.

I hesitate. I usually never would touch something I wasn't assigned, but...it's for the princess? Surely she can have whatever she wants?

I run back to the princess's nook.

"I heeeear you!" she calls out with glee.

When I can see her again, her face turned towards me, although her eyes gaze past my shoulder. She's smiling.

I help her down from the bench, and I fashion a special raised seat, describing what I'm doing the whole time.

"Here you go, my lady." I gesture to her new perch. "A seat fit for a princess."

She reaches out her hand, but I hesitate to take it.

"Where are you? Help me! I don't know where the bench is!"

I can't stand it; I put out my hand and let her glom on. "I don't know if I'm allowed to touch you, my lady."

"Well, who are you? You don't sound like a servant."

"I'm just one of the squires. From Kilkirk village." The lowest. The stupidest.

"Well!" The princess beams. "Then you're one of my father's fosterlings. Of *course* you can help me! You're practically my brother."

I am not sure that her father sees us as social equals to his own children, but I let myself be persuaded and boost her up, moving her hands to show her how to find her bowls and tools. She's delighted, chattering to me about how this table is her new special workplace. It's not too far from either her bedchamber or from the kitchen and solar, so she can do all sorts of useful things for everyone. All kinds of things...she's just not exactly sure what they are, yet.

We do half the bowl together, my hand guiding so hers don't go too high, tilting the pea pods so she remembers the angle. I close my eyes to figure out what she can sense, then open them again to help her.

Once she gets a whole pile of peas in the bowl, she ululates, and I beat my chest and do a high-kicking dance, and we both laugh.

"Now tell me a story, foster-brother Rian," the princess asks. "Please? I love stories."

My heart soars. "I know one about...a girl who lived under a mushroom. Does that sound good?"

"What happened? Did it rain? Was there lighting?"

"There wasn't any lightning, but she had to fight a mouse. She found a hairpin, and attacked him bravely."

"Oooh! That sounds like an excellent story!" She bounces, drumming her feet against the bench.

"But...I shouldn't sit here with my hands empty, either."

She cocks her head. "That's true. Go run get your work, and then you can tell me about the terrible, vicious, bloody, mouse battle. I have a lot more peas, and I'm being very useful."

I run. She's a little bossy and maybe I shouldn't be hanging about with the princess, but I like how hard she's trying. I can help her, and my new room will help me do it.

I like to be useful, too.

***

The head of the castle guard whistles sharply, and all us boys drop our hurley balls and our lunches to stand at ragged attention. Except for me, who was sitting under a tree hiding a book in my lap, and Nessa, who was in the middle of the scrum but is not a boy.

"Squires! Attention!"

"Yes, sir!"

"Which of you was talking about a girl so tiny she could live under a mushroom and fly on a hummingbird?"

Whatever anyone was expecting, this was not it. The boys look back and forth, confused. Nessa glances at me, eyebrow raised—I told her the story too—but I'm too embarrassed and confused to call any attention to myself. It's been nearly a moon since I saw the princess. I hide *Anne of Green Gables* further under my léine and sidle into the shadows.

"What did she eat?" asks one. "Imagine eating a raspberry as big as your head!"

"Could she sleep in a flower?" asks another boy.

"Yes," agrees the guard, not unkindly, "but who was telling the story to the princess?"

Everyone stands up a little straighter, a little more eager. Every night, we hear stories about grown-up warriors saving princesses from all types of evil.

"It was me." Lugaid steps forward, chest puffed out. "Princess Barrdhubh and I are great friends. Already."

The head of the castle guard eyes him up and down. "Leader of the first-year squires, are you?"

"I am! And my uncle is Lord Tadc."

"Hm." The guard appears amused. "Be that as it may, what did the tiny girl do with the hairpin?"

I can't see Lugaid's expression from here, just the way he sets his feet more defensively. "She...put it in her hair. It was a super-tiny hairpin, you see."

The guard raises his eyebrows.

"No!" Nessa cries. "She attacked a mouse with the hairpin! She struck the fatal blow"—she thrusts an imaginary sword—"straight through the ribs! And then poked out his eyes for good measure."

The original story didn't have all that, but the princess kept saying "more, more!" and I kept making up more. When I told the story to Nessa, that was her favorite part too.

"But it's not my story," Nessa adds immediately. "It's Rian's. He told it to me, too."

"Rian of Kilkirk." The guard glances around the meadow. "The king wants to see you. Let's go."

I'm practically shaking as I follow the man into the castle, although he keeps asking questions about the mushroom girl to put me at ease. The other squires try to curry our foster father's favor, but I'd rather if he forgets who I am for a few years. A door opens in front of me, and I realize we've reached the royal rooms already. With a bracing breath, I step inside. The king is sitting with the little princess and her nursemaids.

It turns out that King Cuaodh isn't angry—he's only interested in my stories and how I helped with the peas. He asks a few questions, and then snaps his fingers at the women standing behind the princess, waiting for her to step forward, before refocusing on me

"After you are released from training duties each day, young lad, you are to come and sit with my daughter. Tell her more stories and help her finish her chores." He turns to his daughter. "That goes for you, too, Barrdhubh; you must do your work before stories, do you understand?"

"Yes, Daddy." She sets her little jaw. "I like to be busy. I'm *good* at things, like this sewing."

She holds up a bit of mending, covered with haphazard stitches.

Without speaking, the king raises his eyebrows at the nursemaid. She flusters and curtsies, while the princess stabs her poor cloth again, unaware of the interchange.

"I hear you've been a bit of a challenge," the king tells his daughter.

"An hour!" the nurse cries. "A whole hour of screaming and fussing this morning. And yesterday it took half the morning to get dressed! She kept throwing her nice things on the floor!"

"I want to be helpful," the princess insists, but her head drops.

The king turns back to me, impatient. "The women are busy with their own work. By the afternoon—well, we need someone to come up here. So you are released from carrying messages or helping the tradesmen, do you understand? You are to come here."

"Yes, my lord." I bow, and glance back at the poor little princess, who has now stitched her cloth into a ball and is looking more frustrated than ever. "I'll help her figure things out, I promise."

The king grunts approval, kisses his daughter, and strides away, the nursemaids scurrying in his wake.

I'm alone with the most mutilated mending and the second-most-important person in Theastír. I take a deep breath.

"All right, my lady, it's Rian now. I'm sitting down next to you. How 'bout you hand me that, and I'll take out the thread, and then we can do it again, together."

She thrusts the whole thing towards me, narrowly avoiding stabbing me with the needle. Good thing I'm not a mouse. Slowly, we work through it together, like we did with the peas. I don't do it for her, but I keep adjusting things so she can figure it out.

"*Now* can I have a story?" she pleads.

The sun is growing late-afternoon rosy, and I think we've both earned it. But I haven't worked on memorizing anything new! Well, she can't see anyhow. I pull Anne of Green Gables out from under my léine and start to read. Princess Barrdhubh is completely drawn into the story, and makes comments as though Anne and Marilla were right in front of us. The princess hums with joy when Anne is enthralled by the beauty of Prince Edward Island, and gasps with horror when the Cuthberts are upset that Anne isn't a boy. She leans forward, eyes wide, hands covering her mouth, as I read:

***

"Will you please call me Cordelia?" she said eagerly.

"Call you Cordelia? Is that your name?"

"No-o-o, it's not exactly my name, but I would love to be called Cordelia. It's such a perfectly elegant name."

"I don't know what on earth you mean. If Cordelia isn't your name, what is?"\

"Anne Shirley," reluctantly faltered forth the owner of that name, "but, oh, please do call me Cordelia. It can't matter much to you what you call me if I'm only going to be here a little while, can it? And Anne is such an unromantic name."

"Unromantic fiddlesticks!" said the unsympathetic Marilla. "Anne is a real good plain sensible name. You've no need to be ashamed of it."

"Oh, I'm not ashamed of it," explained Anne, "only I like Cordelia better. I've—"

***

"Oh!" cries the princess. "But I have never liked my name either! Barrdhudh. It's like"—she wrinkles her nose in distaste—"a cat's grumble. Not like a beautiful girl or anything at all."

"It's a—nice name," I say, trying not to say 'good plain sensible,' which I have the feeling the princess would not appreciate.

"It's not! It's a terrible name! I'm just like Anne. I love beautiful things and I want to be called Cordelia. Cor-deeeell-i-ahhhhh!" She rolls the unfamiliar syllables around in her mouth.

I look at the page and realize that I was saying the words as I heard them in my head, which is a different sound than our own language, and the princess understood it perfectly. She also had no difficulty with any of the things that aren't in our world, so maybe the book gave her mind-pictures too. This is a strange and wonderful magic.

"So! Rian! Foster-brother, hey, hey!" She tugs my sleeve. "Greet me!"

I scramble to my feet, laughing, and sweep her a bow. "Greetings, Princess Barrdhubh—"

"No! You are to call me Cordelia! Didn't I just say?"

I laugh and sweep another bow. "Greetings, Princess Cordelia."

She holds out a scrawny little hand. "Thank you, fair knight Rian. You may kiss my hand for luck."

I chuckle and bow over her hand again. I used to play like this all the time with my little sisters.

"So you'll call me Cordelia all the time?" the princess asks.

"Won't that get a little confusing, having a different name just for me?"

She furrows her brow. "I guess it would. I'll have to think about it."

That night, while they're serving dinner in the Great Hall, the king's trumpeter plays the code for attention. When we finally all rustle into silence, the king stands to make an announcement.

From henceforth, he declares, everyone is to call his daughter Princess Cordelia.

12 YEARS OLD

Chapter Four

The Little Prince feels like my first real friend. With his bossy rose in a glass jar, I think he understands how I feel about Cordelia. I have never seen a desert like where he is stuck, but I feel a little bit that way coming to the lowlands. Like my very soul is parched and withering. I read it several times, but can't tell if it ends with hope or not. I wonder if Dreoilín will come back to tell me the answer, but she doesn't, and I move on to other books.

I can't bring Nessa to the library—the hallway just isn't there unless I'm alone—but my library makes a special pile to share with Nessa and Cordelia. Nessa often wants to talk about battles (especially ones that we're going to do in the future, she and I), but she likes stories about women who do amazing things. She wants to be just like Julie of the Wolves, and then has a million questions after I tell her about Amelia Earhart. She finds it not at all absurd that a woman would figure out how to fly a chariot, and then wish to fly it all around the world—we all are learning from the world of the books, just like regular children learn from the bards.

Cordelia's books are usually about other little girls, and they start out pretty happy, like *Betsy, Tacy & Tib*, or *Little House in the Big Woods*. We have a game where I pause the story, and she thinks of the worst possible thing that could happen next until it makes me laugh, and then I come up with absurd things to make everything perfect again and we laugh even harder.

But then, as fall turns into winter and I turn twelve years old, the library comes up with stories about girls going through hard times. The Little Princess had to live in a garret. Helen Keller was blind like Cordelia and deaf too, and we spend the entire month of February reading books about her and her teacher.

The girl in *Roll of Thunder, Hear My Cry* had all kinds of problems, and on the third day of reading the story Cordelia is asking me questions and learns that I am Fir Bolg. It feels strange that all this time she didn't know that.

"May I touch you?" she asks.

"You do all the time," I protest. "And I think the girl in the story is like our Nemed, with the curly hair. Like Fionn mac Cumhaill. " I'm trying to distract her; the palace gossip is alive with how Fionn accidentally tasted the Salmon of Knowledge. Nessa brings him up all the time, because he was fostered by two warrior women before he got the Salmon last summer, and he is supposedly starting a fianna. Nessa plans to have her own fianna once she graduates.

But Cordelia doesn't care about knowledge or warriors. "But I'm curious about you. Can I touch your face?"

I hop down and stand in front of her, embarrassed but obedient. King Cuaodh said that we must let Cordelia touch things, so she can learn things and get confident enough to leave this side of the palace.

"Is it like in the story?" she asks. "Does it make your life harder to have brown skin?"

I shift back and forth on my feet, trying to figure out how to answer. "Our world isn't like the one there. The clans fight each other, but...I don't know. Everyone takes care of children."

"But we don't have many true Fir Bolg here in Theastír. Not that I remember." She furrows her brow, thinking. "But some people say they are more primitive. Not as smart. Oops, did I hurt your feelings?"

"I've heard it before," I mumble.

"I don't believe that, and neither does Daddy. But I shouldn't have said it."

I thrum the pages of the book between my fingers, thinking. "It's not saying things aloud that's the problem," I say slowly. "Maybe that's the lesson of the book."

"Then can I ask you something?"

I smile. "You are." She always is.

"Do you have to think about it, like the kids in the book?"

"Yes...it's not something I can forget, I guess. When I walk into a room, people...notice it."

"I want to walk into a room and have people notice me because I'm pretty. But now I'm not." She takes several thoughtful stitches. Cordelia is a very slow stitcher. "It's hard for both of us, isn't it?"

I smile; it's probably not exactly the same, but I let her make the comparison.

That book takes us a long time to read, because we end up talking about so many things. We agree that we are disappointed that when they have so many things that are more advanced, they are hurting kids because they are brown. I wonder which of my fates could help. Maybe the teacher could show people how to understand each other.

I think the library wants to cheer us up, because then it sends us *The Twits* and *The Witches*. Even though I'm in training for war, some of the scenes make my neck tingle, but Cordelia loves Roald Dahl more than any of the nurse-maids would ever want to imagine. One evening when I am finishing up telling Matilda, King Cuaodh hears all the rumpus and comes into the room.

Cordelia, who can't see the door swing open, keeps on pretending.

"I'm sorry!" I exclaim.

"What, by the gods, is all the singing and leaping for, daughter?"

"Oh, Daddy!" Cordelia spins right into him, and as he swoops her up in his arms and balances her on his hip, while she dives right through the book—the giant cake and the chalk that writes by itself and the boy in the closet.

Now I'm worried that the king is going to lock me up for being mad. These things make sense to me and Cordelia, but she is telling it all out of order and with too many side comments.

Instead, the king smiles at me.

"I haven't seen her like this since before the fever came," Cuaodh says, kissing her hair. "Squire—Rian, isn't it? You're doing well. Keep taking care of my little girl."

I sputter my thanks and assurances.

They both leave, still talking, and I'm left by the fire.

I can't believe it! I helped. I'm doing something good. Maybe I'll have a good fate after all.

CHAPTER FIVE

This summer is the first time I have to kill men and I do not want to.

Clan MacUaithnin is getting close to our village. We have had skirmishes all summer, and King Cuaodh already led out the main troops. Now our training master is bringing the squires, plus a hundred untrained villagers. I am standing on the battlement, supposedly ready to leave, supposedly inspecting my squadron. I am twelve years old and in charge of twelve grown men, and they look at me with a blind hopeless faith because I have been trained.

My men are not yet in place. Unlike me, they have families to hug goodbye.

I do not know which I fear worse. The pain, or killing someone else. Over and over, I dream of a man's face as I raise my sword to his neck. The MacUaithnins have wives and children and dogs, songs that they sing, games that they play. I want to stop this. I want to be a magistrate and make everything fair. I want to be an explorer and leave it all behind.

In the books I am reading now, there is a girl training to be a knight but she fights giant spiders. At the beginning of the story, a monster called a spidren was attacking a nest of kittens, and the girl became so angry that she killed it by throwing rocks, and then she was happy to leave for warrior training where she could defend the innocent against monsters. I like reading her adventures, and it makes me feel close to Nessa even though I haven't seen her all summer. But the book-squire's decisions are easy. In the real world, good men must kill good men.

"Rian? Is my Rian here? This way?" Cordelia's bright voice echoes off the walls, coming closer.

"Here." I croak. I say her name a couple times, so she can find me. Over the last few months, the blind princess has gained confidence through the entire castle, her fingers always brushing the wall.

She stops a step away from me, face turned with uncanny accuracy towards mine.

"Are you dressed for battle?" She sounds eager. "Like a hero?"

"I am too young to be a hero." I can't help but smile. "You just have to pray that I come back alive."

She holds up a colorful pattern of threads, showing me she is already praying. "Tell me what you look like."

"I have lime in my hair, so it is stiff. I have a leather breastplate and backplate. I have blue warpaint on my face."

"What about your helmet?" she asks eagerly. "Do you have bright feathers, or stags' horns?"

I shake my head, smiling. "I'm just a squire. It's just a leather helmet."

"When you are victorious in battle, I will have my father make you a the most spectacular helmet," Cordelia announces.

I grunt, sick again. I would have to prove my worth in battle by bringing my king the heads of our enemies, but I don't want to cut off any heads. "My helmet's fine the way it is."

"May I touch you?"

I take her extended hand and she reaches for my face. Her fingers are feather-light, finding the patterns in the oily paint and not smudging them.

"Rian..." She rests her hand on my cheek. "Are you afraid?"

There is no honorable response, so I say nothing.

"I would be afraid, but I am just a girl," she continues. "Your heart is built differently."

This is patently untrue. She even knows Nessa, and everyone talks about Fionn's foster mothers. I tried to tell her about Kel in my book, but Cordelia likes her stories either charming or completely absurd.

"If you get afraid, you must just think of me." Cordelia smiles up at me, bright as a star. "You wouldn't want me to be hurt! Whenever you falter, imagine those terrible MacUaithnins poking me with sharp things and making me cry. Think of me crying, like this."

She makes a great show of sobbing and hiding her face, until it makes me smile.

"That's enough, lest you break my heart," I tell her. "Why should I think of you crying?"

She is immediately chipper again. "If you are afraid of the MacUaithnins, then think of keeping them away from me. Then you fight with the bravery of a thousand demons."

"Ah." I don't think it's quite that easy, but that is what Nessa says too. We fight to keep the others safe.

The MacUaithnins might love their wives and play with their dogs and sing beautiful songs, but I know what they would do to Cordelia and it is worse than poking her to make her cry. The thought of it makes me sick, but also brings a hot burning anger to the back of my throat.

"The men are here," I tell her. "I must address them."

Cordelia bows her head and stands against the castle wall. I clear my throat, step forward, and say the speech I have prepared. I have put together inspiring things from my books, and pretend I am the characters who say them. I think it came out rather well, and the men gathering for other squadrons draw closer to listen. They cheer and beat their breasts, and I flush with pleasure.

"That was very nice." Cordelia joins me at the balcony. "I knew you would give the best speech."

The thing about Cordelia—she is selfish and prideful, but she is prideful for others, too.

"Princess!" shouts one of the men in the courtyard.

"Our own little Black Beauty!" cries another.

Cordelia smiles and waves outward, although from this close I can see she is flushing and tense.

"You will all fight bravely, for me and Theastír?" she calls, stuttering just a little.

The men cheer, and I'm proud of my little princess. Just at Beltane, she was too shy to address the people.

Cordelia waves again. "And you know you have the best commander in the army?"

The men applaud and laugh good-naturedly, because I am only a squire, but Cordelia turns and reaches for me. "Kneel," she whispers, anxious, and I put myself right in front of her. Her hands find my cheeks, and then she leans forward and kisses my forehead with a flourish.

The men cheer for real this time.

"Our princess!"

"The kiss of luck!"

"We really will come home!"

I hope—either that her kiss has all the blessing they hope for, or that I'm smart and level-headed enough to get them through whatever happens next.

Cordelia has pulled back away from being in view, her breathing fast and her blank eyes are bright with tears. I guess that really was hard for her.

"Thank you." I squeeze her hands. "You did a good job. The men feel better now—listen."

She surprises me by clutching onto my fingers. "Rian..." Her voice trails away.

"Yes?"

She squeezes my hand and steps away. "*Do* come back. I need to know if Alice makes it out of the rabbit hole."

So for the rest of the summer, I push away philosophy, and concentrate on only these things.

Trying to keep soft, silly, helpless little Cordelia safe.

And coming back to tell her stories again.

***

I get back to the castle in the dark of night. I pause a dozen steps away and make our special call so they know I am one of them. Another five steps, and I call again. Reeling with fatigue, I come close to the gate. Good, no one has killed me yet.

I start the first hoot when the latch clatters, the gate opens a hands-width, and someone pulls me through.

"Squire Rian." The first guardsman bows while the others wrestle the lock back into position. "I'll bring you to report—but where are your men?" He isn't supposed to ask, but his voice is raw with longing.

"They're fine," I answer quickly. "Most of them, at least."

The guard draws a shuddering sigh. "Thank the gods. My cousins were in your squadron. Let's go."

We talk about his cousins as I follow his broad back across the courtyard and into the yawning castle. I speak in generalities and broad praise, hoping that no more of them have died since I left.

We are almost to the king's chambers. I will make my report to whoever Cuaodh has left in place.

The guard half-turns to me, a kind smile. "And what about you, son? Did you earn your first honors?"

I shrug. "A few."

He chuckles and nudges me. "That's fine for your first battle! And you just a lad!"

It's like the druids' prediction. I'm becoming a hero and I don't even want to be.

***

Finally. I have made my report, I have bathed, I have eaten two bowls of hot stew. Finally, finally, it's time for my library. Despite my exhaustion, I almost run down the corridor. I crave that little bit of peace so desperately.

There. Everything like I remember. I drop to my knees and thank the gods and faeries, and then get right to making a cup of tea. With sugar! Sugar is an excellent invention. And do they have—oh yes, there are cookies tonight, and little puffy things that might be called patty cakes. I gobble two straight away.

I put the kettle on the fire (it's nice that the fire is always lit for me), and shuffle through the books on the counter while I wait for it to boil. I can't find *Squire*, about the young warrior and the spidren. The library has other plans for me today: *The Strawberry Girl, The Toothpaste Millionaire, Swallows & Amazons*. I turn them over, studying the pictures. I decide the toothpaste millionaire looks too happy for me tonight, and the strawberry girl reminds me of my sister, which makes me sad and I can't hold any more sadness. The simple figures on the last book feel like me, and I like how there's a bunch of them together.

I hope Nessa's not dead. Oh, gods watch over her.

Reading will push away this haze of pain and fear, like the fire melts the aches on my body. I can read until I am asleep, and then there's no time to think about—a burst of fluttering startles me. I spin around—there's the wren-faerie again, and the lid to the table is gaping open.

"Well met, Rian of Kilkirk," Dreoilín chirps.

She came back! But I'm really exhausted—but it's a real fae, paying attention to me—but I'm hardly in any condition to have a conversation. "Good evening." I bow and try to push my face into a pleasant expression.

"Look!" She flutters towards the table. "Your astragali are back. You can roll again!"

I left before sunrise and by now it has been dark for hours and hours. I have been running and hiding for the entire day, and the day before that we were fighting, and I have scrapes and sores and bruises but it's nothing compared to my aching heart. I left my men in pain, moaning, bleeding.

"Must I?" I come towards the table, slowly. There are all the figurines. They're so beautiful, I don't want any of them to go away.

I don't want any of my choices to go away. I can't bear to lose anything more right now.

"But you have been doing things, this last year," Dreoilín scolds. "You are older now. You understand yourself better."

"I don't really think so."

"But the bones know. Go. Go!"

I hated the battle, the stink and fear of it. Maybe the fates will know that, and the sword figure will dissolve this time. That will prove that the druids were wrong, and King Cuaodh can assign me another job. I scoop up the astragali and roll them before I can think again.

They come up three green sides and a triangle. I don't know what that means.

"Which one, which one!" Dreoilín trills, as though this is exciting.

Three breaths pass. I clutch *Swallows & Amazons*, wishing I could have friends like in my books. That's what I'd choose.

Then the tiny jar with the tiny lid crumbles away to nothing.

"But I want to be a healer!" I cry. Think how much I could fix!

"Oh, my poor dear boy!" Dreoilín sings a sad little melody, spreading her wings as though she could wrap me in a hug. "You look so tired and weary, and you sound so sad. Tell me about what happened. Tell me all your stories. I'm listening, dear chick."

No one has fussed over me since I left home, but I hesitate. I've been at Cuaodh's castle almost two years, and learned what we don't say.

"I have never had a human chick," Dreoilín says. "Tell me why you want to be a healer. Would that help you do good in the world, like you so desire?"

Maybe there's magic in her words, or maybe I just need to tell someone. "The men—my men after battle. It was... awful. We prepare for the world beyond death, but don't talk about the pain..." I shake my head, but can't find the words. "I did what I was told in the battles. There weren't many of us, so they had me stay at the narrow spot. We blocked the MacUaithnins escape. We did it." I wipe my eyes. "My men were brave and we held it long enough for some of the real warriors to catch up. But they were...all bloody and stuff."

Dreoilín sings a mourning little melody. "You got them out."

I shrug. "That was my job. When we waited, I had scouted out a hut that wasn't far, and a farmer to bring us his cart. We loaded up the men and brought them there." The guilt. The shame. They were hurt and I lived. Why didn't the stupid warrior figurine disappear?

"Did you leave them there?" Dreoilín asks.

"I was supposed to!" I exclaim. "I wish I could have been a healer and made them better! I didn't know what to do, so I made a lock for the door, and sneaked through the enemy camp to get back here to make my report, and the lord is sending someone with supplies and I hope my men aren't all dead! Why can't I become a healer?"

"Because you left them there," Dreoilín answers.

"But I had to! I did my best!"

"You did. And you made things better."

"I didn't! I couldn't heal them!"

She flutters down from the sconce. Standing on the edge of the table, she brushes her wings against my arms. "You helped by keeping your head in battle. You helped by building a lock for a hut. You helped by using your skills to sneak and your stamina to run all the way back to the castle to get help. You did all those good things, little chick."

I am so tired, I bawl, like a child instead of a man.

"But you did not make the choice that a healer would make. You made the choice that would fit a leader or an explorer or a warrior. Do you not see?"

"I didn't mean to," I snuffle.

She sighs. "This is the way our fates are sealed, little chick. One choice at a time."

13 YEARS OLD

CHAPTER SIX

The spring that I am thirteen and Nessa is sixteen, it is so cold for so long that they hold the Trials late but the forest is barely putting out buds. Some of Nessa's age-mates leave for new positions a year before they receive their knighthood, hoping that the kingdoms on the sea are faring better; Prince Ardgal leads a small band, trying to root out attacks before neighbors decide our castle is ripe for plucking.

A messenger arrives one morning over breakfast. Since the King is already busy, Lord Tadc is the highest noble left in charge, and he accepts the messenger's address. Lord Tadc, Lugaid's uncle, is still at breakfast, because he is the sort of man who is pleased to pay his way with lavish compliments and very little work.

"You are very lucky," Tadc tells the messenger, pitching his voice to carry through the room. "We happen to have one new knight who is still stationed with us. He will be happy to vanquish your problem. Or rather, I mean...*she* would be happy."

His voice drips with scorn, but Nessa perks up. She does like to vanquish problems.

Tadc gestures, and Nessa bows low before him. I bristle, but don't make a sound. Lords have precedence over the warriors, but I think Tadc just enjoys making a princess bow to him. She is wise and brave and clever, *and* she was born a princess, and *most* importantly she works hard and takes blows for king and country. Tadc just sits around.

"Warrior Nessa, this fellow will take you to his village. They have a boar who is causing injury and stealing the last of their supplies. Go and kill it."

"Yes, my lord." Nessa bows again, a smile sparkling in her eyes. "I will choose my crew and gather supplies."

Tadc holds up one finger.

Nessa waits, almost quivering with eagerness to lead her own party. "Yes?"

"One."

"One...what?"

"One man. We can spare you one fighter only."

What? Is he just outright trying to kill her?

"But my lord"—the messenger twists nervously—"it is a very *large* boar."

"Nessa is a very brave fighter." Tadc grins, showing too many teeth. "You wished to prove your worth, did you not, my pretty?"

Nessa's chin jerks up at the endearment. "I can manage."

Lugaid laughs, quickly muffling the sound.

"I will be fine!" Nessa snaps. "One warrior is all I wanted."

That's a bald-faced lie; boar hunting is always done in a large group. With big men.

Nessa spins and marches away from Tadc, scanning the room. She jabs her finger towards me, then vanishes before I can follow.

I catch her halfway to the back pens. "Are you sure this is best? You should choose someone big."

"You're the only one I trust," she snaps.

It worries me that she has not found someone to trust among her age-mates. I realize I have not asked how she is doing in months, or at least, I have not insisted that she tell me. I hurry after her, brow furrowed, thinking through the men she trains with. I've never liked the way they joke about Nessa.

"Is anyone bothering you?" I ask as we come out into the cold spring air. "Are they touching you?"

Nessa waves her hand. "Never mind about that. Quick, we need to choose the dogs before Tadc thinks of that too. With the best boar-hounds, we'll be fine."

***

On the day's trek into the hills, clearly the messenger does not think that one newly-minted warrior, one not-yet-grown squire, and half a dozen boar-hounds are going to be enough. He barely speaks, sparing us only the occasional mournful glance.

"Maybe he's one of the ones who doesn't like the Fir Bolg," Nessa says as he rounds a corner, voice heated. "He thinks you're slow and backwards of mind. Never you mind, *I* know you're the best in the palace!"

Maybe he doesn't like woman warriors, especially when they are beautiful with long golden hair. But I don't speak out loud—I don't think any of us need to hear it.

The dogs run forwards and back, snuffling after trails and nudging our hands. They, at least, are happy.

***

We spend a cold night in an abandoned hut. The villagers try to pretend that they honor us with our own space, but their avoidance is so palpable that it dims even Nessa's enthusiasm. They are all Milesian here, every one, so perhaps they do believe the stories about my people.

Or perhaps they don't want to bother with making friends before our certain death.

In the morning, the messenger takes us down a small path, until he says he is sure we can find our way, practically running back to the village. Indeed, the dogs are perking up their big ears, and Nessa and I can see hoofy prints in the muddy path.

As befits tradition, Nessa makes an inspiring speech.

Equally befitting tradition, I whoop and beat my breast. It doesn't convince either of us, really, but at least I'm a little warmer.

Nessa sets the lead dog on the trail, keeping the others behind us. "We'll ambush him," she explains, going into a long and complex strategy which she is fully convinced will make the two of us as useful as a dozen full-sized men. We both carry heavy boar-spears over our shoulder and knives in our belts.

The forest grows denser, the dogs fan out, and I watch Nessa's bright head bobbing ahead. Tadc has the same battle sense as his fool of a nephew. Nessa is brilliant at sword-work, and I'm quick and unexpected. We are the least suited to send after boar, which just takes big heavy blows.

"Have you ever fought boar?" Nessa calls back. "I've gone a couple times."

"Never," I reply.

She laughs. "All the better! Then you won't be burdened with expectations!"

It's so ridiculous that I burst out laughing too.

The boar leads the dogs in a wide circle. The animals are all better than we are in the dense forest, and we are both wearier than I like by the time we hear them baying. Nessa perks upright, and adrenaline floods me as I make a wide run to her right. (I've learned that word from my books. I can recognize a lot more feelings now that I read so much.)

As Nessa predicted, the boar takes a stand in a small clearing. I position myself along the natural line of escape, the dirt already churned with boar-prints. I slip behind a bush and make the soft whiffling noise in my teeth, letting the dogs know where to drive the quarry.

Not that I actually want a boar running straight at me. By myself.

But it will be injured by the time it gets here. Halfway to bacon and ham. It's just a pig, right?

Nessa calls out, the dogs start a frenzy of barking, and the boar—whoa. That's a deep sound! How big is this thing?

Adrenaline freezes into sheer panic, but I have to hold my ground. I've got to carry out Nessa's plan.

Nessa ululates her battle cry.

Barking, snarling, enormous grunts.

Nessa screams, and my heart stops.

But there's more barking, and Nessa yells. Not nearly as confident now, but definitely alive.

There's a crashing in the brush, and I brace for my blow. Here they come!

The thing is *huge!* I put all my weight into my spear, but can feel that the blow just glances off muscle and bone. The boar turns to snarl but the dogs harry it, and as they run as I use the momentum of my thrust to roll behind a tree.

Well, that's not going to work. Nessa and I could each poke the boar a dozen times and it would be no more than annoyed. *Very* annoyed.

We need to go back and demand a crew from the village. With the King's warriors to strategize, some of the farmers could be brave. Right now, the important thing is that the farmers are *larger* than us.

Just about anyone is larger than Nessa and I.

Nessa is a natural leader, and she would have done it if the villagers hadn't been so suspicious of us, and Nessa was already feeling defensive about me—and me about her. We probably were a grumpy pair, but—

Now is too late. I hear Nessa and the animals make another stand. The dogs will not be called off their quarry, but they need us to deliver the killing blows. The woods shake as they drive the boar to Nessa, who yells. There are several thumps, which means she didn't land a single solid blow.

I hear the lead dog turn. They're coming back my way, and fast—I duck behind the tree and they thunder by.

That was cowardly. But I can't afford to be injured, or the boar will take Nessa down. She sounded hurt.

I tug my spear from the underbrush, going through Nessa's instructions. My commanding officer.

But none of them will work.

This winter, I have been reading beautiful, lonely books like *The Secret Garden* and *Black Beauty* and *Blue Willow*. They make me feel like I am not so strange and alone, but not a single one of them had any advice about keeping a mean boar from killing your commanding officer, who is also possibly your only friend.

I wish I could drop an avalanche on it!

Or one giant rock. That would do, if I could climb a tree and drop a boulder.

The thought is absurd, but it gives me an idea. There's no boulders around here, but maybe a loose branch! That tree looks sturdy and easy to climb—I run fast, before the dogs turn the boar again.

The master has trained away my fear of heights; he made me go up and down trees for an entire month. I cried, I stumbled, and eventually I got really good at it. So up I go, like a red squirrel with a spear on its back. I'm working on the dead branch, getting it free—

Nessa screams again. Pure fear. And here I am, like an idiot, three men high in a Scots pine where I can't run and help her. She didn't tell me to climb a tree.

One of the hounds howls in pain but the bushes shake. The dogs have got the boar moving again, and they remember where I am. They're trained to bring it to the hunter.

Here they come, and I'm not ready—but next they'll take it back to Nessa, and she's hurt.

I shove the branch, which cracks and tumbles in a leisurely sort of way. It's not going to hurt anyone, but it comes down in front of the boar, who rears back, huffling and shuffling.

It's right below me, and there's one other heavy thing up here.

Me.

I brace my spear and drop.

This blow goes deep but the boar is a mountain! It shakes me off and I fall into the mud, rolling desperately away from those hooves. Claws scrape my hip, but it's one of our dogs, over me, defending me. The boar swings around, crashing through bushes, the dogs at its face. I push to my knees, frantic, but my spear is gone. The boar's wounded, blood foaming from its mouth.

But I can't kill it with a knife. No one could get that close. It's slow and stumbling, and this is when a big untrained man could do a lot of good.

The boar breaks through the dogs, heading for me. I draw two knives and brace in fighting pose, which is hopeless but better than lying in the mud.

There's a flurry of movement. Nessa runs forward, spear braced in front of her, and makes a flying leap at the boar's side. This second blow knocks the beast down and Nessa flies over his back, tumbling safely into the woods beyond.

Now the dogs rush in, grabbing his ears and who-knows-what. I hope they'll finish him off, but the gesture isn't right. The lead dogs looks at me, his ears as excited as Nessa's original speech.

Fine.

It is not graceful, but Nessa and I manage to finish the beast off with our knives. Really, disgustingly, painfully not graceful at all.

Only when the lead dog flops to the ground do we realize it's over. After all, the dogs were the only ones who had any idea what was going on here.

Nessa stares at me, mouth gaping, hair tangled. I'm sure some of that blood is hers. Nessa is usually so confident and beautiful, I've never seen her look like this.

I'm not sure anyone has seen Warrior Princess Nessa mac Euchaid look like this.

"Very well," she gasps, "good job, men. Now just"—she spins one finger—"tie his hooves together. We'll put a long stick through the loops and carry him back to the village. I'll take the head side and you take the tail end."

She stares for one more second, and then we both burst out laughing. She reaches out her arms and maybe she fell into me or I flopped into her, but we are both holding each other up and laughing hysterically, and then even together we can't stay up. We sink into the mud, half laughing and half chocking. We can't get any dirtier than we already are.

"It was just a pig, Rian," she says. "All that for a stupid, stupid pig." And she lays her head on my shoulder and sobs.

I wonder again what her story is. "I want to see my mother again," I mumble, because that is always my story.

"I want you to see your mother too," she wails. "And me—I need to fight the evil men. Not a stupid pig."

The dogs come over and lick our faces.

Nessa's leg is hurt, we both have cuts, and three of the dogs are injured. But everyone can walk, and there is no help for it. Even at full strength, I couldn't carry Nessa, and even together we couldn't lift a boar-hound. We wash in the stream and limp back to the village. The dogs know the way, and this time, Nessa does not even pretend to lead.

"Never again, Rian," she says as the sky goes purple.

"Never what?"

Nessa pauses, bracing one hand against a birch. "Never again am I letting their prejudice and their tricks force my hand. They fooled me, making me think it was about bravery."

She meets my gaze, her blue eyes steady—and sorrowful. I've seen Nessa in all kinds of moods, flashing anger to laughter to curiosity to pride. But never this.

I have to say something. "Even bravery doesn't mean you can do something, when you just can't."

"It doesn't make us six big men each," Nessa agrees bitterly, and limps on.

"You've got to use the skills the gods give you," I say, mostly for myself. "Make that into your weapon." I wonder about those ivory figures. If a boar gets me, then there's nothing else.

"Never again," Nessa mutters.

We are exhausted and limping and covered in boar's blood, and neither of us know how we have set our fates in motion that day.

CHAPTER SEVEN

Lugaid is having his buddy sneak around to capture the silver cup, even though he's the biggest and slowest of our group. The boy he assigned to look-out has bad long-distance eyesight, although he's always trying to hide it, and Lugaid left me to guard the escape route although I'm the smallest and sneakiest. This is always the way he plans things—all about the job he thinks is important and who he thinks is important, not about who can do what the best. I'm getting kind of tired of it. Maybe I'll just beat him at the Trials next spring, even though he'll work with his buddies. I want to get back at his uncle Tadc, too. Neither of them have two brain cells to rub together.

That expression is one of my new favorites. On the other hand, someone with a large brain is Sherlock Holmes. I would much rather be a Sherlock Holmes than a Tom Sawyer, although I don't think there is much call for mystery-solving in my world. If someone ends up dead, we all know exactly who killed him because he's doing a victory dance in the village square. I am intrigued by a world where killing people is not the solution to everything, but Sherlock Holmes and Tom Sawyer still seem to encounter an awful lot of problems, so maybe it doesn't work very well.

This is beastly boring. No one is coming my way, probably because Lugaid and his buddy mucked it up at the very beginning of the plan. I wish I had a book, but my library is far away—we're on one of our bandit raids to the coast. The bandits were easy, so the training master decided we would have some practices in a new locations. Two teams of squires, competing to steal the silver chalice from the hut where the knights are staying.

I peer around the rock, but there's no one there. No one anywhere. Frankly, I rate the possibility of that lunkard actually getting out of the hut unseen at somewhere around zero, so my day isn't likely to get any more interesting for a while.

I stand on the rock, staring out to sea. That was what Prince Caspian did—go out to sea, off the edge of the world. I love to imagine being him, although then I read *The True Confessions of Charlotte Doyle* and I'm not so sure.

What's that—down around the cliffs? In a few moments, I figure out that it's a girl with baskets, probably coming back from gleaning at the tide. I scan for any of my faux-enemy (or real enemies for that matter) but the meadows and dunes are empty.

I hop down to the sand and greet the girl. She's about my age, with a sweet face. I offer to carry a basket and she smiles right up at me which...feels kind of good.

"What is a stranger like you doing in our little village?" She sounds eager, not suspicious.

I explain how I'm one of King Cuaodh's men, and she's gratifyingly impressed. Outside of Theastír, I guess that means something. I walk a little taller. She lets our arms brush. I smile at her, and she giggles.

I set down the basket, deciding she's not going to mind if I stop and act like a warrior. I stand on one of the boulders and survey the dunes. Still no one.

"Are there bandits?" she asks. "Is it dangerous?"

"We got rid of the bandits," I tell her, and explain about the training drill. Other guys brag to girls, so it's not a secret, really—especially since Lugaid's plan has definitely failed by now.

She asks me lots of questions, seems impressed at all the answers, and giggles an awful lot. We go back to her cottage, where her mother seems impressed by a visit from one of the king's men, and her father seems amused by our flirtation and sends us to mend nets by the shore.

Her mother brings us some special dishes, and I savor the salty flavors. We all know I'm leaving when the sun starts to set, so we just enjoy the afternoon together. The sun is warm on my hair, the waves are crashing below us, and the conversation is fun. I think she is likes the attention from someone she feels like is unique (and maybe handsome?) and I like the way she makes me feel like I'm someone who matters. We let our hands brush and I find ways to make her giggle.

This is nice.

***

When the harvest comes in, there is plenty to eat for the first time in months. Everyone celebrates, but I can't stop thinking about bigger things.

It's almost my birthday. Dreoilín is coming back any time now. Or is she? If she comes this year, and I roll the astragali and one fate crumbles, then I'll know for sure the way this works.

Besides, I'm looking forward to telling her about my year. I'll pass the squire tests at the Trials next spring, so that would be a great time for King Cuaodh to give me a new job—if the warrior token happened to dissolve this fall, that is.

The healer disappeared when I didn't do anything with it, so I try to encourage the other non-warrior fates.

The magistrate—when I hear that some maids have been treated unfairly, I listen to their story and bring their case to King Cuaodh, even though it makes my heart pound. But it doesn't turn out scary. He glowers as I explain the situation, the poor girls cowering behind me. But then he simply sends his guard to catch the man, search his room for the trinkets he stole, and dismiss him from service. That's it.

The teacher—I overcome years of avoiding the other squires and offer to help with the newest boys. Now I run the basic drills with a wooden sword for the third period of each morning.

The adventurer—well, I went to the south coast this summer, and sailed on a boat, and went on assignments halfway to Dun Ailline and to the western coast.

The scholar—I'm not sure what this is, but it involves books, and I love my books!

I'm sure I'm not meant to be a leader. The lover is a little embarrassing, but I wouldn't mind when I'm older. But that still leaves plenty of good non-warrior possibilities.

And then—it happens! She's here! As soon as I open the library door, my eyes always go straight to the sconce, and tonight there's the little green wren-woman. Dreoilín chitters a greeting and I bow, and when she demands that I roll the dice, I'm happy to obey.

I tumble them in for a long time, letting them absorb the heat from my hands. Let it be a good one! Finally, I spill them onto the velvet.

Dreoilín trills and we both stare at the row of figurines.

The mast crumples. Then the ivory sail sprinkles away, and by the time it's gone, the edges of the boat are blurry, then gone. Once the beautiful figure is nothing but a pile of dust, I look up at Dreoilín.

"But I *did* adventuring this year!"

"Oh, do tell me!" She flutters her wings. "Where did you go? What did you see?"

So I tell her about the ocean, and she asks all about the curragh and how it was sailed, and I describe walking on the top of the cliffs, how the wind buffeted my body and I sang and it carried my voice away. I have a lot to say.

"But I guess I don't get to go back," I conclude.

"The fate doesn't say you can't go back," Dreoilín chides. "You sound happy about seeing new places, so maybe you will! Maybe you'll be a warrior who travels, or a leader who conquers new lands, or a magistrate in a place we've never imagined. Who knows!"

This is heartening, that even one fate can be so many things. I fiddle with the other figurines, imagining possibilities. "But why did it go away?"

"Well, little chick, look into your heart. You were curious about the boats. You were thrilled to feel the wind. You were amazed by the beauty of the ocean. But how did you feel about coming home?"

"That was the best part! I missed this library—"

I spin and swing my arms to encompass everything, and Dreoilín preens.

"And Cordelia had so many stories to tell me. And I still owe King Cuaodh my service. And Nessa wants me to join her fianna one day, so..."

"So you will go out into the world, and always come home."

I smile and caress the other figurines, smooth and full of possibility. I like this. I'll do my best this year, and Dreoilín will come back, and I'll be one closer to my destiny—the fate that I am choosing, myself.

14 YEARS OLD

CHAPTER EIGHT

The castle lawn is filled with trestle tables piled high with spring flowers, with jugglers and bards circling to entertain the crowds. I am seated at the Honored Table, and King Cuaodh has given me a silver-decorated breastplate and a fine wool cloak for passing the Squire tests, and a large gold brooch for beating the other boys.

I am grumpy.

I haven't been home in three and a half years. I've passed training that makes me better qualified than most fighters, and I could get a position as a guard or lead the volunteer squadrons in a village—like my *own* village. But no. Everyone expects me to stay for the knight training, and I owe King Cuaodh my duty until I am eighteen and officially a man.

Other than duty, no one wants me here. Everything's changing. Nessa will be leaving soon to take a position with someone else—and knowing Nessa, she'll be rushing headlong into battle and get herself killed before the year is out.

Princess Cordelia sashays past our table. The other boys stare, but I turn my gaze to my goblet. I don't know if Cordelia acts this way because she can't see the way the boys react, or because she wants them to do it. This winter, she's begun spending more time in the women's solar and I see her less and less. When she's with me, Cordelia is clever, curious, and enthusiastic. When we're alone, I like her.

But I'm not supposed to be alone with her any more. She's only twelve and she's still tiny, but she's getting curves and the king is planning for her marriage. Even though I'm her foster brother and leagues below her in rank, one of the ladies has taken to hovering at the edge of the room while we work together, and Cordelia gets silly and simpery when the others are there.

Nessa has gone all feminine lately too; tonight she's dressed in a bright saffron léine and richly embroidery inar. She's at the king's table acting as though she's interested in politics—or Prince Ardgar, who is definitely interested in her.

She'd better be careful. Now that the MacUaithnins are subdued, King Cuaodh is stronger than ever and Ardgar will only take a bride who would enhance his tactical position. Nessa was born a princess, but I think her kingdom was one of the ones that was taken over by another king. It happens all the time, but it doesn't make her a strategic marriage.

Ardgar leans over Nessa, his smile oily, his arm across the back of her chair. She pats his hand and smiles back.

I glower at them both.

Nessa catches my eye and scowls—then bares her teeth in case that wasn't clear enough. Then she looks up at Ardgar and laughs. Maybe even she *giggles*. Yuck—who wants a warrior like Nessa reduced to mere flirtation? She'd rather talk about the heroic feats we will do together in a few years, when I am a knight too and she has formed her own fianna—even better than Fionn mac Cumhaill's. She paces and strategizes, she doesn't flirt. Why does Argdar even want her like this?

I think they're all being foolish. I take my last sips of wine, shaking off my mood, and head down towards where they are building the bonfire. I do like dancing, and it's going to be an excellent celebration tonight.

***

Now that I am a knight-in-training the king has generously awarded me my own tiny stone cubby. I figure I had better make a show of using it for at least a few days, so I trudge up the stairs. I usually go to my library, but it's too late to read anyways.

Voices catch my attention. I'm used to ignoring rustling in the corridors, but that's Nessa, and her tone is oddly high. I step into the shadow, head cocked. It takes a long moment to hear the other person reply—Prince Ardgar.

Now that I'm focused, I can make out Nessa's words—"wait—it isn't—please don't—" and fury erupts in my belly. I rush down the corridor. No one, not even the prince, should be forcing himself on a woman, and *no one* should hurt Nessa.

Just around the corner, there are two figures barely visible in the light from the arrow-slit, the larger one holding the saffron-clad one against the wall.

"Stop!" I demand.

They jerk away and turn, their faces pale circles in the moonlight. Nessa's léine slides down her arm, her inar gone.

"Who is it?" Ardgar laughs, unkind. "Go away, little boy. You have mistaken who I am."

"I know who you are, my lord." And I don't care. "And I know the vow you've taken to your fellow warriors, to respect and defend—"

He growls at me. "This is not about a fellow warrior! Men and women can treat each other how they wish."

"But she does not wish—"

"Go away," Nessa says, her voice high and tight.

I know she recognizes my voice. I know she does not want him.

"Leave us alone," Ardgar growls. "If I have to catch you, I'll find out your name and have you publicly whipped."

"Hurry," Nessa snaps. "Leave me. *Run!*"

When I hold my ground, Ardgar advances, his hands fanning in the dark.

I am a warrior trained to obey my commander and ask questions later. I run because Nessa told me to.

***

I race the rest of the way to my little room because Nessa might find me there. She has to get away! I slam the door and howl. I seize a wooden bowl and throw it against the wall and beat my breast and let out a yipping war-cry which turns into nothing but a sob.

I hate this world. Whatever Nessa's story is, she's had enough tragedy in her life.

She doesn't need to be held against the wall.

She doesn't need a baby in her belly.

I hate myself. If I were a true friend—if I had reached my growth yet, I would take Ardgar by the shoulders and slam his head and kick his knees, and once he was down I would strip him naked and—

I collapse on my bed, head in my hands. He's the prince. If I did that, I would be dragged to the village square and put to death. Slowly. Messily. And Ardgar would still have his way with Nessa, who would have one less friend.

I wish I was older, and noble born. Or maybe I could be enough of a hero it that my king would give me honors, and then I could marry Nessa myself. I wouldn't expect anything of her, I'd let her assemble her fianna and run free. I wouldn't even bed her, because children would slow her down and I suspect she doesn't want to bed anyone at all.

Even as the fantasy comes to me, I realize that it wouldn't be pleasant. For me, that is. I want a wife who is kind and gentle, and who actually wants me to kiss her.

But that isn't the point. If I could protect Nessa, I would—even at the cost of my own happiness. I have done the work. I have taken long marches and spent nights in a tree and honed my reflexes—but it still isn't enough.

I have to watch her hurt.

I pull my furs up around my shoulders. I am accustomed to the library bed, where the mattress is deeper and the blankets are cloth, so my furs are barely worn. My mother caught and tanned them for me when I left to foster at the castle.

It seems like another lifetime. My mother could be dead by now.

My door slams open, then closed.

"You *idiot*," Nessa says. "You stupid *child!*"

"I am not—" I cut myself off, confused and startled.

"What good did you think you were doing? You, confronting the prince?" Nessa paces to my window and back. It is barely three steps, her léine flapping around her. She is like a hawk in a cage.

"You don't want to kiss him." I mean it as a question, but it comes out flat.

"No, of course I don't want to kiss him. He's grabby and harsh, and always gets sweaty even right after a bath."

"Then I had to say something!"

"It's not your job to defend my honor!"

"Someone ought to defend you!" If she's going to act like a woman, someone should treat her like a woman!

"I can defend myself!"

"But you weren't. You let him—"

"I did! Because I made a decision!"

"Do you think he'll marry you?"

Nessa snorts. "Of course not. I think he'll screw me."

I spring to my feet, rage quivering through every muscle, burning across my skin.

"Do you remember when they sent us after that boar?"

I grunt. Of course I remember.

"I vowed to use every weapon in my arsenal." Nessa comes to a stop directly in front of me, her face inches from mine.

Through her flowery perfume, I can smell her sweat. It's sour and acid; the smell of fear.

"There's so much I can never do, as a woman, no matter how well I fight. You don't even understand how much I can't do."

"There's plenty I can't do either, a Fir Bolg in this castle of noblemen." My voice is hot.

"I know, but you"—she makes a gesture of frustration. "You choose not to do so much. You don't sleep in the room with the other boys. You could hear what they say. You are faster than anyone but you don't join the races. You tell your stories to the women and draw a whole crowd hanging on your every word, when you could be putting the other men under your thrall. If you just took Lugaid down in a fistfight a couple of times, all of them would flock to you, but no! You could be"—her voice is rising, sharp—"the undisputed leader of all the youths, not just the squires. But no. You just go off by yourself, a lone wolf. A waste!"

I am stunned. It has never occurred to do things just to prove that I can. "Lugaid hasn't bothered me in a year or more."

"Exactly!" Nessa throws up her hands and bursts into motion again. "Because he knows you'd win! You could bother Lugaid!"

"But what would be the point?"

"The point?" Nessa slams one fist into her palm. "Power."

"Enough power to protect you from Ardgal?"

She hisses. "I don't need your *protection*."

That stings. "But he was holding you down and—"

She shoves me. "And that's one weapon I *do* have. My sex. Let me use it."

"Don't!" I yell. I realize—even if I had all that power she wants, she wouldn't marry me. Even just for protection. Even if I never touched her. It's like a blow, chilling me.

"You don't understand anything," Nessa cries. "Just leave me alone!"

"I can't leave! You're in *my* room. Ruining your reputation for nothing!" For someone useless as a man and useless as a friend.

"Fine. But let me manage Ardgal how I *want*."

Her voice goes squeaky and quavery but she bangs the door.

***

Fine! Even Nessa doesn't want me! I bundle my personal belongings, my hands shaking but the gestures drilled into me. I don't even know where I'm going, but this isn't it. There's no use in being honored in the Trials and at the special table if I can't *do* anything! Or *help* anyone! Apparently I'm just a stupid child.

I race down the stone stairs, through the corridors, and down further. To the heartbeat of the earth. To the place where I belong. I burst into my library, and maybe I could have cried myself to sleep and woken up and pushed all my feeling down, and I could have been a knight-in-training on his first day with my mouth closed. Maybe that's all I wanted.

Instead, something flies into my face. I yell, windmilling my arms and dropping my bags. It's all wings and hair and needle-like teeth, and I have to shout "friend, friend!" to suppress my instinct to attack. My hands and feet are ahead of my mind, and I'm braced with a knife in my hand before I can think. Dreoilín collapses on the carpet, tiny green hands clasped over her head, twittering.

"Gracious!" I stare at my knife, but can't quite manage to sheathe it again. "I didn't—hurt you—did I?" My chest is heaving.

"Are you going to kill me?" Dreoilín chitters from the floor. "Are you? Poor me, poor me!"

"No. You just—startled me."

"No?" Dreoilín swoops upwards in one gesture. "You won't hurt me? Then roll the dice, you must roll the dice, roll, Rian, roll!" She races in a little circle, flapping her wings and rising into the air, repeating the words over and over.

"Tonight?" I put my free hand over my ear, trying to think straight. "I'm not born in the spring."

"Doesn't matter! One per year! Tonight! Tonight!"

"What happened?"

"I don't know! Roll, Rian, roll!"

This doesn't feel right, but I can't think anything with her wings and hair everywhere. Dreoilín is screeching and crying out instructions, and Nessa's voice pounds in my head. *Leave me. I don't need you. Stupid child.* I shake my head and grip my knife. I know Dreoilín won't hurt me, but it makes me feel better. More real.

"Roll, Rian, roll! That's it! Open the table! Look! Open!"

I want to yell at her to just sit down, but I manage to regulate my voice and ask nicely. She perches on the sconce, then leaps to the food cabinet, then the bookshelf. I grit my teeth and throw the astragali.

Dreoilín gasps and freezes.

I rub my hand over the figurines, too impatient to wait for them to dissolve on their own. There, one is breaking—

"No!" I hold it closer, the little people crumbling into my palm. "I wanted to be a teacher! I was working on it. I'm helping the younger boys. I am teaching already! I *am!*"

Dreoilín stares at me from the bookshelf, green eyes wide, wings undulating slowly.

"This is my fate, right?" I gesture at the table with my knife, which apparently is still in my hand. "Mine! And I'm choosing it. That's what you said!"

Dreoilín doesn't answer.

"What if I want to be a teacher? I've done all the things right. These *bones* don't decide how I feel about things. I do!"

She still doesn't argue with me.

I close my hand and the ivory dust seeps between my fingers, and then I see it. I decide, me!

"This is exactly what I'm doing," I say, tense. "I'm going back to my own village. And I'm going to use my skills to teach them how to fight. All those people—I'm going to help them. I'm going to help!"

"Are you sure that's a good idea?" Dreoilín sounds tentative. "If the bones are warning you..."

I snort. "You can call it being a leader while I teach. Or maybe I'll marry our rí túaithe's daughter and be the lover and the teacher. That's what you told me last time, right? You can just do one thing and call it another."

Dreoilín ducks her head, letting her hair cover her face.

I know that isn't what she said and I know that isn't the way fate works, but I'm tired of this. If nothing I do matters, then why not do what I want?

"Right then. I'm leaving." I glare around the library, regret clenching my stomach.

Because apparently I've been *hiding* in my library while Lugaid rules the boys and Ardgar takes what he wants. I don't deserve any of this.

"According to the laws of my people, I've earned my manhood," I tell Dreoilín.

She doesn't answer.

I fasten my new cloak around my shoulders, tidy my bag, and take a moment to bundle up the muffins and cookies. I should leave now, under cover of dark.

"Thank you for everything," I tell Dreoilín. "Goodbye."

She still doesn't answer.

I leave anyways.

CHAPTER NINE

After four days of walking, I crest the hill and Shy Mountain is the bright green of early summer. Below me, round houses nestle into the forest, beside dark furrows with their baby crops. The faerie stream is to my right. The round fort is in the next meadow west.

I put my hand to my mouth and ululate the cry of my people, and then I let my feet free and run.

***

Coming home is everything I have dreamed of, these three years and more. My parents embrace me, my elders bless me, my brothers and sisters beg me to swing them in the air. My mother has two new little ones, and my arms remember the way a baby fits against my shoulder.

But with life comes sorrow. There was a fever and a few faces in my village are missing. My brother Euchu died after a terrible accident. Our neighbors had a fire. But this time, when I weep and pray and beat my breast, I am not alone.

My whole village brings me from house to farm to tree, showing me what is new or beautiful or sad. The boys build a bonfire and the women each bring food to share, and it is familiar and good. Our bard sings the song of our people so we all remember, and then sings the last three years so I know it. I promise to tell them my story tomorrow.

But as the fire dies down and we head towards our huts, the bard puts his hand on my arm.

"Little Rian." His face is becoming wizened, but his voice is still as smooth as honey. "Does our king know you are here?"

The "our" throws me. I forgot this territory is claimed by Cuaodh too, perhaps in part because of the bargain he made to foster me.

The bard steps back, shaking his head sadly. My hesitation told him too much.

***

I have an important job, just like Nessa said. I am here to organize and lead Kilkirk's defenses. Everyone is happy about this, and they tell me stories of other villages which have been raided or burned. I speak with the builders and tell them how to erect a palisade of wooden logs, pointed with the tips facing outward, and how to construct the gates. I meet with the blacksmith and explain the latest technology in weapons and fasteners. And that afternoon, I gather all the strong villagers together and make a speech about training for battle.

I make a speech and start them on some drills. That's the thing about these home armies—they're all enthusiasm and no technique. The country people's weapons are heavy and slow, so certain gestures will break through sword work, but when they flail around it's easy for a trained warrior to block. I go down the line, adjusting stance. Look at me, teaching—and they are doing better already!

"Good, that's it!" I tell a boy a little older than me.

"Thank you, sir." He bows, flushed and pleased, and turns away.

"Wait—where are you going?"

"Home, sir. You told me I had it right!"

I'm flustered. "Yes, but now you must do it a hundred times in a row."

His mouth falls open. "That many?"

"Yes…" The type of blunt orders I followed won't work here. "So when you are scared or confused, your body strikes the blow even if you don't have the chance to think about it. Remember how we worked on getting our feet in position?"

He nods. "That really helped!"

"So do the sequence a hundred times, and you'll be able to do it even when you can't take the time to get your feet right."

"Ah, I understand. It's all right; I can do the weeding tomorrow."

I sense a problem here. "But you need to do the same move fifty times tomorrow, and then I'll show you a new one."

"A new one?" This is the man to our left, shocked.

"You do need more than one set of moves," I explain.

"But I thought you said that this would block their sword blow!"

Everyone is watching me now.

"It will." I sigh. "But the warriors know more than one move with their swords."

The villages hem and ahh.

"Thank the gods we have a real warrior to train us!" a woman cries, and the others agree.

"How long will we need to spend?" the boy asks me.

"We'll start with half-days of training," I answer, thinking fast. "After our first couple weeks, perhaps…an hour a day."

I thought that was minimal, but my new army is shocked and overwhelmed, and there are rumbles of discontent.

"I'll try," the boy says. "But I have a lot of work at home. My wife is having our first child in a moon or two."

The world tips. The rivers might be in the sky and the stars at my feet for the way I feel. "Your…wife?"

He smiles, and tells me her name and how many cattle they own (one) and points in the direction of their house.

I think I manage to smile and nod before I hurry over to the water barrel. I drink from the dipper and splash my face.

My world did not wait for me while I was away. The children I grew up with have become men and women with their own lives, while I was swinging a sword and telling stories to a spoiled princess.

At the castle, I am too old to chat freely with Cordelia, but not nearly old enough to court a woman. Home in my village, the girls are already marrying off. I am really not sure I should have come home, especially without telling anyone.

I am not a hero like the druids predicted. I cannot even protect Nessa.

Besides, I miss my library.

CHAPTER TEN

"There is a visitor for you, Rian." My aunt bows towards where I am working with the gate. She keeps her eyes lowered, which I am not sure if she means respect towards me or that she is hiding something.

"Thank you, auntie." I bow and follow her.

She leads me to our bard's hut. Half a dozen men are sitting in a circle, talking, mugs in their hands. Their body language is serious but not angry. One of them, with his back towards me, has the light hair of the Milesians, but I don't recognize him.

My gut clenches in anxiety. My secret heart hoped for Nessa, come to join forces and laugh and boss me around. But what stranger would walk four days into the hills in order to speak with me?

I pull my shoulders tall and walk up to the group like I am a man. I still haven't had my growth and I don't have a beard, but I have done a man's training and have a man's job now. I flip quickly through the characters in the books I have read recently, discarding the Hardy Boys as too cocky and Sherlock Holmes as just plain useless in the real world.

The bard pours me a mug of ale, and we all solemnly discuss the possibility of rain.

"Galchobhar has come all this way to give you a message," the bard tells me.

"An invitation," one of the elders clarifies.

I make a seated-bow to Galchobhar. I recognize him vaguely; he is an older man who works in the women's wing. Doing repairs, mostly.

Galchobhar slips forward onto his knees, bowing his head to the grass. "Knight Rian," he says, looking up at me. "Foster son of our great King Cuaodh."

Next to me, the bard hisses through his teeth.

Galchobhar lowers his head again. "I seek you out at the command of the Princess Cordelia."

Apparently I am supposed to reply. "Ah. Cordelia." As soon as the words are out of my mouth, I realize I have skipped her title, which makes me either sound too familiar, or like I am claiming the high titles that the messenger has flattered me with.

He and I both know it is mere flattery.

"What does the Princess Cordelia wish?" the bard asks mildly, keeping the conversation moving.

"I am woeful to interrupt the training program you have told me about," Galchobhar says, "but the princess wishes Rian to become her personal guard. He has just passed the required tests, and at the same time she has come to her womanhood and is allowed to choose her private staff."

"Allowed?" asks the elder on my right.

Galchobhar shrugs. "What Princess Cordelia wishes, it is best for Princess Cordelia to have."

"That's hardly a good way to raise strong, obedient women," grouses one of the elders. "Now, for my daughters—"

He rambles on, but we all ignore him. I don't think King Cuaodh is looking for parenting advice.

"I am honored to be chosen for the princess's personal service," I say slowly. "Surely, she gave me the summer off to spend with my family. As a reward for passing my Trials."

It is a test, to see if the man knows anything.

He shakes his head, quick and firm. "I am terribly sorry." He licks his lips. "I am sure she meant you to have the summer away, or you would not have been dismissed. But her womanhood came on...rather quickly. And she wants her personal staff...now."

"Hm." I lean back on my chair, keeping my body calm and neutral while my brain races.

Cordelia knows how much my family means to me. She is selfish in a petty, foolish way, but she does not cause harm to others. She wouldn't want to hurt me.

Or would she? Am I just seeing her through rose colored glasses and imagining her to be better than she is? Am I making her into something kinder—more like myself—the same way I did to Nessa? Maybe I don't understand either of them at all.

I push aside those psychological considerations for later. The strange part is definitely that her womanhood "came on" mere days after the Beltane celebrations. I know that girls' courses is the official beginning of womanhood, but it's not really something that needs to be made public. Fathers usher their daughters into womanhood at the big festivals, not four days afterwords. This is just strange.

And besides, it's not like I'm staring at her, but I do spend a decent amount of time with the princess. She just started, ahem, budding like a rose, this last autumn. I don't really think that buds go to fruit quite that quickly. In people.

"When do you need to leave?" the bard asks.

Galchobhar glances at the sun. "Tomorrow."

The elders glance back and forth between the messenger and I. Their mouths are pressed in, or their brows furrowed slightly. None of them protest this ridiculous timeline or ask that I might complete even one more day of my training program.

They have figured out that something is wrong.

They know I have lied to them.

***

Galchobhar and I leave early in the morning. I hug my mother, but disappear into the forest before the village is even awake.

I wanted to be helpful. I wanted to protect them. I did!

We walk and walk. I think through telling this all out to Dreoilín and admit, inside my own head, maybe I was being selfish. I do care about my village, but maybe I also wanted to feel important. I wanted to show them that I'm worth something after my training. Maybe I wanted someone to admire me, and Cordelia doesn't need me any more and Nessa doesn't want me.

Was that so bad?

But the shame clings to me the way the fog clings to the river valleys.

Galchobhar is a good walker and does his fair share of the work when we set up camp, but he is not much for talking. There's nothing but me and my thoughts, and I miss my library something awful. I think about the books that I have read, and what could help me learn what to do next. I want to be a better person, like the ones in my books.

I'll do that, I decide. I imagine telling it to Dreoilín, having a great attitude towards whichever figurine crumbles this year. There's still plenty left! I'll learn from my mistakes and be better. I'll be patient with Cordelia, who is probably just going through a phase. I'll be a good friend to Nessa, no matter what she chooses. I'll study until I earn my knighthood, or maybe this is the year that the astragali will show something different, and King Cuaodh will give me a new assignment and I'll work hard.

Everything will work out, just like it does in my books.

***

On the second day, we hear another party down the road, and Galchobhar sings out our code. He whistles it again as the other group breaks through the trees, putting out his hands as though he is holding me back.

I recognize two palace guards and one older warrior, although I don't recall their names. Their eyes glaze over the two of us but they do not smile or meet my eyes.

The leader holds up a coil of rope. "We are here to apprehend the traitor."

For just a moment, I think they are requesting that we join their search party. We're all King Cuaodh's men.

"Hand him over," their leader says, and at the same moment—

"I am under the orders of Princess Cordelia," Galchobhar says.

One of the guards steps forwards, glowering at both of us. He jingles the slave chains at his belt.

Is this to do with *me?* Slave chains? Am *I* a traitor?

"Princess Cordelia required that I bring this man to her." Galchobhar's voice quavers just a little. "I am sworn to obey the princess. She is just such a *little* thing, my good fellows. If she wants something, her father wants to make her happy. That's all. The little princess." He drops his gaze.

My throat has gone hot then cold then parched. I never meant any disrespect to my king! But I suppose I left, in a hurry, and I didn't explain. I didn't get permission.

He thinks I'm a deserter. Disloyal.

"We're here under the king's orders," the leader snaps. "If Rian were a full adult, he would be banished. As it is, we are to bring him back to the castle for punishment."

"He's a sneaky little devil," adds the large guard. "We're to use these." The chains again.

"And we have full permission to treat a deserter as we see fit," the leader snaps. "I know what *I* think of serving in an army with men who don't take their vows seriously, and he won't be so pretty when we get in."

I didn't mean to. I was just mad at Nessa, and scared, and it didn't feel like I fit in anywhere. I just wanted to be useful, and now they will beat me and starve me, and my foster father will—

But Galchobhar is spreading his hands helplessly. "The princess said to bring him just as he was. She wouldn't like him coming back all black and blue, wouldn't like it at all."

"The princess needs a loyal guard," snaps the leader.

"I will always be loyal to Cordelia!" I cry.

"See?" Galchobhar shrugs. "She wants him like this."

They argue on and on. Eventually, I sink to the ground, wrapping my arms around my knees. My head is throbbing with fear and self-loathing. How could I do something so terrible? I only wanted to help.

No, I wanted to fit in. I wanted someone to appreciate me, and I guess I wanted it so bad that I was willing to die for it.

Eventually, another party comes down the road. These are some locals, and they have the village magistrate among them. He hears the arguments between the search party and Galchobhar, humming and nodding along. I huddle on the ground, no more important or capable than a bundle of grain.

"I cannot think of an exact law that applies to this situation," the magistrate says eventually, "but do you all agree to be bound by my decision?"

Each of the four men gives him their word and the special hand gesture.

No one looks at me. I have no say in my own fate.

"You will all travel together," the magistrate declares, "sharing all your camping goods and supplies. After all, you all serve the same king. As Galchobhar requests, no one will harm the boy. He will be fed his fair share of rations, and allowed to bathe. However, you may put the collar on him, and lead him with the rope. After all, it is your duty to bring him back to your king, and he might otherwise run away again. You may take his jewelry into your keeping, but you may not cut his hair."

The guards immediately start arguing over who gets what.

My new brooch and fine cloak! They show that my king honors me. I have come to take it for granted that I do well in every Trial and battle, and to simply expect the king's rewards.

But the magistrate waves his hands, stopping them. "No, no, no! You don't get to keep them. Just hold them until the king decides—"

The guards burst out again.

"Has a boy really that much fine jewelry?" the magistrate asks Galchobhar.

"He is a very promising young warrior," Galchobhar replies. "But perhaps you had better keep it all yourself."

So that is what happens. I must take off my ear-bobs and rings and anklet, not to mention my brooch and cloak, and put them in the keeping of this random magistrate. Everyone at the castle will immediately notice that I have been stripped of my honor.

And then they put the slave collar on me. It is sticky leather against my neck and shoulders, heavy with chain that slows my every step.

I want to stop thinking. I want to just disappear into actions and animal desires, the way some of the men seem to.

But for the rest of that day, and the entire next day's march, I cannot turn off my mind. It's a worse torment than the collar.

CHAPTER ELEVEN

On the fourth day after leaving Kilkirk, one of the guards hurries ahead. He is going to warn King Cuaodh; I am sick with fear and shame.

I recognize every turn of the road now. I remember how fancy everything seemed the first time I came to the city from Kilkirk village, but I have gone to these houses on the king's errands many times. I have grown confident in my station—now how far I have fallen.

I wonder, will all the ivory figurines will crumble this time? Am I no longer worthy of wearing the armlet that holds my fate? All my possible fates may be already sealed. Done. Finished. Life over. Nothing accomplished. Even if the King doesn't kill me, banishment would mean certain death. In our world of constant clan warfare, no man can survive alone—he serves either a king or a fianna. It's not like my books. Oh, my books. What if I'm never even free to return to my library again?

***

The guards do not take off my collar when we enter the village. Everyone calls insults, and boys throw stones.

I do not have a single example from my books of someone who was led back to their home in a slave collar while people threw stones, so I don't know what to do. I hold my shoulders high and do not look to the right or the left, because that's all I can think of.

The stones hurt.

My guards lead me through the village, through the castle gate, through the courtyard, and straight into the Great Hall.

My foster father—my king—has prepared for my return. Cuaodh is in his great throne, dressed in brightly colored robes and wearing his bracelets and circlet. Guards in the castle colors line the wall, spears propped on the ground as they stand like statues. The castle magistrate and bard sit at a table to one side, faces pinched and cautious.

And there—my heart swoops and falls and bursts. Two grand chairs across from the king.

In the first, Prince Ardgar. Behind him stands Nessa, spear in hand, wearing the castle colors and Ardgar's personal insignia. She has given up her own dreams to become his personal guard, and probably his concubine too.

In the other throne, Princess Cordelia. She looks grumpier than any of them, chin in the air, her little feet already drumming her over-large chair.

I have planned one thing—I burst forward to prostrate myself at King Cuaodh's feet, my forehead touching the floor. "I am sorry, my lord. I did not mean you any disrespect."

I have startled everyone, including the guards who dropped my chains to the floor with an ominous clatter.

Cuaodh stars to speak, and stops.

Cordelia's voice pierces the brief moment of silence. "I want him for my guard. Do what you must, Daddy, but then give him to me, whole and healthy."

"He is a traitor," King Cuaodh declares, his voice echoing through the room. "He swore loyalty to his training master and to me, and deserted without informing either of us."

"But he's been fine for years," Cordelia says. "It doesn't really seem worth all this fuss."

I judge it better not to speak again, but I do push myself onto my knees so I can peer around the room.

"He could have been bought by our enemies," Cuaodh says. "Or stealing our gold."

"Oh for heavens' sakes, Daddy!" Cordelia shakes back her hair. "You know that's ridiculous."

"I cannot give you a traitor for your personal guard!" Cuaodh roars.

Galchobhar, the guards and I all wince back, and even the row of guards on the back wall half-jumps.

But Cordelia laughs.

There is a long silence.

"This is *Rian*," Cordelia protests. "Don't you remember—the peapods? The girl the size of a mushroom? He helped the maid whose silver comb was stolen; why would he steal from you?"

King Cuaodh glares at her, but Cordelia fluffs out her sleeves and doesn't notice.

"Rian of Kilkirk!" He swings back to me. "Why did you desert myself and break your own vows?"

"It was my own childish emotions, my lord. I was always loyal to you, but I was overcome by missing my family. I thought I could serve you better if I trained them in the lessons you have been kind enough to give me, thus increasing your blessings ten-fold."

"Nonsense!" Cuaodh grumbles. "No one is a sensible soldier for years and then suddenly runs off to his mother. Something happened here."

Nessa shuffles. I meet her eyes, and her expression is like after we fought the boar. The horror of it all.

"It's probably something that doesn't matter to you or to me." Cordelia cocks her head, fiddles with her hair. "He got jilted by a girl at the bonfire or some such. Those are the things boys his age get upset about."

Cuaodh considers.

"Ple-eeease," Cordelia whines, then sighs gustily.

"I could give him a chance to earn you," Cuaodh growls, spearing me with a look. "One year of hard labor outside the village, and then one year working in the castle. Hauling water, chopping wood, fixing the walls. After that, if he shows his loyalty and you still want him—if you still remember him—he can be assigned to your guard."

There are men who both serve in the palace guards while also completing their warrior training; after all, these are exactly the types of positions we train for. But what Cuaodh suggests is expelling me from everything. I would lose my place in the warrior class. My library.

And what if Cordelia no longer cared about a servant boy when it's over?

"Dad-dyyyy." Cordelia sighs and rolls her eyes, all her theatrics in full force. "You haven't been listening to me! I am a woman now. Look behind me!" She sweeps her arm towards the blank wall. "No one. No one to protect me!"

"Every soldier in this land will protect you," Cuaodh says. "I will let no one harm a hair on your head."

"Ha! You're not even here half the time. And you're far too busy. I want Rian!"

Cuaodh sets his mouth in a hard line.

Cordelia drums her feet. "What are you doing, Daddy? Remember I can't see you! I don't have any protections. I'm helpless!"

"He must prove himself worthy of you." Cuaodh glares at me. "Two years."

"Ugh!" Cordelia hops down from her chair and makes her way towards her father, doing the fish thing with her arms again, like she did when she was younger.

I had doubted, but now I'm sure of her. Cordelia knows her way around this room.

So if she is play-acting, I must help. I leap to my feet and burst over to her, pausing a respectful step away. The chains clatter on the floor behind me, so I know she knows exactly where I am. Without speaking, I make a low bow and extend my arm.

Flawlessly, Cordelia's hand lands upon my wrist. She bursts into a wide smile, bathing the room in her sunshine. "Forward!" she cries. "Bring me to my father!"

I lead her to her father's throne, setting her little hand on the armrest. I step away, bow, and clasp my hands behind my back. The very picture of awaiting my next orders.

"Daddy." Cordelia flutters her eyelids, but pitches her voice to carry. "In two years, you shall be preparing my wedding feast. But I am pretty now, and pretty is dangerous, is it not?" Flutter, flutter, head tilt, hands clasped. "I need a guard. And I will have Rian or no other."

The king grunts. "His hair shaved. His jewels confiscated. No more access to the training yard."

There is a collective gasp from the room, and I don't dare look towards Nessa. Honor means everything to her.

The "warrior" token will crumble now, and suddenly I realize that I didn't hate it. I hate the wars, but those won't disappear no matter if I can fight.

But Cordelia clicks her tongue and leans onto the throne. "It would be dishonor me if a common soldier has access to my private chambers. He must stay your foster son."

She's asking too much...but she is his darling.

Cuaodh hesitates.

Cordelia steps back, swooshes her skirts, and throws back her hair. Imperiously, she reaches a little hand into the air, and I obediently insert my wrist beneath it.

"He must train with your warriors," Cordelia announces. "The druids have said he is destined to be a hero, and I want a hero for my personal guard!"

"Do you get everything you want?" the king asks, as though he is not quite sure.

Cordelia raises her little chin. "When I turn fifteen, I will give up everything to submit in marriage to whoever you choose. If I am beautiful and you are strong, then you can double your kingdom with that one alliance. I will please my husband, no matter who he is, because that is my duty to you, and I ask for so little in return, Daddy! Just Rian as my guard. That's all."

"I give you dresses and jewels!"

"Those are for your sake, to make me look desirable. I can't even see them."

"I give you everything you want."

"Well then, it's settled!" Cordelia swings forward, letting me support her, and laughs.

The king glowers. "These are questions of men and loyalty and honor. Far beyond the ken of a girl-child."

Cordelia narrows her eyes. "I. Want. Rian."

Cuaodh looks at her, then me, and sets his jaw as he frowns at the far wall, beyond us both.

My arm is held out stiff, supporting the princess, who keeps her blank gaze fixed slightly to the wrong side of her father. I hardly dare breathe, waiting to be thrown out of the walls, worrying that Cordelia's demands will make everything worse.

The king flings his hand to the side, dismissive. He still stares at the wall, his jaw fixed.

"You heard the girl!" he roars. "Take off the chains! No foster son of mine will be treated with this indignity."

The room rustles with a collective gasp, but Cordelia and I do not startle. She lifts her chin, a tiny smile in place.

I lead her back to her chair. I hold my shoulders high and do not look to the right or the left, because that's all I can think to do.

***

Within hours, everything goes back to the way it was. Like I had just read a scene in a book about a prisoner and a slave collar.

I am clean, fed, and back in the private room that I was assigned for the second half of my training. I have sparred with the other squires, reported to the head of the castle guards, and acknowledged my own direct reports. My erstwhile guards have been sent back up towards the mountains to retrieve my jewelry from the magistrate, and the king has given me more so that no one can doubt that the princess's guard is a successful warrior.

I am too emotionally exhausted to visit my library. I did not know such a thing was possible, especially when I was so certain I'd lost it.

Besides, I am ashamed. I tried to argue with the fates and see where it got me.

Everything goes back to the way it was, but I am changed.

15 YEARS OLD

CHAPTER TWELVE

The year I am fifteen years old, I finally hit my growth. It seems like the cobbler must make me new shoes every month, and the training master shakes his head and says he will only let me use loaner swords until I am done with this growing nonsense. My shoulders strain the loose seams in my tunica and léine, and I can carry more and run faster. My black hair flows halfway down my back and Cordelia pays for bronze beads to be braided in, and I am relieved that the king did not shave my head.

My appearance brings honor to Cordelia. She tells me to stand in the middle of the room so the ladies can tell her how I look, which I find embarrassing but I know that to her mind is a compliment. The ladies flutter their eyelashes at me, and I know this is a compliment too—although I'm not about to soil my own nest by flirting with the girls who are my daily working companions. Cordelia spends her money on fine fabrics and silver jewelry for all of us, and we make an elegant procession with our tiny spitfire sashaying in the lead.

Nessa despises Cordelia; I don't know why. Nessa tells me that she has heard for a fact that the little princess has not started her courses, and all her tantrums about getting her own court was just selfish posing.

"You shouldn't be lowering yourself to work for a spoiled brat like that," she spits. "When I have my fianna, I will hire you immediately. You will be my first knight, earning battle trophies right and left!"

"But I am not yet a knight," I avoid mentioning that Nessa doesn't have a fianna, she had no way to save me from Cuaodh's anger, and that she herself is working as for Ardgar. If we're criticizing the royal family, I don't think much of him, either.

Cordelia may not have her courses—or she may, I really don't care—but she is growing up. She waves away the stories about Anne Shirley and Pippi Longstocking, and my library starts offering something very different on her shelf.

She likes what they call "horror." Green eyes on the covers, haunted houses, serial murders, lurking vampires. I have long made it my policy to read a few chapters in a book for her before I settle into my own stories, and then work through telling them out loud when I see her. Well, now I see Cordelia every day, and her books give me nightmares.

So I wrap *Frankenstein* and *Carrie* in a cloth with purple daisies, and bring them away with me in the morning. The library always has more books, and new ones. I think they're coming from another place and time, and when they vanish, I assume they are just going back again. I haven't seen *The Borrowers* or *The Mixed-Up Files of Basil E. Frankweiler* for years now.

But just to take extra care of the books outside the library, I stitch the colorful cloth into a bag, and ask the druids to put a spell on it, to protect anything that is inside. I have plenty to offer for the spell; I am already one of the richest men in Theastír.

In the late afternoons, I tell stories to Cordelia and her ladies. All our hands are supposedly busy, but some of the ladies are frozen in place as the story creeps towards yet another gory death. Cordelia hems with quick fingers and a small smile.

"She's a monster herself," Nessa says, after she asks me to tell her a story and then begs me to stop. "Only a heart of evil could appreciate such evil deeds."

I shrug. "The princess has always liked intense emotions."

"She's cataloguing ways to kill us all!"

I think if these books actually taught innocent women to build monsters and drink blood, someone would have stopped making them long ago. Or...far in the future. I wouldn't have them, at any rate.

As for myself, the books are the only thing that understands me, and I retreat more deeply into my personal world. When Cuaodh has visitors and feasts, I must attend Cordelia for the night. When the training master leads night drills, I attend those too, and when Nessa is free sometimes we stay up late talking, although there remains a distance between us—something that has never come back after that night in the hall.

But if no one requires me, I retire to my library and I lose myself in books. The time pauses and I read until exhaustion, desperate to keep the real world away.

I read Haruki Murakami and Jack Kerouac; *The Bell Jar* and *The Color Purple*. I spend a long time with *To Kill a Mockingbird* and understand why it didn't come to me a few years ago, even though Scout is a little girl. I raise my face and can practically feel the wind on Jane Eyre's heaths, and then lose myself in the jungle heat of *One Hundred Years of Solitude*.

There is a physical Rian and a shadow Rian. The physical Rian grows taller and wears bronze beads in his hair; defeats older knights in training drills and wins awards from visiting lords.

But Shadow Rian has all the feelings and never belongs.

***

Princess Cordelia is learning to entertain her father's guests, but she refuses to travel to visit other kings. At home, she has memorized all the rooms and forbidden the servants to move the furniture, so she moves with confidence. That's how she wants to be seen, bold and pretty.

A couple of times, I am sent on trips with the Family. With Cordelia back home with her women, and Ardgar busy with courting *his* women, Nessa and I have time together. It's been over a year since our argument, and we've learned to avoid certain subjects and find a new rapport. We don't mention it, but we still are both outsiders, and neither of us have real friends among the other warriors.

Nessa has learned of an enclave of women druids in Ui Néill, and asks for a day's outing for both of us. We stride along the road, talking and joking, and other passers-by give us a wide berth. I know we're striking, with gleaming swords at our hips and gold sparkling on our hair and fingers. I'm as tall as Nessa, now, and I'm worried that I'm going to grow too much and lose the fighting advantages of being fast and compact.

The women druids live in a series of stone houses built into the hills. I wait respectfully while Nessa completes her transactions, looking around and imaging what stories might take place here. She bargains for a knife encoded with spells, a handful of white stones, and has her fortune told.

"Do you want yours too, while we're here?" Nessa asks me.

I know my fortune, or at least the five ivory fates that are left for me. "The druids told it for me when I was ten," I say truthfully. I don't mention that I have long since discarded their words. I am crafting my own future.

The women druids of Ui Néill warn us that it is too late and dangerous to walk back to the village, and offer us a tiny hut built into an oak. Very tiny.

"Do you need a second room?" they ask Nessa.

She shrugs. "As long as two palettes can fit, it doesn't matter."

So after dinner, we bathe and lay down side by side.

She's cheerful, chatting happily about her fianna. The one that doesn't exist yet, but she's so sure it will. I let her plans wash over me, thinking about how there are two Nessas, too. One of them, I know so well—her laughter and the way she feints to the left in battle. But I still don't know why she wants revenge on the druid Cathbad, or in what country she was born a princess, or how she will raise the funds to pay for a fianna.

"What about Ardgar?" I interrupt.

"What about him?" Nessa sounds only sleepy, not defensive.

"You're sleeping with him...?"

She shrugs, brushing my shoulder. "He gives me what I want. What does it matter to you?" Like the long-ago Nessa in her stillroom, she is not judging but curious about my meaning.

"It means something to me because *you* mean something to me," I answer, finding my words slowly. I sense that it is very important to make Nessa understand that I do not crave her body. "I want a man to treat you well. How do...do you like it? Does he give you any joy?"

Nessa shrugs again. "It's bodies. They move together. Sometimes there's joy, I guess, the same way you feel good after you have a good fight."

When I find a woman, I don't want loving her to feel like a good fight. "And...a baby, Nessa? Do you have any...?"

Nessa goes still. "Ardgar doesn't want a child on me any more than I want to deal with a brat. He takes precautions."

We lay in the dark for a while. I try to think of any questions that she might answer, but I sense that this was as deep as she'll go.

"I just want you to be happy," I say finally.

"I will be," she answers. "Just as soon as I get my fianna. I'll be happy as a dove in her cote when as I watch Cathbad writhe in pain and draw his last, shuddering, bloody breath."

Yup. Nessa's definitely done with emotional conversation for one night.

***

A man tries to assassinate the princess and I kill him.

I'm shocked how easily it happens. It's the festival of Lughnasadh and the castle is full of visitors, so I trail Cordelia everywhere. She is turning fourteen years old, and she flirts and flutters and giggles, and I thought I was bored. But I see the movement out of the corner of my eye, and before I can think twice I have knocked Cordelia behind a chair and dealt with the man. The other guards don't even have time to raise their spears.

King Cuaodh puts me beside him at the feast afterward and gives me the best cuts of meat. It drives the other kings mad with jealousy, but anyone at our castle could have told them that Cordelia always comes first with him. Tonight, I'm just the conduit for his wild, desperate love...and I can't wait to leave.

It's most of the way till morning when the King Cuaodh goes to bed, but still I go down to my library. I glide my hands across the smooth wood, turn the gas lamps on and off (the vases with glass hats are called lamps, I now know), fluff the pillows and straighten the coverlet. Just to reassure myself that this is here, I am here, this is my place.

I stare in the fire, too unsettled to read. Or am I?

I used to vomit after battle, wracked by with nightmares about the pain my sword might have caused. I used to think about the men's families. This afternoon, I didn't hesitate. His blade was stained with poison and heading straight for Cordelia, but I am stronger and faster, so I killed him.

I test my mind. My thoughts. My nightmares.

Yup, I would do it again.

No, I don't want to puke.

Maybe growing up into warrior wouldn't be horrible. Perhaps I could do good in the world that way, because the gods know I am good with a blade.

High on the feeling, I open the lid of the velvet table by myself. I glance at the sconce, but Dreoilín does not appear.

I slide the armlet up my bare skin, surprised how loose it is still. Then I study the ivory figures, holding each one in my hand, seeing how it makes me feel.

The lover.

The leader.

The warrior.

The magistrate.

The scholar.

The dead man was important. The reason I killed for Cordelia is important—I am not even sure I like her, but I am sure she deserves her chance at life. The reason I may or may not follow Nessa is important; I do like Nessa, but I can't imagine living my life powered only by the desire for revenge.

I run my finger over the figures one more time, then close the table. There's nothing else I can do. I bank the fire and climb into bed.

CHAPTER THIRTEEN

At Samhain, Nessa dresses in all her finery and goes down on her knees to King Cuaodh. She begs him to release her from his service so she can claim her birthright, vowing before everyone that she will never raise her sword against any of his people.

From Ardgar's stormy expression, I guess that he didn't know his lover was leaving. Clearly he only cares about her spear and her bed—this isn't a surprise to anyone who ever bothers to have a conversation with her.

But the king is delighted with Nessa, making a long speech in praise of her beauty and her prowess as a warrior. He declares that he is proud to have trained her, and he has full faith that she will defeat her enemy—who is, of course, his enemy as well—and find her own place as a great queen. There is much cheering.

That night, I go upstairs to my lonely little room, because I expect that Nessa will want to talk.

I'm right.

"Move over," she hisses. "It's freezing."

I tuck my furs around my back and press up against the wall, making space for her. It's a narrow bed, but we're both skinny. Nessa is all elbows and knees and little burst of impatience.

"I'll miss you," I risk saying.

She ignores this. "Listen. I know you're not old enough to leave, but it was time for me. So about Ardgar?" She rolls on her side, her eyes boring into me.

"What about him?"

She snorts. "They're planning his wedding. He's only nineteen, but he wants to be chosen as Cuaodh's heir so he's ready to consolidate his power. That's why he's leaving right after this, to finish the negotiations."

"Leaving without you."

"He wants me to come along! Can you believe it?" Nessa flops on her back, pulls up her knees, tugs the covers over, and then puts them all back down again.

"Stay as his..."

"His everything. I don't care if he wants to screw me." Her voice is hard. "It doesn't matter to me. But he's willing to take some innocent girl to wife, and screw her *and* me. Having a concubine is one thing, but having two princesses at one time is just an *insult*."

So she does care about the way Ardgar has treated her.

"I'm sorry you don't have a father to defend your honor, but I could fight him for you," I say, keeping my tone teasing so she can take it the way she will.

She laughs. "I'd like to see that! He was the best knight in his class, but I think you'd beat him. You're getting good."

"You could still beat me."

"I could. I can beat Ardgar, too."

I wait. "Do you want me to challenge him? I will."

"Nah." She adjusts the pillow and turns back on her side, facing me. "It's not worth it. You'd just hurt your political chances, and he's still the prince. Just an angry prince."

"Like an angry badger?"

She giggles. "*Exactly* like an angry badger."

"You still think I could be a leader? You used to tell me I was bad at it, not talking to the boys and stuff." But still, the astragali didn't take it away.

"You're the calm, silent type. But the men envy you, and the boys follow you, and the women want you. Of course you could be a leader."

Could I? Nessa was born to be a leader; she's just been preparing all these years. In our world, leaders have to be warriors first.

Then I remember the ivory heart-and-circlet. That's the other way to do it; I could be the warrior while my wife made the decisions. That sounds easier, and more like me.

"I came up with a present for you," Nessa says. "Look."

Nessa wriggles around, pulling something out of her pocket. She presses it into my hand; it's round and smooth. A chain. A pendant.

"What is it?" Pendants are usually spelled, and most often worn by children.

"Look! Oh, I need light. I'll have to show you." She hops out of bed and produces a softly glowing lamp.

It's a magical light, not a real flame. Nessa has been busy.

I sit up and hold my pendant near it. It's a moonstone, swirling slightly like milk.

Nessa shows me a similar one, hanging beneath her robes. "Look, they're connected together. I have a couple more, too. They're for my fianna. With that"—she taps mine—"you'll always be able to find me. Let's try."

We experiment for a few minutes. If I hold the moonstone by the chain and think about Nessa very hard, then it twitches lightly in her direction. Since my room is so small, she makes me try it down the hallway until I can figure out which way she's gone, then up and down the stairs. At that point I put down my foot and say we're both cold and tired.

I wondered if she would return to her room, but Nessa climbs back into my bed. She's not as careful with her limbs this time, and she rests slightly against my chest and knee. It reminds me of sleeping with my next-in-age sister, running all day, melting together at night.

I want to protect her, the way I do for Cordelia. I want to knock away the men who would hurt her, and give Nessa her own space where she is safe—both from the men with swords and the ones who make jokes about her body. I'm not sure which is worse.

But Nessa doesn't want to be protected. So I settle for this, one last night of being close. Of knowing that she trusts me enough to let her elbow sag against my chest.

"I'm going to miss you, too," Nessa says.

"I always wanted your story," I answer.

She is silent for a long time, but I can tell by her breathing she is still awake.

"Cuaodh knows, but I don't tell it any more," she says, finally. "That was the deal we made, that I would join his squires and start all over again. Assa is gone."

I shift on the mattress, getting comfortable. Focusing on her.

"I was named Assa," she tells me. "Assa—the easy, the good. My parents loved me as much as Cuaodh adores his daughter, but I rewarded them with my diligence. I practiced the harp, I spun the finest thread, I helped with healing in the village."

Assa had her own figurines, then. Her own drawer full of possibility. And here was the harp she mentioned, years ago when I told her my story.

"I did so well, with so many things, my parents wanted to give me every opportunity to learn. So they sent me to foster at the Loch na Eagna, with the twelve Fir na Eagna—the men of wisdom. I lived there for five years."

Her voice breaks. Almost unconsciously, my fingers curl around hers, and she holds on tightly. The way Cordelia did years ago, when she was still scared of her blindness.

"I did everything they asked. I studied one task with each of them, feeling like the tiniest beginner next to their wisdom. I learned music and history and painting and weaving and beekeeping and...oh, it doesn't matter." She pulls away from me, flopping so her back is to me. "The raids came through now and again. We retreated behind the walls, we had guards. My foster fathers told me to hide in a certain cubby, under the stairs in our tower. I always did. And then..."

I can guess what's coming next—why she wants revenge. "Cathbad?"

She grunts the affirmative. "All twelve. All..."

She can't say it. Nessa, the fearless warrior, can't manage the word "killed."

After a while, she sighs and rustles and twitches the blankets and turns over to face me. "I was the only one left, but some farmers came the next day and found me. Apparently fever went through my father's kingdom, and my cousin was on the throne. The farmers thought he wouldn't be very happy to find out I was still alive, so they brought me along with to their own king. That was Cuaodh, who remembered me from when my mother and I stayed with him one winter. So—it doesn't matter. Anyways. I made the deal with him, and joined his squires. He oversaw my training, and he has kept my mother's jewelry for me, until I'm ready to make use of it. And now I am! That's my story. Here I go, off to start my own fianna!"

"And your name?" I ask.

She stiffens again. "Ni-Assa. Not easy, not good. I became a warrior. I became..."

I can sense her smile in the dark, and she curls up, nestling into the pillow and bumping her knees into mine.

"I became trouble," says Nessa mac Eochaid.

I smile too, and tuck the furs around her shoulder, not quite touching her. I can imagine it; Nessa and her twelve ivory figures. Cathbad messed up her board, so Nessa crumbled eleven herself. There's been only one left, long before she turned eighteen.

Nessa is a warrior—and she's trouble for anyone who crosses her.

***

Without Nessa, the castle is cold, and I am grumpy. Cordelia tries to tease me into a good mood but I retreat into formality. In the training yard, I accidentally rip the padded armor when we are dueling for first touch.

I can't wait to retreat into my library that night, but of course Dreoilín is waiting for me.

I bow respectfully, but I do not open the table when she flutters eagerly. I have some questions first.

"Why are there no books about war?" I ask her. "I know it happens in these other worlds, like when the Pendergast children are staying in the countryside and find Narnia. But I've searched, and there's no books about tactics or weapons, or even stories set in wartime."

Dreoilín cocks her head.

Maybe she won't even answer, but I'm tired of all these people who say do this, do that. At some point, either they like who I am or they don't.

"It's too close to your own life," she says finally, hesitant. "I don't really understand how it works, but that's the rule. You can learn, but you can't take the answers from another time."

There is a rule? "You mean...there are others like me?"

"Well!" Dreoilín swings back her hair, rather like Cordelia but green. "I happen to think you're pretty special, myself. But that might be because you are *my* human, so I'm rather vain about you."

When I first came here, I would have been terrified to think that I belong to a faerie. But now I am only amused—not because I don't take the fae seriously, even ones who are only the size of my hand. I certainly do. But it's getting a little funny how many people think they own me, and they're all wrong. Shadow Rian cannot be held.

"But there are other libraries? Other youths with their own astragali in their hands?"

"I should think not!" Dreoilín exclaims. "I came up with the library myself! I spent years searching for the right thing, as soon as you were born and assigned to me!"

"Well...thank you. I really like it." I'm really miffed now. "Does...every person have their own faerie? And—"

"Don't be foolish. You know most people don't have anything to do with the fae. I got in"—she flutters and blushes a darker green—"just a wee bit of trouble. And so I was assigned a person to keep me busy. I could have kidnapped you or done your chores at night, but I thought this would be more interesting."

"This is very interesting, to be sure."

She preens and clucks.

"Where did you get this room from?" Does that person have a hole in their house, I wonder?

"It was nearby, and it finds the books itself. It's *time* that folds and shimmers, not *land*. I couldn't have brought you a Greek library, even if you wanted one."

"I...think this one is just fine. Excellent." I decide not to get any more technical, although I don't understand. Probably what's confusing for humans is as clear as day to her.

"But you asked about people, didn't you?" Dreoilín chitters. "Yes, people go through the Veil. You're probably met one, although you didn't know it. Once you have your adult fate, your armband will take you through."

"Like—the druids? Do they come through the Veil? Maybe the special ones, where Nessa bought the moonstones?"

"I wouldn't know, I don't pay the least attention to druids," Dreoilín answers airily. "It's more likely to be the people who do things."

I know some druids who would be devastated to hear this perspective.

"Speaking of which!" Dreoilín flutters so hard she ascends. "Open the table! Roll the astragali! Let's see your new fate—and then tell me all about your year. Oh, I can't wait to hear! This is the very best part, hurry!"

I open the lid, but don't notice any sense of foreboding. Just exhaustion, overlaid with amusement.

I cast the dice and wait.

Almost immediately, the set of scales dissolves.

"The magistrate," Dreoilín says thoughtfully. "It's a position of power and respect, and would have allowed you the family you desire. But it's a position of judgement, and you do not judge. You have not tried to train Cordelia to be calm and wise; you simply admired her determination and imagination. You have not tried to convince Nessa to give up on her plans to lead a fianna, although you know how men will try to turn her into a sexual object. You have suffered Cuaodh at his worst, but you still respect him for what he does well."

"But that doesn't mean anything!" I cry. "I couldn't have changed those people if I wanted. I can't make anyone be who they are not!"

Dreoilín grins, showing all her shiny teeth. "And those, my little chick, are not the words of a future magistrate."

"They're not," I agree. I'm ready to move on, touching the remaining four figures. This is the first time that I haven't immediately regretted the one that disappears. I can see how that would have left the most time for an ordinary life and family, but the others suit me more.

The warrior, of course. The expectation everyone has for me.

The lover; being half of something greater than myself, like I have supported Nessa and Cordelia.

The leader, where I could make the greatest difference.

And the scholar. After the books I have read, I now understand this one. It is not a withdrawal from the world, it is digging more deeply into the human psyche, which is the one place we truly touch people. As a scholar, I could change the world from the inside. By spreading understanding, I could spread the peace I yearn for—not immediately, but slowly and surely.

Justice. Patience. Understanding. It sounds good.

"Now!" Dreoilín sings her wren trills. "Tell me about your year! You are growing so big and handsome! Do tell, do tell!"

I hide a smile. "Most certainly. But first, I need a cup of tea."

Dreoilín flutters about the room, turning somersaults in the air, watching my every motion. I don't mind making her wait. I know that she's seen everything, it's just that the joy is in the story.

I happen to agree, myself.

16 YEARS OLD

CHAPTER FOURTEEN

The next time I come back to the library, I speak to it firmly.

"Thank you very much for all your excellent books," I tell the bookshelves. "They have been beautiful and thought-provoking, not to mention contain many fascinating lessons for murder. But that is quite enough of that. What else is there to read?"

I start to make tea, but turn back. "And as for Cordelia, worry a little less about her. What about all the other ladies in waiting? You are such a clever library, why don't you find some stories they would like."

I go straight to bed, to give it a chance to settle itself, then stay away for a day, in case its feelings are hurt.

When I return, there is a P.G. Wodehouse waiting on the shelf. The illustration is simple and playful, yet somehow not childish, and I can't wait to dive in.

***

The library outdoes itself and produces actual plays for the princess and her ladies. It takes me an entire week to figure out how they work, and that there are unbound pages for each lady-in-waiting, with colors for the different characters. I hesitate for a few more days, worried this is too unbelievable, or it won't work, or they will all run off and tell their fathers.

I decide to trust the library and that women know how to keep secrets. One rainy afternoon, when it is too wet for the practice yard and too dark for fine sewing, I close the women's solar and distribute the little unbound books. The girls touch them, curious.

"There are stories in here," I tell them. "I know it doesn't look like much of anything when you first see it. But don't think too hard, and just look at the little black marks. The story comes into your mind, like someone is speaking."

Several giggle, and I think it won't work. But someone cries out, and someone else begins saying words. She is not really *speaking* them, she is saying them in a row like clumsy beads. But then someone else starts saying her part, and she makes sense of it.

"Wait wait!" cries Cordelia. "Where's mine? I will be the best! I am *good* at saying words out loud!"

"I think—that is—"

"My lady, the rest of us shall say the story for your joy and benefit," one of the ladies interrupts me smoothly.

"But—" Cordelia drops her head. She knows the one argument she can never win is about her eyesight.

"I have one more," I offer tentatively. "You could touch it."

She perks up. "I definitely want to touch it! I will understand it then."

Books don't work that way, although this one is oddly stiff. I don't remember it being like that. I pass it to her, and put my hands on hers to show her how to turn the pages.

"Here are the words," I say. "They look like little black dots, but—"

"I   can   feel   them!"   Cordelia   cries. "In—the—bleak—midwinter—I—was... Listen to that, Rian! It's just like you said, the words came into my head."

I am beyond amazed. The books have a little texture, but I don't know how she can—still talking, both about how fascinating this is and reading her lines, Cordelia pulls my hand towards her book, showing me in the only way she can. And she's right! Her book is something different. It has little raised dots, and when I look closely I can see they are arranged in patterns. It makes no sense to either my eyes or my fingers, but when Cordelia touches it, the story comes into her head just as well as the printed words do for mine.

Her victory is so intense that it freezes my body in place and brings tears to my eyes. She used to dance and ululate when we got to a good place in the story; now she just sits very upright, her face sparkling as she says each line. I am tempted to grab her hands and swing her around, letting our bodies free in dance and joy.

But we are growing up now, so I let her ladies praise her, standing off to the side, smiling to myself. Oddly lonely.

Through that long winter, I find one play and another, and distribute the parts among Cordelia and her ladies-in-waiting. Now, instead of being the center of attention, I listen to them perform, which is definitely easier. I have more time to read my own books at night.

It is clear now that the supply of books is infinite, so I get pickier with them. The library provides a variety of books which are clearly intended to be funny, and I like some better than others. *Three Men In a Boat* is a pleasant meander, but I find David Sedaris too bitter. Erma Bombeck and Patrick McManus I absolutely adore, especially the stories of a bumbling boy trying to fish and explore in the woods. At least we can be friends when I'm reading. These books feel like walking into a stranger's house and listening to them ramble on about everyone in the village whom you have never met, and that feels...friendly.

Then one evening, the book I find has the same bright cheerful colors, and my eyes catch the words "brilliant and funny and the most delightful writer" so it sounds like the others. There is a man kissing a girl on the front, and I don't look too carefully because I suppose it could be funny. But *Love, Theoretically* does not feel like a rambling story about someone's neighbors. It feels like I am right there, eating cheese with the main character and feeling her feelings, which is my favorite thing about really good books. I rustle through my cabinet, and indeed, it helpfully provides cheese for me to eat while I read. So I settle into my chair with my blanket and tea and cheese, and prepare to read as long as I can before my eyes close in spite of me.

And then...I come to a part that means I'm not falling asleep at all. Other books have mentioned bodies and kissing. But this has 63 pages (I go back and count) of things that the man does that make the lady feel wonderful. In great detail. Lots of detail. I read on, find even more scenes, finish the book, and go directly back to those scenes again.

Now I'm truly exhausted, and grateful that time doesn't go the regular way while I'm in my library, or it would probably be morning and I would have gotten no sleep and fail all my training drills in the morning. I'm going to be bad enough as it is; I don't usually read this long. I shuffle towards the bed, but manage to mumble my thanks for this new offering.

It's not that I didn't know about sex acts; the gods know that the squires and the guards both talk about them plenty. But I've never heard anyone talk about the *feelings*. I've longed for a wife of my own, but I haven't even known what it would be like.

Now that I've read Ali Hazelwood, I know what it would be like to fall in love.

***

By spring, Cordelia agrees to travel with her father. She is still extremely reluctant, and her entire retinue must come along. Concerned about both the previous attempt on her life and also how Cuaodh's increasing power makes her more of a target, I receive permission to hire two additional guards, so there is always someone near Cordelia. I search far and wide to find women who can use weapons, and teach them additional skills myself.

I keep close to the princess in crowds, and I assign the female guards her night shifts. That seems respectful.

With Cordelia is protected, I can take a little time for myself. There's a house in the center of Vodie where I have noticed people gather in the evenings, drink ale, and sometimes there is dancing. Maybe some of them women here will think that I'm handsome, and I like dancing. No one knows me here, so even if I embarrass myself I can just go home and do my job.

I don't know what to say, but being strong and silent seems to work out fine for the men in the Lisa Kleypas and Mary Balogh novels I've been reading lately. I walk through the gathering, pausing among the tables on the lawn.

I feel eyes watching me and hear feminine giggling, and this time I don't mind.

"Do you want to come and sit with us?" The girl smiles and pats the bench beside her, and her companion giggles and moves aside to make room for me.

"I don't mind if I do." My voice comes out deeper than I expected. I bow slightly, and then on second thought I kiss their hands. All the girls at the table giggle and offer me theirs, too. There are a couple young men on the other side, cuddling a pretty lady each, and they reach out their hands with the gesture of truce, which I return. One of them pours me some ale while the others introduce themselves.

They know what I am by my clothing and Cuaodh's family crest, so I ask about them. That's not hard, and soon I've got them talking and giggling about their families and their jobs. All the young people are friendly, the men and women both, but I'm here on a mission. I choose the girl on my right, the one who spoke first. I like that she picked me out, but she also has a sweet playful smile, and some nice soft curves brushing my arms and hip as we all eat and talk.

I turn to her, hiding my nerves under a cool smile, just like Sebastian, Lord St Vincent. "Do you want to…take a walk with me?" We don't have fancy balls and house parties like they do in *The Devil in Winter*.

But the pretty blonde is happy enough with what we have tonight—and what we make of it together.

***

That summer, we have no major clan war, but Cuaodh's outer villages are constantly harried by bandits. We're all tired, using the late hours of summer light to get into the next position instead of to rest.

One day when he is holding an audience, Cuaodh calls me forward in the throne room. I haven't been singled out since that awful day more than two years ago. So much has changed, but I still come forward with my shoulders high, looking neither to my right nor my left. My lord can do what he will, but I know that I have done everything that is honorable.

"I know you are young," Cuaodh announces, his voice filling the room, "but your training master has said you are besting even the other knights. We have need of your services to serve my people, Rian of Kilkirk."

He draws a sword from a shimmering cloth, and behind me, people cheer and ululate and cry out praises. I bow and accept the sword, turning it in my hands. It is forged with the finest techniques, which will hold up to endless work and sharpening. A perfect circle is on the hilt, which is forged in the particular style of Theastír's blacksmith. A pattern of winding leaves is etched into the blade, and I know this sword was created just for me, the quiet boy from the hill-country.

I swear my fealty, and Cuaodh puts his hands on either side of my face and kisses my forehead. I remember what Dreoilín said, that I saw Cuaodh at his very worst, retaliating in anger because his pride was hurt. He almost destroyed me, but I've seen his goodness and it weighs more than the bad. He works tirelessly to defend his common people; he took a chance on a farmer's son like me; he took in Nessa when she was orphaned and terrified.

"I continue your fosterage in name only, until you are eighteen and a fully a man in the eyes of every magistrate in the country," Cuaodh says. "But in this household, from this moment forward, you have full duties and responsibilities of a warrior. You will report to my generals now, instead of the training master."

"And the castle guard?" I ask. Am I being removed from my position with Cordelia?

"You have no guard to report to." But Cuaodh's eyes are sparkling, and he gestures beyond me.

The entire castle guard comes forward, their ranks neat behind the head of each division. Then they kneel—the Guard of the Gates, the Guard of the Doors, the Travel Guard, the Personal Guard of the King, the Prince, and my own two companions for the princess. I don't realize what is happening until the Head Guard hands me his keys.

"I'm an old man," he says, smiling, wrapping the keys between our hands as he holds mine tight. "I have known you were special ever since you were a wee lad with a great story. Welcome."

He steps back, leaving me alone at the front. Pride swells in my chest as the guards cheer, and I can see that they are happy that I am the one chosen to lead them now.

So I go down the line, accepting loyalty from each guard while the crowd ululates. I keep my palm flat and fingers raised, while they flick theirs in.

The ivory circlet downstairs flashes into my mind, and wonder if leadership has been my fate all along.

Chapter Fifteen

"Rian? I know you are here." Cordelia moves confidently through the dark.

"I got back at sunset. I was going to report to you in the morning, my lady." We are at the rear of the castle, towards the bathing rooms. I have just finished scrubbing off the dirt of travel and was looking forward to bed.

"But I have missed you. I wanted to say hello." Cordelia's voice is charming and petulant, affectations she does not usually bother with for me.

"Hello, Cordelia." I do not exhale even the ghost of a sigh, since she would hear it. I wait in the dark corridor, which is only polite so she knows where to find me.

But this time, she doesn't stop a polite distance away. She comes all the way to me, close enough that I smell her floral perfume and the honey on her breath. She rests her palms on my chest.

"I am wearing a blue and green checkered léine," I say, as though she just wants to "see" me with her hands. "My hair is wet and tied back. I have a scratch on my neck, but it's healing fine."

"You are taller than you used to be," she says. "And square across here." Her fingers flutter across my chest and shoulders, and she laughs. It's lower and richer than the giggles she uses on her father and the other men.

This time I let her feel my sigh. "I'm tall for a Fir Bolg, but ordinary height among the Milesians. Any man who trains with a sword has shoulders like this."

Cordelia touches my cheek. "You're still clean-shaven."

"I prefer it." My voice is curt. Warriors and nobles go either clean-shaven or wear a full beard; only ordinary people wear a mustache alone. "Cordelia, I will see you *tomorrow*."

"It's so busy tomorrow." Her fingertips brush across my jaw, down my neck.

I take her hand away, folding it firmly in mine. "We are not children anymore, Cordelia. This does not work."

"I know we are not children!" She snatches her hand back. "Next year I turn fifteen and I will have to marry. My father will choose someone important, so he will be old, and he will be a warlord so he will be stern and cruel! Have you seen those men?"

"Your father wants you happy. He will choose—"

"I just want to know what a kiss is like, Rian. I just want to kiss a handsome, kind man before I am bound in my fate."

Cordelia's fate—I had imagined the Family would more choices than any of us, but perhaps Cordelia never had many at all. Perhaps they crumbled years ago when she was the only princess who lived, and the last of her choices vanished with her eyesight. All but this one.

She slides her fingers to the back of my head, but I don't lean towards her.

"Please, Rian? You kiss other girls. I know you do."

"I do."

"Why not me, then?"

I don't answer. I move her hand away, again.

"But I am so lonely. And I like you. And I *trust* you." Her voice breaks on the word, and I know this is not Cordelia the flirt or Cordelia the calculating. Her wants are as deep and raw as mine.

"I'm sorry." I wish I could bring her to her own library—or maybe a theater. If we were in the one of the worlds that loves the stage, Cordelia would be admired for who she is. She could be bold and dramatic and pretend to be someone different every night, and everyone would think she was brilliant instead of spoiled.

"Kiss me. Please."

"No."

I wait for her to throw a tantrum, threaten to tell her father, fire me on the spot. Cordelia has a great deal of power over me.

She has both palms against my chest. Head bowed, leaning in slightly.

My hands hang at my sides.

"I wish I was other girls," she finally says, bitterly. Resigned. "I wish I could just go out and *do* things. I wish I could *see*."

I sigh. "I wish you could too, but I can't give you any of that."

"I know." Cordelia leans forward, onto her tiptoes, and aims her face as high as she can. I know she's given up, and I let her say goodbye in the way she needs. Her lips barely graze my chin. "Goodnight, Rian."

And the princess turns and walks away.

I am not sure I will see my childhood friend—the girl who asked for my help with the peas—ever again.

***

My birthday passes. Harvest fades into winter storms. Ardgar marries. I attend all the negotiations, either behind Cordelia or in my position as head of the palace guard. I take a lover from among the bride's ladies, although we both agree it is not forever and are careful to avoid pregnancy. In the evenings, I am relieved to escape to my library and the ever-more-broad selection of books I can find.

I miss Nessa. I hold the moonstone on its chain, and it twitches—slightly different directions but towards the north, which is to be expected. Most of Ireland is north of us. I figure this means she is still alive, but still on the move, which means Cathbad is still alive as well. Some days I am tempted to go to her, but I only care about protecting Nessa, not killing Cathbad. I am not sure she would be satisfied with that.

Dreoilín is late this year, and it gives me too much time to think. The leader, the lover, the warrior, the scholar. I am all these things, and I don't know what the astragali will choose—or decide I have chosen. I've made decisions this year—quit fighting the things that I'm good at.

When I slip away from the Yule festivities on the shortest night of the year, Dreoilín is huddled in front of the library fire. She is unusually subdued, wrapped in a cloak made of beech leaves.

"You are coming into yourself, Rian of Kilkirk," she says. "Whatever the dice choose, I am proud of you this year."

"What about you?" I ask. "You don't look well."

"It is nothing. I have been trapped in the winter cold, that's all." She shivers into the cloak, which rustles. Leaves go dry this time of year, so it's not much protection.

I bend to add logs to the fire, prodding it to send flames higher. I turn back to her.

"Who trapped you?" I ask, but she looks away and doesn't answer.

Instead of opening the table, I go through the chest in the corner. There, I thought I'd seen something big enough to warm Dreoilín. I ask her permission, then wrap her up in layers of cloth, and settle her in pillows on my squashy chair.

She is more fragile than she looks.

I make a strengthening tea, and pour some into a saucer for Dreoilín, and bring her a scone as well.

"Are you sure, Rian?" She cocks her head.

I remember all the stories where feeding a fae binds it to you, where once the pooka has a coat it can escape from the house where it had been bound to help.

But she's cold, and maybe sick.

"I am sure," I answer.

She eats and drinks and does not leave.

When her color seems more like leaves' new growth and she is asking me all about the festival tonight, I open the table. Dreoilín chitters and flutters, and while I am waiting for her to settle on the sconce, I slide on the unfinished armband. Somehow, it still doesn't fit.

"Do I really have that much more growing to do?" I spin it slightly on my bicep.

She trills laughter. "You have many years ahead of you. The chicks always think they are grown after they make their first flight."

I am somewhat insulted, but it's not worth arguing. Even Cuaodh said I was basically a man! I cradle the astragali in my hands, letting them slide back and forth.

The scholar, the leader, the lover, the warrior.

I roll.

Nothing happens.

I cradle each ivory figurine, and finally, finally, feel one crumble as my thumb slides across it.

"The lover!"

"Are you disappointed?"

"Just surprised. After all..." I think of the girl upstairs.

"Rian..." Dreoilín trills a song, and swoops from the sconce to land on my shoulder, fiddling with my hair.

Those are a lot of very sharp teeth very near my ear, so I pick her up gently and bring her back by the fire. I settle her in the chair and perch on the ottoman beside her.

"You could have had Cordelia," Dreoilín tells me. "Not just in your bed, but if you had given her a little of the love she craves, she would have fought her father for you. You're not a political match, but you're the most promising warrior he has. He would have eventually approved the marriage, and with his daughter always close and reminding him how valuable she is, Cuaodh may well have passed the crown to you."

I am so surprised I laugh, but then I remember the rumors my new lover tells me. Ardgar has been losing his temper with the wrong people. Cuaodh could choose another one of his sons, but they are in distant positions, and it is true that the king focuses on the people he sees frequently.

"And Nessa? You easily could have had Nessa. Cuaodh would have been delighted to loan you men to defeat her cousin and reinstate her to the throne, thus having a neighbor king so deeply beholden to him, but Nessa is young and clever and would outsmart him in the end. You thought of Nessa, but you never even suggested marriage to her."

"Because she wouldn't have wanted it! She wanted revenge, not her throne back."

"Nessa is a strategist. Unlike, clearly, yourself. And Rian..."

"What else?"

"You could have had me. I was bound to come back here by the solstice, even after the trouble I was in. You must have guessed I have a human form which would give you power among the humans. But instead, you fed me."

"Did you want to marry me?"

She rustles indignantly. "Of course not. You are a little chick. But I would have helped you if that was your fate."

I don't know what to say. I get us both more tea instead.

"None of those are love," I finally explain. "It's a trap. You never wanted me, but you would have served me. I could never give Cordelia the adoration she craves because I don't want her like that. And Nessa? She doesn't want anyone at all."

"So you think love is like your books? All charming coincidences and burning gazes?"

I stare into my tea. "No. But…"

I understand it then, although I'm too shy to put it into words. I want a partner who sees me. Who understands there is a Shadow Rian behind the man who moves so easily through the room. Who cares about the reasons why I do what I do; who will still accept me even if I make a mistake. Marrying any of the women in my life now would mean giving up on that forever.

Even though each woman likes me, I have never given any of them the real me. I have always been careful.

"I don't mind letting that one go," I say.

Dreoilín spreads her wings wide and laughs.

17 YEARS OLD

Chapter Sixteen

Since the scholar has made it through all these years of rolling the dice, I figure I had better try it out. I ask the library for more books, all kinds of books, hard ones as well as good stories.

One night, I find a small volume called *A Modest Proposal*. I start it happily enough, but then—the proposal is to eat the Irish children—my stomach roils and I throw the book across the room, heart pounding. The pages are crumpled where it lays on the floor. I have never treated a book badly, but this one I consider hurling in the fire.

Children. Children! Not meat. Not vegetables. Not fish. Children!

***

I crawl into bed and sob, partly for the story that I am slowly realizing is not real, and partly for my siblings who are very real. Some of them are nearly grown, marrying and starting their own farms. The Fir Bolg do not wait until we are eighteen. I love them, and I have missed so much of their lives.

That question leads to more, so while I am seventeen I make my way through Irish literature. There is no history, no explanation—I guess that would be too close to my reality. But from the different novels, I come to understand that Eire is defeated, subjugated, defined as a whole, and somehow rises again. I also find books by Maeve Binchy and Sally Rooney, and their Ireland seems just fine.

It's the scholars who kept it all going—and maybe, with the knowledge I have, I could be a scholar who helps history go a little more smoothly, at least for the children. The scholars held onto our Irish language and culture; they wrote things so that we could never be dismissed entirely. That's something worthwhile in the world, certainly.

I carry that knowledge with me as I go about my day, making friends among the older men. The other boys my age move away; Lugaid goes to serve another king, and I don't feel anything to see him leave, not even relief. He is too petty and foolish to matter to me any more. The retired head guard, it turns out, is somewhat of a philosopher himself, and he has a friend who is a retired bard. Some nights, the three of us sit around the fire talking about ideas. I wonder if the bard is one of the ones who has come through time; he speaks of things that aren't quite real. Yet. When I answer sensibly, he raises one eyebrow. We never speak of it, but we can talk of kings and countries and carriages together.

Meanwhile, there's a betrayal among the palace staff. I don't apprehend the traitor, but I help Cuaodh reorganize the ranks to prevent it from happening again. The training master brings in a new set of squires and I help with their lessons. Cuaodh calls me to his council room where he hears that Ardgar has been captured and jailed, and we are still debating strategy when another messenger arrives: it is his wife's father who has taken Ardgar. So I guess that new marriage has fallen apart already.

I listen while Cuaodh's lords and generals vent about all the mistakes Ardgar has made. I was not the only one who was angry about the way he treated Nessa, it turns out, although some shrug and think a weakness for women doesn't mean much at all. When it is time to make a decision, Cuaodh expects me to speak. My heart is skittering, but I keep my voice low and calm and give my perspective on how the proposed plans will affect the castle guard. After every man in the council room has spoken, Cuaodh rubs his hands over his face.

"I let him cool his heels in prison," he says, looking old and tired. "If he makes it out, maybe he will learn this lesson before it's too late. If not..." He sighs. "I have other sons."

The leader, the warrior, the scholar. I am seventeen, and I am all of them.

***

Cordelia celebrates her fifteenth birthday at Lughnasadh, and the rest of southern Eire celebrates by sending their unmarried kings and princes and generals. King Cuaodh calls home his next two sons, and those of us who were in the council room do not tell why. Theastír Castle is nothing but a parade of visitors, filling every spare room, camping on the lawns. Fist-fights break out in the meadows, and I am too exhausted to even bother to pick girls to flirt with. I never kiss the girls in our own village; it makes things too tricky later, once we learn how little we care about each other.

Well. I think most of them would be delighted to marry me if I made the slightest hint. But none of them have any particular interest in anything besides my face and wealthy prospects, and I find them boring quickly. None of the girls can have conversations like the old guard and the bard, or even Cordelia back when she talked freely to me. I am careful to set my expectations clearly, and there's plenty of girls who are happy with something quick and fun.

My position is tied to Cordelia, and everything is changing now. Soon she'll be wed, and her husband will hire her personal guard. Never mind the ivory fates; it's time for me to make some practical decisions.

During all the festivities and meetings, Cordelia sits at the high table, drumming her feet against her chair, listening to every word of her father's negotiations. I hate watching this, Cordelia's bright personality sealed away like amber. But it's not my business, so I seal myself away too; talking little, letting my face show less.

Not even two moons after her birthday, the engagement is announced. Princess Cordelia will marry King Móenach of the Vellabori. Like she predicted, he is gray-bearded and a known as a fierce warrior. But he also seems ready and willing to dote upon a new little wife, and he finds her sass and pouts adorable. He is vastly wealthy and offering her a very comfortable life.

Also, he hates me.

***

King Móenach of Vellabori wants a private meeting with me, Rian of Kilkirk, son of a farmer. My king spends two days negotiating the terms. Eventually, we meet: the door is closed but there is a bell is in the center of the room to ring in case of emergency; we leave our swords with the magistrates from both households, but everyone knows we each have multiple knives concealed about our persons. I don't know what Móenach wants, but I would strongly prefer not to have to use mine.

The door closes behind us. Móenach starts to speak, but spins on his heel and paces before a word leaves his mouth. Despite being slightly stooped at the shoulder, he is tall even for a Milesian, with a wide jaw and full hair. Right now, his eyes are wild. He reminds me of an injured animal—ready to lash out at any movement, irrational.

With my attention on him, I stand with my back to the wall. Shoulders up, looking neither to the right nor the left. Cordelia seems delighted with her match, which is as much as I ever wanted, so I have no quarrel with Móenach of Vellabori.

"You!" he finally snarls. "*You* are my wife's lover!"

Sherlock would have said "elementary, my dear Watson." I choose to bow slightly and keep my voice level. "I am not."

He snorts. "You have unbridled access to her private rooms. You are in charge of her guard, and made sure you are the only man on it. She has been seen kissing you farewell before you leave for battle."

"Yes. I am her foster brother, and if you ask your sources they will tell you that she has given me the good-luck kiss every year since we were children. It means no more than it did then."

He glances away, and I know this is exactly what his sources told him.

"But you have access to her rooms," he growls. "You spend hours there some days."

"With her ladies in waiting. We are never alone."

"Never, huh?"

"Never." I have been careful since that night in the corridor, but Cordelia has not asked me twice. "But I have greater evidence for you than just my word."

"Do you? Hah!" Móenach crosses his arms, glowering at me.

I do not like the role he has assigned to me—the little fool from the country—and his accusation is an impingement on my honor. Since I am *not* Cordelia's lover, and her night-time guards would corroborate this, I could call him out for single combat if I chose. I pace towards him, keeping my movements lithe and smooth like a big cat. Always facing him, never letting his hands out of view. If he reaches for his knife, I will be on him first. I am faster.

But it will be easier for everyone if I win this with my words.

"Listen, Móenach. I am not just a guard here, as you well know. If I wished, I could marry any woman in this castle, including Cordelia."

He startles at that.

"And let me tell you"—I circle him, slow and smooth—"if I were Cordelia's lover, then I would insist on marrying her myself." I let that sink in. "If I told her to, she would beg her father for me. Cuoadh wants my loyalty and would give me her hand if she begged. But you see"—I spread my own hands, wide and empty—"I have not asked. The Family has made a political connection instead, because *I am not her lover.*"

Móenach considers. Clearly, he's a slow thinker.

"Then you are on my side?" Móenach asks, finally.

What sides? My mind flips through possibilities, and I quickly decide that if Móenach wants me to reassure him then that is in the best interest of everyone involved. "Of course. We are two men who wish to protect Cordelia."

Móenach scratches his head. "Then—one warrior to another—whose child is she carrying?"

That's news to me, but it's not so surprising that she got her kisses; Cordelia always gets what she wants. Hm, she is not showing through her léine, but she did hurry the engagement. Midway, perhaps. "If you tell me what you know, I can help you find the answer."

He snorts like a bull. "She won't admit it. But as soon as the wedding date was announced, she came up with this plan to go directly to the woman druids at Ui Néill, and stay there for several months. For prayer and a greater understanding of womanhood, she so claims. But tell me!" He flings his hands into the air, pacing again. "Why would a new wife go directly to a community of druids, and only attend her husband months later? And then! I tell you—and *then!*" He has to shake his head and grumble for a few trips up and down the floor before he can speak. "I caught her by the waist and demanded one kiss. Her ladies were there and they"—he swooshes his hands, meaning they shooed him out—"but I could feel what I could feel. She's carrying."

Móenach is on his third wife; I don't doubt him. Cordelia has been moving differently lately, now that I think about it, but I have had no wives so I didn't put anything together.

I shake my head and cluck in empathy, thinking quickly. It will be a great embarrassment to everyone if the wedding is called off now. Móenach wants his trophy bride, Cordelia wants her life of luxury, and everyone wants to ally the kingdoms.

Cordelia saved me once. I will do one last thing for her.

"As one warrior to another," I reply, "it seems to me that you have about the best possible situation."

He turns to gape at me.

I shrug slightly. "For marrying a girl as pretty as her, that is."

"She's very pretty."

Good, he's already defensive about her. Cordelia can use that.

"But I don't see how this is good! It's another man's child! It's—"

"A healthy young woman, you can't ever really be sure she is celibate, can you? With your experience, you understand desire, I'm sure." And with my books, I can at least talk about it.

He sputters a general agreement.

"Really, the problem would arise if she were just a little bit pregnant, hm? Enough that it might be yours or it might not. It is her first; she might not even be sure, herself. But this way, she has made plans so you won't be raising another man's child!"

He considers this.

"Or what's even worse?" I go back to circling him. "If she were barren. You don't know what else the fever did besides her eyesight, do you?"

He jumps, and I can practically see the lightbulb spring on above his head—a joke between me and my books.

"So you have the proof that she can bear a child. And she has the proof that it's not yours." I spread my hands again. "She goes to Uí Néill, they place the baby in a safe home, then your lovely wife comes home to you with an empty belly and much gratitude." I lean closer. "And you know what?"

"What?"

"I have been to the druid women at Ui Néill. They will take good care of her, but when Cordelia returns to you, she will be very, very grateful for fine sheets and good wine. Very...grateful."

He likes that.

"It gives you a few more moons to get everything ready for her, besides," I add. "There are all kinds of ways you can set up your castle to make it welcoming for a blind woman."

"Her ladies-in-waiting have been explaining that," Móenach mutters. "You're right, it will take some time..."

"I have never been her lover, but I can give you some advice." I press onwards. "Warrior to warrior."

He nods again. "She's very young. I want to make sure she is not tempted to stray again, so—"

"So you must be very kind to her," I say firmly. "Here is one thing about Cordelia: she is loyal. If you give her what she wants, then she will not stray."

"Like a man?"

Like any human being, I think. "Somewhat," I say out loud. "But there is more you can do to care for her."

Now that he is thinking in terms of keeping his new wife in his bed, Móenach is eager to hear my advice.

"She's very delicate," I explain. "And you know women—they are very malleable in their thinking. So you must always explain everything to her. Discuss your plans in great detail, so she can understand them."

"I thought women did not care about such things. I could just send her presents and come to her room at night."

"Cordelia may not understand, but she will be flattered that you spend the time with her. Whoever her lover was, I am sure he talked to her a great deal. Women liked to be talked to. Cordelia especially."

Móenach sets his jaw. "I can talk to her as much as he ever did. I can do better!"

"I'm sure you can. You will have a great deal more time, after all. Talk to her at breakfast. Join her for stories in her solar in the afternoon."

"Stories?"

"Didn't you know how well Cordelia can tell stories? Ah, you are in for a treat."

"Can a blind woman tell stories?"

Whatever lightbulb is glowing above his head, it's not a very bright one.

"This one can," I assure him. "Now you have won her heart, and all her stories too. And her sons." It seems worthwhile to belabor the point a bit. "As long as you treat her well!"

"I will treat her at least as well as you have!" Móenach declares. And then, without even saying goodbye, he bursts out of the room and away.

I go to the window and push the horn frame out of the way, looking down at the back gardens. It is misting today, but there is the bench where Cordelia likes to sit in the sun.

"I've done the best I can," I say out loud, although she isn't there and she won't hear me. "He's going to tell you all about his political plans, which is the best chance I can give you to manipulate him. The more time he spends with you, the more he's going to like you, and the more he likes you, the more he wants to please you. You've got to run with that."

I drum my fingers on the stone sill, looking out over the world that has been my home. "If he listens to you tell stories," I say softly, "he might even fall in love with the real Cordelia. What more could anyone want?"

I turn to fetch my things, but pause and chuckle to myself. I flick my fingers out the window, a final salute to the girl who has tangled her youth with my own. "And, my crafty little princess...you've got a couple hundred ideas from my library, should you decide you have to kill him."

***

A couple hours later, one of the servants brings me to attend King Cuaodh. He is alone in the council room, and as soon as the door closes behind me his shoulders slump and he rubs his temples.

"I can't keep you on as a guard," he says immediately. "Móenach still doesn't like you. And did you know about my daughter?"

I sit at the table across from him. "I did not. But I don't guard her room at night."

"The other guards won't say anything at all, and I hardly blame them. Loyal to their mistress first." Cuaodh's tone is proud; even though it puts him at a disadvantage, he values loyalty above all.

"Is Móenach keeping the engagement?"

"Yes, but on the condition that I dismiss you. He's gotten sulkier as the afternoon goes on."

"And I make an easy target?"

"Yes—but never fear that I will desert you."

Again, I think. Desert me *again* as soon as I am not in your face, reminding you of my value.

"I'll just give you a position where Móenach can't see. For a little while. A few years. You are almost eighteen, are you not? Any day now."

"Any day," I agree.

"I know it seems like I am divesting you of honor," Cuaodh says hurriedly. "But I have something even better."

I raise my eyebrows.

"My son." Cuaodh drops his voice and leans forward. "Ardgar has escaped from prison. His wife has left him, but he is gathering men and has asked for my help."

"A fianna?" I ask.

"No, he has a fort." Cuaodh describes the place, a corner of his kingdom where I have patrolled sometimes. "I want to see how he does before I trust him with any more men. So I have agreed to send him a few, and I would like to send you as the leader."

"That's hardly a position worthy of my service," I point out. "I oversee dozens of soldiers on a daily basis, and an entire battalion in the summer battles. Now you're giving me one squadron, reporting to a disgraced prince?"

Cuaodh shakes his head and taps his own chest. "No. You're reporting to *me*."

I figure it out. "About your son."

He nods.

"You are sending me as a spy, into enemy territory."

He shrugs. "He is not precisely the enemy. Or if he is, you must tell me."

Some version of loyalty this is. "He is your son."

"So he has the most to gain from killing me. Or, if he is simply a fool, the greatest chance to ruin me."

I fold my hands and consider this. I think through the possibilities; Cuaodh against Móenach and Ardgar, the next two princes against Ardgar, Móenach who is just clever enough to know I'm a threat, Ardgar against everyone, Cordelia looking out for herself. I blame her the least, but they all make me sick.

"If you release me from my fosterage, I am joining Nessa's fianna," I tell him.

Cuaodh watches me for a long time. Like Sherlock Holmes, he is a smart man.

"I won't be able to change your mind," he says eventually.

"You won't."

We are silent again.

Cuaodh holds out his hand, one finger held in. It is the symbol of bargaining between equals. "Then make me promises about when and who you will fight. Whatever fianna you join, whatever king you serve, I will give you trade rights if you agree not to let your leader fight my men."

I put out my hand in the same symbol, and we spend the next few hours bargaining.

I gave Cordelia what I could. This is my last gift to my foster father, who in many ways is a good man.

#

I have packed everything before I go down to the library. I have been awarded a horse, and we will leave at first light.

Dreoilín is not here. I call her name, but wait only as long as it takes to put tea water in the kettle.

I open the table. I slide on the armlet, but it is still a little loose, and I don't know how to put on the terminals to keep those little screws from stabbing me. It doesn't matter; I'll leave it here.

I scoop up the astragali, and glance at the sconce. She's still not there. I don't know if the magic will work without her, but I don't have a choice.

I am choosing to leave, both the books and my position of power. I am planning to travel across the country alone, where I might be set upon by bandits and enslaved. I might lose all three ivory figurines tonight.

In truth, I am not afraid of the bandits, although I know I should be.

I roll the dice.

Immediately, the circlet crumbles. I expected as much; I could have negotiated a position of power in Móenach's household or Cuaodh's, or I could have surprised them all and fallen in with Ardgal, whom I fully expect to take at least one throne. I'm leaving it all, and the fates will never give me this opportunity again.

I touch the little ivory quill pen and scroll. I know what they are, now for certain.

They are cool and solid.

Nothing happens. I test the ivory sword, too. Solid.

I am still seventeen years old. Dreoilín told me I would not lose the last fate until I reach manhood, so maybe I have one more choice left.

One more chance to grow into the armlet.

18 YEARS OLD

CHAPTER SEVENTEEN

The autumn leaves go from tawny to dusky to empty, and I travel across Eire without incident.

If the scholar's fate is still with me, I am confident that the library will travel with me too. I keep the daisy bag wrapped deeply among my possessions, more treasured than my gold jewelry—which I do treasure; it will buy a house for me and my wife one day.

In the evenings, sitting at my little fire, I stitch three tiny padded bags. One for the ivory sword, one for the ivory scroll, and one for the astragali.

As for the armlet, it will follow me if it will, or I will live a normal man's life and death. I leave that to Dreoilín.

***

I can tell I am close when the moonstone is giving different nudges every minute or so; I hold it out in front of me as I lead the horse. A man jumps from behind a tree, but immediately registers what he sees and points to the moonstones in his earrings. We introduce ourselves, and he shows me to their hut, and teaches me the calls so the men in the fianna will know I am one of them.

It looks like Nessa's fianna is holed up in a little hut, halfway up a cliff in the territory of Cruachan, in north-central Eire.

But something is wrong. Not all the way wrong; this *is* Nessa's fianna, so Nessa is alive, and has secured a place for them to stay, which must mean she has a contract with a king in Cruachan for the winter. But it is not quite right.

I store my belongings where I am shown, spread my blankets on the palette I am allotted. I tether my horse where I am told, a meadow with a shed and two cows and stalls for another horse. Two cows is wealth. Something is right.

But I still have a bad prickle down my spine.

Evening comes early this time of year. The grizzled man and I both perk our heads when hear voices coming up the trail.

I go outside to wait, standing on an outcrop of rock so they will see me immediately. Better not to get killed, that way.

A small group comes around the corner. About eight of them, Nessa's bright hair and voice in the center. I recognize a couple other faces, and the insignia from a two royal houses. Younger sons. That's a good sign for her fianna, that they will come into power.

A man in red walks beside Nessa, laughing at her jokes. He puts out a hand in a proprietary air, which Nessa ignores. She does not look up until she is close to the house, and then her face lights in a smile—which she shuts down immediately.

"Rian of Kilkirk—welcome." She bows. "Please meet the others of our brotherhood." She gestures to the man in red, standing too close. "This is my husband. Cathbad."

CHAPTER EIGHTEEN

I spend my first year of manhood in an assortment of cramped and dirty hovels; chasing bandits, raiding enemy camps, and stealing cattle from one party and delivering them to another. It's the stupidest thing I've ever done, but I stay close to Nessa.

In the evenings, I bring out my books and read, telling the stories out loud if anyone wants to hear them. At first, Cathbad questions me often, but it soon becomes apparent that my magic begins and ends with taking books out of a bag covered with purple daisies, and he loses interest in me. As for the other men, accustomed to Cathbad's constant illusions, predictions, and potions, they find my "boxes of stories" hardly even worth mentioning. I don't have a squashy chair or gas lamps, but the library continues to deliver new books to my bag. No matter how tired I am, I read something every night. I need to show the fates that I am not abandoning that choice.

It will break my heart if I am stuck in this life forever. Everything else is gone, so I want to be a scholar.

It soon becomes clear that this state of petty mercenary work is temporary, at least for Nessa—and therefore myself. She, too, is increasing, although Cathbad puts an illusion on her whenever she leaves the camp. She appears vaguely masculine and distinctly not-pregnant, although if you're accustomed to watching sword work you can see how she's compensating for a large and inflexible midsection.

More than two moons pass before I manage to speak to Nessa alone. Our group is managing little boats when a sudden storm comes up and the other men are caught on the shore. Instead of going back, which would be the sensible thing, Nessa plunges her oars forward, towards an outcrop in the middle of the lake. By the time we stow the curragh behind a bush and creep into the cave, I understand that it is not Nessa who has been trying to delay us talking. She curls into my side like no time has passed since we said goodbye that night in my room.

"Some of the fianna I can trust, and some I can't, and I don't know which ones." Like always, Nessa leaps into the heart of the conversation. "My men! *My* fianna. Hmph."

I wrap my wool cloak around us both, and she presses up against me for warmth. I'm not sure where to go with this next. I have too many questions.

"You were right, weren't you?" she says. "I wanted to use my womanhood as a weapon, but it was always my weakness."

"You're not weak. It's just...you underestimate how much men desire to take down a strong woman. It draws them, like the most luscious herd of cattle."

She laughs, like I meant her to, and relaxes slightly against me.

"All he had to do was catch me alone," she says softly. "His magic was like a net, and his manhood...did the rest."

Anger boils inside me. "I should have married you."

She turns to smile at me. "I wouldn't have taken you, back then, although I should have. But I'd never make you happy, Rian."

I don't argue. It's true.

"But I'm getting something out of him, Rian."

She touches the swell of her belly. I wouldn't have thought a child would make her happy, but she is complex and—

"I made Cathbad tell me the prophecy of the day," she continues. "He said, 'this is a good day to conceive a king.' So! Cathbad gets me. I will get a king."

So much for motherly feelings; she's jumped straight to politics.

"Does Cathbad have a kingdom for your son to inherit?" I ask.

She shrugs. "No. I assume I'll have to kill him and marry someone else. But I'll keep Cathbad around long enough to make the child legitimate, and make sure he gives the baby a prophecy."

There are so many holes in this plan that I wouldn't trust anyone besides Nessa to carry it out.

***

When Nessa's time grows near, the leaves are same bright green as Dreoilín's hair and we are completing jobs along the River Conchobar. My flowered bag has been producing books like *The Midwife of Hope River*, *The Birth House*, and a whole set of *Call the Midwife*, but neither Nessa nor Cathbad shows any interest in connecting with a midwife who actually exists. I assume this means I'm meant to deliver the baby. I ask the bag multiple times if it could possibly, just maybe, find some non-fiction on the topic, but it just pops out with *Hello Stranger*. I don't even bother to open it; it's another Lisa Kleypas, so although the back cover promises a midwife, I'm sure I'll find good sex scenes and not the least bit of practical advice. Oh well.

Nessa wakes me in the early morning, her mouth pinched with pain, and we walk down to the river together. Cathbad hurries after us, pulling on his red cloak.

Nessa spins and puts her hands on her hips. "Well, husband? I demand a prophecy for our child. He is coming."

Cathbad glares at me, but I don't move from Nessa's side.

After some grumbling, he goes to work, arranging river rocks and checking the patterns of bird flight and such druid-like things. Nessa and I walk back and forth.

Given how much battle strategy she's still discussing, I think this is yet the early stages of labor.

Around mid-day, Cathbad joins us, pleased as punch. "My beloved!" He kisses her cheek.

Nessa makes a face.

"The powerful signs are all around us. If you can wait to deliver your baby until tomorrow, he will share a birthday with Jesus Christ!"

"Who's that?" she demands.

Cathbad purses his lips. It's clear he doesn't know.

"Never mind." Nessa waves him off. "It must be someone important. I can wait, and then besides, we get another prophecy for a new day."

"Nessa, if the baby is meant to be born soon, you're only hurting yourself and him by attempting to obstruct your body's needs," I protest. The books have taught me that much.

"Nonsense." Nessa takes a slow, painful breath. "My body obeys me. Now go away, both of you—I'm going to take a nap."

She naps, she eats, and Cathbad won't leave her alone. She makes it to nightfall with no more than gritting her teeth and grumbling, but her contractions increase with the darkness. She's determined to make it till the new day dawns, but I think the baby has other plans.

"Breathe through it," I suggest. I'm not sure what it means, but the midwives in the books say it.

Nessa promptly does the opposite. She holds her breath, staggers around trying to hop on one foot, and hoists her belly upwards with all her considerable strength.

I sit by a tree and sink my head into my hands, roiling with frustration. Maybe it's just as well we didn't call a real midwife. At least I'm used to Nessa's antics by now.

"You're nothing but trouble," I call across the meadow.

"That's me!" Nessa agrees.

Oh, by the gods' blades. Now she's propping her knees over a big log and flopping her shoulders on the ground. Yup, so she's as upside-down as possible.

I don't know if the baby cares about being upside-down, or if a first labor just goes slowly, but she manages to make it through the night. Cathbad has a good sleep in his tent, and then joins us in a little meadow by the river, where I can dab Nessa with cool water.

By then, I've spent hours rubbing her back, holding her up, and stroking her hair when she swears the baby is going to rip her apart from the inside. We are both sweaty, snotty, and bloody, but Cathbad is as fresh as a daisy. I'd happily kill him myself, just now, except I'm a little busy.

The first rays of sunlight tip over the trees. Nessa screams, lands backwards in my arms, and drops into a squat. I grunt, just barely keeping her from hitting the ground—and a squashy, bloody blob drops out of her and right into the shallow water.

Nessa collapses against me, silent.

I yell.

Cathbad snatches the baby from the water, ululating with joy. He attempts to raise the baby into the sunlight, and I lose my temper completely.

"They're still connected! Do as I say, now, or they're both going to die and you have nothing!"

To my surprise, Cathbad does. I lift Nessa in my arms, he carries the baby, and we lay them both on blankets safely away from the river. Nessa is clutching my hand and mumbling about the prophecy, so once she's all settled I send Cathbad off to do more of his ridiculous stones and birds and prophecies. I can't believe either of them care about such things at a moment like this. There's a real live baby, right here!

The baby is wiggling and kicking, and Nessa is asking me questions already. Good thing they both seem healthy, because I certainly don't know what I'm doing. I've managed to glean enough from the books to manage the basics, tie off the cord and sever it, deliver the placenta, and put the baby on Nessa's breast. I've got them all wrapped up and am lighting a fire when Cathbad comes back.

He's delighted. He spews out some long song about the son of a son and kings and fates. I light the fire, check on the baby, and fetch food for Nessa.

Nessa falls asleep smiling. I'm not sure which one of us has pleased her better.

***

I order that a tent is set up around Nessa, and make the men cook and heat bathing water and otherwise stay in the other camp. Cathbad still doesn't want anyone else alone with Nessa, but I refuse his orders point-blank. I am not leaving her side, and I am letting no one else stay—especially not her husband. Cathbad argues, but to my surprise the entire fianna takes my side.

We have our privacy. Nessa, baby River, and I.

I hear the men around the fire far into the night, drinking and toasting Cathbad. Let them! Nessa deserves their praise, but she doesn't care about any of it right now.

The moon is bright enough that I can see the soft shapes beside me. I brush the hair of Nessa's cheek, and tuck the blanket closer around her. River fusses, and I rub his back, delighting when he leans into my touch, sighs, and settles back to sleep.

They aren't mine. This moment is going to end, but I want to hold the memory forever.

I fall asleep with my arm across them both, waking every time the baby fusses or Nessa moans. I care for them through the night.

It's the one thing I can do.

***

Nessa wakes me with the first rays of dawn, when I figure the men of the fianna must have only just gone to sleep. I light the fire and we tend the baby's needs. I roll up one straw palette against a tree and help Nessa get propped upright. She cradles River as he nurses, studying him, running one thoughtful finger across his little skull. It pulses with each suck. I make us both tea and porridge and settle beside her, arm wrapped around one knee.

"I need one last thing from you, Rian." She looks up at me, her face swollen and tired.

I sigh.

"Do you remember the stories of Fionn mac Cumhaill? He was raised by two warrior women. I want them to raise my baby too. Fionn has just settled with his fianna in a castle near Dun Ailline. I need you to bring River to Fionn's foster mothers."

Well, that's quite a plan, but I don't bother to argue. "When?"

Nessa glances towards the other camp. "Before they wake up."

That's *quite* a plan. I drop my head onto my knee.

"I'm far too busy to raise him myself," Nessa chides. "Besides, I might be a bad influence, given how I must kill his father and all. I can take him back when he's—oh, what age do children become useful? Eight or ten? And I need to marry a king first."

Oh, Nessa. I spare a moment for all the fates she didn't choose; the ones where she would be resting on pillows with a women attending and a husband who adores her. The fates where she didn't have to send her newborn away, along with the only person she can trust.

Never mind. We make the best of what we have now. "What about the milk?"

"That's why we have a nanny goat."

"Do you know how to feed a baby from a nanny goat?"

"No, but I'm quite sure you can figure it out. People do it all the time. Look at that, the strong boy! He's done nursing."

"You have to put him on your shoulder and burp him," I say, tired.

"How do I do that?"

"I'm quite sure you can figure it out," I tell her dryly. "People do it all the time."

I turn away and busy myself packing my bags. She's probably right. This is the best for little River. She's already put him upside-down and dropped him in the river, and that was before he was even properly born. She'd be a terrible mother.

I'm grumpy and angry. I dive my hand into my panniers and find the little cloth bags. I touch them: the scholar, the warrior. Still there.

By the time I have loaded up my horse and put the goat on a lead line, Nessa has eaten both our breakfasts.

"Good job." I drop to a crouch by the fire, tickling River's little foot poking out of his swaddle. "You've managed to make it through a whole hour of motherly nurturing."

Nessa laughs. I re-wrap the swaddle and start another breakfast for both of us.

"Are you sure?" I ask her.

She sighs. "I wish it didn't have to be like this, but I think I'm out of choices. Or rather..." The birds sing and the fire crackles while she thinks. "My choices have come down to whether I submit to Cathbad forever, or do I fight for my own life. Any life."

Taking the baby to Fionn mac Cumhaill—who most certainly will *not* want to raise a child who is destined to be a great king—is an audacious plan with little chance of success. But if Nessa is going to go down, she's going to fight every last inch of the way.

That's my Nessa.

"I know," I say.

I finish the porridge, and we talk of commonplaces, our shared memories, the pig. We laugh. I eat and tidy, but don't dawdle.

I put my hand in my pocket just as Nessa says, "There's one last thing."

I hold out the moonstone. It was already in my hand to return to her.

"Yes." She takes it, and turns it over in her hands, not meeting my eyes. "You're not coming back. I release you from our loyalty."

She puts up her hand and we both make the gesture. The cutting off.

I knew this was coming. I was going to tell her that I had to leave her fianna, but now that it is here my heart is breaking.

She still doesn't look at me. "You're too good, Rian. I can't ask you to help me in what comes next."

I want to sweep her up along with the baby, take then both somewhere safe. I am strong enough to carry Nessa now, and I could kill any warrior who tried to stop me. But I won't. I have never obstructed her own decisions, even through all these years of watching her pain.

Nessa finally raises her face, meeting my eyes. "You didn't want to be a warrior, and I told you that you could use your sword to defend the innocent. I was thinking of my foster fathers laying dead, and you were thinking of your family so very much alive. I only wanted revenge—but you took my words and made them into something better."

Nessa takes a slow, shuddering breath. "You learned to be a warrior so you could help people. And now you can. You are strong and powerful and have a whole life ahead of you. Now go, Rian. Go away. Hurry. Take my baby and leave." She pulls her knees to her chest and buries her face in them, her bony shoulders shuddering.

I bundle up the sleeping baby, hoping he's content for a while. I've seen women make a pouch in their léine with a belt over top, so I try something like that, although it doesn't hold him up and I have to keep my arm around him too. I untether my horse and cluck to her, looping her lead rope between my elbow and the baby. I yank the goat away from her grass and get her moving.

But then I go back to Nessa, and kneel beside the one person who saw a battered, lonely, frightened little boy and cared for him. I only have one hand, but I use it to lift her face.

I kiss her forehead. The blessing. The farewell.

Through her tears, she smiles at me.

Neither of us can manage any more words.

I go.

CHAPTER NINETEEN

It turns out that transporting a newborn baby and a nanny goat across Ireland is both the most ridiculous and the most difficult thing I have ever done.

One or the other of them makes a siren call of deliciousness to every predator in the land. If River is willing to sleep in the sling, the nanny goat wants to stop and eat a bush. If the nanny goat is willing to trot along, River needs his nappies changed. And neither of them like any part of the process of feeding him, although River likes being hungry even less.

There were nappies in my books, but none of them had to deal with a goat on top of it all.

Good thing I'm stubborn.

After a couple awkward one-handed fights with unpleasant beasts, I try to attach ourselves to a party of anyone, going anywhere. We are highly inconvenient, so I demand as little as possible, which means I go with other people's plans and we criss-cross and scatter-shot in a vague and meandering way. Heading generally south, eventually closer to Dun Ailline, but taking ten times as long as any reasonable course.

I prefer to spend our nights with farmers. River can't drink as much as a nanny goat produces, so usually the goat's extra milk and a couple hours of my labor is enough to trade for a place on their floor for us and a place in the stable for the animals. The wives show me how to sling a baby properly, how to burp him, the right songs to sing.

Staying in these homes, I figure out my own story to tell. I'm a free warrior who had a contract with the king of Crích Rois and brought along my new wife. Tragically, she died in childbed, and I am bringing our child back to her parents to raise. As they ask questions, my imaginary wife becomes almost real, the love and memories hovering between us like butterflies. After all, the child is certainly real, and he wants milk and clean nappies.

So River becomes my son. Snuggled against my chest, talking and singing to him, watching him change day by day. Sometimes, the farm wives offer to take him at night, but I keep him by my side, his breath against my shoulder. I sleep, but I am always aware of him. No one else could watch him so carefully.

I loved Nessa as fiercely as my own sisters, but with reservations. I loved Cordelia and her father, but also with reservations. I always kept some part of myself back, for they didn't want it.

River—I love without hesitation or pause. He swallows my whole heart and soul, and with every little baby chirp and happy kick, he gives everything back to me. What else is fatherhood, really?

****

It is midsummer by the time we come to Fionn mac Cumhaill's territory, which is actually past Dun Ailline and almost back to Cuaodh's kingdom. No one else is coming this way, so we are on our own: my patient horse, my silly goat, and my little child who is holding up his head and smiling when I talk to him. So I'm chattering baby-nonsense when a man drops out of the tree.

"Halt, in the name of Fionn mac Cumhaill!"

I hold up my hands, away from my sword. Several more men gather around, blades out, studying me suspiciously. They wear matching colors and carry fine swords; they look well fed and pleased with themselves. Nothing like Nessa's fianna.

Ah. So the rumors are true, and Fionn is on his way to become a king.

"What is your purpose for trespassing on our land?" their leader demands. "You are clearly armed. Fionn has not requested your presence."

I bow. "I come to ask a favor."

"With a baby? Why is a warrior carrying a baby?"

I refuse to negotiate with the front guard. I bow and request to be taken to Fionn.

They agree, but first they take my horse and sword and bind one wrist with chains. I insist on keeping the other free, that I might have a hand to keep River secure.

With the baby, I cannot fight and I cannot flee. I expected this before I entered their lands, prepared both to suffer indignity and to use my wits as best I can. As I am led towards a king in chains for the second time in my life, I wonder what I will do if the foster-mothers aren't here, or Fionn refuses us shelter. I can't go back to Cuaodh, who will know just who this blond baby is and quickly turn him into a pawn in his own political games. I would only bring trouble to my family if I escape to Kilkirk, and no one there can protect us. River deserves a lifetime of choices, but mine are running out.

Unlike Cuaodh, Fionn is waiting for me outside. He is scarcely older than me, with a grand chair, fine dogs, and druids waiting on him. He gestures casually, and the guards unbind me.

Two older women with well muscled arms and the distinct look of knives under their léines sit off to one side. These, then, are the ones I want—Bodhmall and Liath Luachra, the foster mothers.

My heart flinches because even if all goes well, I'm going to have to give River up. But that is also what fathers do—whatever is best for the child. The life I can make for River, scrounging and desperate, is so much less than what they can do. I have to try to make them take him.

I bow to Fionn, but not too low. One warrior to another.

"Your name and your training, young warrior," Fionn drawls.

There's no harm in giving it. I tell him my true roles in Cuaodh's household, then repeat the story that I was working in Crích Rois.

"Up there...we've heard stories of a dangerous fianna." Fionn narrows his eyes at me, testing my reaction. "Led by a woman. A woman with a vow of revenge against all men, and a fate that promises her more power than her father ever held."

"Is that so terrible?" I ask. "Many of us will hold more power than our fathers. Mine was only a farmer."

"What about taking revenge against all men?"

I shrug, one-shouldered so I don't bother River. "I doubt she could be so powerful."

"She has killed one king already." Fionn watches me.

I don't react. "I didn't encounter any blood-thirsty women."

I've watched enough in Cuaodh's council room; Fionn is trying to see if I will say her name and reveal that I know more than I say, or show by my shock that I was loyal to a newly-dead king. I wonder if she has killed Cathbad or someone else, but it is equally possible that Fionn is lying to trick me.

Fionn shifts in his chair, stabs a finger towards River. "Why do you have a baby? Why are you bringing him to me?"

"With your permission, my lord..." I turn and bow to the older women. "I have come to request that he is fostered with Bodhmall and Liath Luachra."

The darker-faced woman stands and comes towards us, smiling and clucking at the baby. "I am Bodhmall. May I?" She stretches out her hands.

I don't want to. I might never hold him again, and he has my whole heart. But I reach into the sling with a now-familiar gesture. River is delighted to feel fresh air on his little limbs, and kicks eagerly. Bodhmall chuckles and cradles the baby in her arms. He grabs her chin and blows bubbles, and she brings him back to the other woman, who touches River's forehead and palms.

"He was born under a good star," Liath Luachra announces. "We could raise him, and he would become something."

Fionn turns back to me. "But my druids tell me another rumor." His tone is sharp now. "There was a baby born, somewhere towards the north, who will become a great king. I am supposed to become a great king, too, and this baby will come along right as my beard turns gray. I don't want the trouble, Rian of Kilkirk. Do you understand me?"

"I understand," I answer. My shoulders are straight, I look neither to the right nor the left, but my heart is pounding. How much does he know?

"This child is born of a woman warrior called Nessa," Fionn tells me.

He pauses, but I still don't react to her name.

"The prophecy says Nessa's son is the child of a king and the grandchild of a king. Have you heard anything about him?"

"My lord, look at me. I have been busy for months. Have you ever tried to lead a nanny goat through the woods with one hand?"

The men laugh, and even Fionn relaxes. Just slightly.

"Is the child yours? Wait." He gestures to one of his druids. "Put the truth spell on him."

The man gestures, and a sparkling sort of purple surrounds me.

"It will choke you if you dare to tell a lie," the druid warns.

I read a book about this. I focus on the truth: River who would not be comforted until I came back to the farmhouse, River's first smile, just for me, the feel of his little body settling in to sleep on my shoulder. On me.

"He is mine," I tell Fionn and the druid. "No one on earth loves him as much as I do."

The purple shimmers around me, soft and happy. This is truth.

"So who is his mother?" Fionn demands. "Are you Nessa mac Euchaid's lover?"

"I am not," I answer immediately, and then gather my thoughts. I can't say exactly what I have been telling the farmers, about the contract in Crích Rois and the death in childbed, or the spell will catch me and Fionn will kill his rival while my River is but a helpless babe.

"Do you recognize my name?" I ask instead.

My change in attitude catches their attention. Some of the men chuckle, that I am speaking back to Fionn mac Cumhaill.

Fionn furrows his brow, but clearly doesn't recall. One of his men steps forward with a bow, Fionn gestures, and he whispers in his ear. Good grief. This leader is so proud of himself that he must say every answer himself, even when we all know who thought of it.

"You were the leader of King Cuaodh's entire guard," Fionn recites, pleased with himself, "and the personal guard of his daughter. You left his service just before her wedding last winter."

"So I did." I bow slightly, then lean forward. "And do you want to hear a story?"

I know the power of those words. I don't think there is a single Irishman who can resist, and Fionn is no exception. He leans towards me, eyes glimmering.

"Some say"—I drop into my story-telling voice—"that Princess Cordelia was the most beautiful girl in all of Southern Ireland. I can tell you for the truth, she was the most passionate. The most strong-willed. And one night, this beautiful girl came to me in the hallway. She trusted me, as her childhood friend. As the guard who saved her life. And she asked me...for a kiss."

There is a collective gasp, and I give them a moment. I know the way men's minds race forward after this declaration of manhood and then the word "kiss." They will come up with all the lies themselves, and Cordelia is now a powerful queen who couldn't care less about their suppositions.

"It is not widely known," I continue slowly, "that when my princess was married, she was already growing as ripe as a pomegranate. Her new husband—allowed—her to go to the women at Ui Néill for a few months. Until her maidenly figure returned. But as I was the only man with access to her private rooms, I was sent away."

All the truth, every word of it. The spell sparkles happily. They had better not ask too many questions, because the timelines don't match; Cordelia's child will be several months older than River.

I fall back into storytelling to distract them. "My Cordelia had long hair, as smooth as a river, and eyes that sparkled with mirth and joy." Especially when listening to horror stories. "I had trained as a warrior, led the bravest charges, defeated the other knights."

"It's true," adds the informant. "His fighting reputation is well known."

"But nothing I could ever do would make a farmer's son worthy of Princess Cordelia." I shake my head sorrowfully, and the men cry out their commiseration. After all, a fianna is composed of landless sons and those hoping to raise their social class; they all understand the story of not being good enough. I made them think of *their* Cordelia, the woman who is considered too far above them.

Fionn cocks his head. He wants to feel superior, so I hand it to him on a platter.

"What could I do?" I spread my hands helplessly. "Cordelia is lost to me forever, gone to the far west. I have traveled around Ireland since I was dismissed, living by my sword. Now I have spent these months bringing you this helpless child, who has no one but me to love him. I beg you to raise him as befitting his brave heritage. I beg you to raise him as I never can—landless, jobless, and friendless as I am."

Every word of it is true, and the purple mist shimmers and evaporates.

I fall to my knees, the men cheer, and Bodhmall bursts into tears. Fionn raises his chin and smiles, gloating.

Aha. I have him where I want him. When he thinks he has won.

Chapter Twenty

Fionn's castle is only half-built, the inner walls still mud, the palisade unfinished. They assign me a room on the upper story, but I tell them I prefer the heartbeat of the earth. They insist, but so do I.

Fionn has offered me a place in his fianna, and why not? I have nowhere else to go, and if I stay close to him I will see River again. Bodhmall and Liath Luachra will raise him across the water in Scotland, but they are frequent visitors.

I descend the lowest stairs, one pannier over my shoulder, my daisy bag in one hand. With my baby gone, there is a cold place on my chest and my heart is lonely underneath. I pick my way down the hallway, mud squelching underfoot, water dripping in the distance. This is nothing like Cuaodh's castle, but Fionn is only going to rise in power. His time will come, and now mine along with it.

My fingers brush a door, fashioned from scraps of wood. Holding my breath, hoping, I push it open.

Bookshelves line the walls and a fire crackles merrily. I heave a great sigh of relief and close the door behind me. My library has found me again—but still, I miss River so much it hurts. I hoped this would make me happier, but I only feel blank.

This room is larger and a different shape than the one in Cuaodh's castle, so the bed is off in a dark corner and the squashy chair has its back to me. I set my pannier on the bed to unpack in a minute. Everything is familiar;

the same blankets, the close-stool tucked to the side, the jars of tea lined up behind the water jug. I note it with my head, but Shadow Rian feels nothing. I go to the fire to retrieve the kettle—

And something catches my eye.

She is sitting in my chair. A woman clothed only in her green hair, far taller than I, and if she unfurled her wings they would stretch from one wall to the other. She grins, and her teeth are not like needles. They are knives.

My heart clatters like a runaway freight train, but I only bow my head. "Well met, Dreoilín. I have something to give you."

"Welcome, Rian of Kilkirk, my little chick." Her voice does not so much come through her mouth as rattle in the walls, echoing in my bones, but at least she is still talking to me. "Are you surprised to see me?"

"You are very large." And terrifying, my head says—but my heart feels nothing but loneliness.

She laughs, and the stones rattle in the walls. "I warned you not to feed me, but you did. I warned you that you could capture and marry me, but you didn't."

This is true. I wait.

She cocks her head, gnashing her teeth. "I have been waiting and waiting for you. Aren't you going to roll the dice? Roll, Rian, roll!"

For an answer, I reach into my pockets and retrieve a little padded bag. I check the shape. Yes, this is the one.

I draw a shuddering breath. I am closing the last door. This is not what I planned, but I know better than to show any fear.

I slide the scholar figurine onto my palm and extend it to her, realizing at the last moment that I am not sure how she will take it. She bobs her head towards my hand, like a chicken pecking at grain, except it's all those sharp knives coming right at me.

I brace myself and stand firm.

At the last second, Monster-Dreoilín puffs out her breath and rears back. My hand burns, and the ivory scroll evaporates.

"So." She laughs, and the bookshelves rattle. "You didn't want that one?"

"I did. I wanted them all."

She laughs again, but her expression is different. "I know. I watched."

Beyond the firewood is another rack, glimmering dully. White.

It's bones. There is a pile of gnawed bones in the corner of my library, with teeth-marks the size of the knives grinning at me. But I did not give Fionn mac Cumhaill the satisfaction of my surprise, and he held my child's future in his hands. I don't react to the bones, either.

I look straight at Dreoilín and answer calmly. "When I looked at my child in my arms, I knew I would do anything for him. And what can I do? I can defend. I can save. So...I will be a warrior."

"*Your* child?" she mocks.

"Mine," I repeat. Families are made in more than one way.

"Keep the astragali, then," she roars. "Your son might need them someday." She spreads her wings, knocking vases to the floor and books from their shelves, and rears towards me, baring her teeth.

"Is this it, then?" I ask. "Seven years of raising me, and now you're going to kill me?"

She raises her wings and laughs. More books tumble and another lamp goes out.

I'm a little annoyed. I put my sword on the bed, but would it do any good? There isn't much reach in here. I should care more, but I am numb with the loss of River. I need to survive to hold him again, to show him he is always loved and treasured, and I'm not going to let even Dreoilín stop me.

"After raising you, I have the right to keep you as my slave," Monster-Dreoilín roars. "Or eat you—I'm sure you're delicious. But you fed me and did not bind me. With your care, I could escape the magic that kept me helpless, and now I am strong enough to return to my home in the underworld. So in thanks, I will let you live your little human life, with your little human sword and your tiny human love. And"—she flaps her wings and the fire goes out—"you may keep the library."

"Thank you." It's all I can think of to say. It would be better if she left.

"And I brought you this. You earned it." Dreoilín tosses her head, and the armlet clatters on the rug at my feet. "My little chick—my little hawk." She laughs and the walls shake.

"Thank you," I repeat. "Thank you for everything. Goodbye! Good luck in the underworld!"

"My home," she rumbles, glancing up. In a tornado of feathers, she gathers herself together and leaps—straight through the ceiling, through the room above, through a half-built tower, and exploding into the sky.

My reflexes spring me backwards, leaping behind the bed as a shower of stones come tumbling down. Stones are rolling. Men are shouting, but in fear, not in pain.

It's just fae logic, to get to the underworld by flying upwards.

When the cacophony stops, I count to twenty and peek over the mattress. The evening light pours through a cloud of dust. Small and large stones, plus a small wooden chest, a chair, and a hoe have collapsed into my library, but it seems basically intact. Since this room is larger, there was a clear space in the middle, and the construction of the walls protected the furniture, which is now almost hidden behind rubble. I have to look carefully. Yes, the bookshelves are fine, my squashy chair needs only cosmetic repair, a couple lamps are broken but the jars of tea and bread are still in place, and—

The table is broken straight in half, its velvet interior gaping open and looking like it is seared by lightning.

"Halloooo?" A face pokes through the gaping roof. "Anyone there?"

"It's me, Rian of Kilkirk," I call back.

"He's not dead?" someone asks.

"He vanquished the monster!" someone else cries.

"Did you vanquish the monster?" the face asks me. "It's eaten two servants already. We've been so scared that we've been shoving livestock into the cellar."

They did warn me not to go down here.

I think for a moment, climbing over the bed. I'm disappointed that my once-sweet Dreoilín has been eating people, but you never can trust the fae. "The monster was waiting for me." I put my hands on my hips, looking up through the gaping hole. A few more faces join the first. "But I knew what to do. She won't bother you anymore."

A cheer goes up. I hear Fionn, demanding to know what is going on, and everyone answering at once.

"Well, where is that boy?" Fionn's face appears in the hole. "The monster is gone? Prepare the feast! Call the bards! Come, Rian of Kilkirk, and sit by my right hand!"

"I'm coming, my lord," I call. But first, I put the books back in their places, delighting in their smooth covers and that special, papery smell. Some romance, some French literature, some horror. A nice balance. Much better than book after book about midwives. I brush off the bed, and decide it will be fine to sleep in tonight. I've missed this bed.

Finally, I pick up the armlet. It glows with the soft warmth of amber jewels, and the terminals are little patterns of—what is that among the leaves? Little ruby hearts.

I slide it onto my arm. After these last months of living by my sword and working for my dinner, it fits perfectly. One last gift from Nessa.

"Don't worry about it!" the man calls down. "We'll all help you fix your room, if you still want to sleep in the cellar. You come and relax."

"I'm on my way." Whether or not I like Fionn personally, this is a good group; they take pride in their work and don't hesitate to give credit.

I let my sleeve fall over the armlet. I don't need to show it off; I know it's the promise of adventure and love.

From above, there is more cheering, the roll of drums. They know how to celebrate, too. I'm looking forward to dancing.

That was an excellent first day on the job, if I do say so myself—I've put Fionn deep in my debt, securing River's future and much more. I chuckle—it's one last gift from Dreoilín.

Now we see what comes next. I'm a warrior. The fates always said I would be a good one.

The End

AUTHOR'S NOTES

I have incorporated as much history into this story as possible, but there is so much we don't know about third-century Ireland, and in the end, this is fantasy.

Nessa:

Nessa is a real character from Irish mythology, although I confess I have taken her from the Ulster cycle and inserted her into the Fenian cycle. There is extremely little about her—not even her full name. She is only Ness/Neasa/Nessa, the mother of Conchobar mac Nessa. She is a female warrior, creates her own fianna in order to enact revenge for her foster fathers, is in some way subjugated by rape/marriage (the Irish stories like to do that to their women warriors) and bears a son...and then reappears some years later conniving to get her son into power, which he wields so successfully that an entire mythological cycle is written around his adventures.

The castle & warrior training:

There are no castles surviving today that were built in Heroic Ireland, so it is possible that the castle where King Cuoadh lives is entirely a figment of my imagination.

On the other hand, we know the Irish managed to build large stone structures thousands of years before this story takes place. I think they could easily have had large defensive structures where a king would house his significant court and best warriors. This is also why I allowed Theastír Castle to have hallways and corridors—since defensive action is the priority, they allow warriors to get around a large structure quickly and easily.

I was able to find very little detail about their warrior training, other than it was common for boys to be fostered to receive it. For the structure and complexity of the Irish armies, it seems reasonable that some lords would have particularly robust training programs with multiple levels. There were indeed professional warriors as well as ordinary soldiers, who might also be farmers or artisans.

By this period, the warriors were the second-highest class, directly below the nobility, and quite wealthy; but in this time of constant fighting, the nobility owed their power to their warriors. It was indeed a great opportunity for Rian to be fostered with the king—but later, the king had a strong incentive to overcome his personal pride and allow the promising young warrior a second chance, rather than risk Rian joining another king's army.

The races:

There were three major waves of immigration into Ireland during these several hundred years, and only the third one—the Celts or Milesians—were white. Many scholars claim that each race wiped out the previous one, so there was only a limited time of overlap, but others have found similarities in dance, art, and facial features from modern day Celtic culture to the North African and middle eastern cultures where the early Irish originated. It appears that there was plenty of intermingling as the cultures slowly combined, so that is what I depicted.

Structure of Irish/Celtic society:

Most of the details around Rian's life are based in history. The Irish wore brightly colored clothing, jewelry was common for both men and women, their society was war-like but also constrained by many specific rules which required magistrates. They had access to ocean trading routes which extended all over Europe and especially to the Mediterranean, so the wealthy had access to wine, olive oil, precious gems, and anything else that was known in Europe.

THE KNIGHT AND HIS MAGICAL ARMLET

DEDICATION

To all those who are fighting injustice and striving to make the world a better place....and who are tired. So tired. You deserve some care and kindness, too.

Reading Notes

Rian = Ryan

Ailbe = Ava

Guaire = no modern equivalent; approx. "Gwee-duh"

Clothing:

Léine - the primary garment for both men and women; a long sleeveless drape of linen similar to a toga. Men belted it at their knees with trousers underneath, women wore it longer. The sleeves of the undergarment (tunica) showed through, which for the wealthy were draped, slit, ribboned, and highly decorative.

Inar - men's short-sleeved jacket, worn over the léine, richly embroidered and decorated for festive events.

Mythological basis for the story: This volume is not a complete fairy tale or mythological retelling. It continues to tell the story of Nessa, mother of Conchobar mac Nessa, when she marries the King of Uí Néill and tricks her way into becoming one of the most important behind-the-scenes monarchs in early Ireland. Conchobar is, indeed, the name of a river; I left his name generic so the focus of these stories remains on Nessa.

This also includes part of the story of Fionn and his first wife, Saba, which is continued in my book *The White Deer of Kildare*.

The armlet is my own invention, but the concepts around the Veil, the flexibility of time, and the fae world are all taken from Irish mythology. Rian belongs to the highest class of a society of warriors. However, there are no battles shown on the page.

Content Warning

There are references to children not raised with their birth parents, and who has the right to make decisions for a child. However, fosterage was a normal way of raising children in this period. In this story, River was always loved and cared for by both Rian and his foster mothers.

CHAPTER ONE

I come out at the edge of a field. In the rain. With my left foot in a puddle, and that's the one they just patched up. I shake out with a grimace and try to figure out where I am before starting what promises to be a cold and dreary walk. I should be glad to be home again, but God's wounds, I'm weary of this whole rigamarole.

The change is always disorienting. In 1971 we were having a bright and windy day, lots of coming and going in the hospital, tinny speakers playing American Christmas carols. Now my ears are pounding with silence as I scan the open meadow in front of me, wondering why I came out here. When I'm done with a job, the armlet doesn't really care where it sends me, so I can make hints for the Veil to pull me back to where I want to land. This time, I needed to get home in time to see my son.

I brace my hand on the aspen, which shakes water down my neck. As I move to pull up my hood, I remember the tokens in my hand. Bare oak twigs and green holly. My breath catches as I check the signs around me—did I make it back in time? The trees are leafless, the barely visible slant of sun clings low to the hills, but I can't tell if Solstice is passed...

Aha. The clatter of men and pack horses emerges from the trees below, one voice rising above the rest—King Fionn mac Cumhaill, my boss. I guess this is close enough to where I ought to be.

I'm going to assume the oak and ivy did their job—like calls to like—so I kiss them to thank them for their service, then set off across the field, towards my fianna. Most of the men nod without a second thought, assuming that I've just come back from scouting or fetching or a hundred other normal assignments.

"Ho, Commander Rian." One man peels away from the others—a spring in his step, hood fallen back from his curly hair and medium skin a shade lighter than my own. He flicks a salute, turned so only I can see the formal greeting.

Guaire would know how long I've been gone, but first I have to pause to help pull the cart around a tree-root, chatting with the cartier. This is the way it always works; people see what they expect to see, and the Veil blurs their memories to fit their expectations. When my armlet pulled me away, my fianna was on the way to pay a diplomatic visit to a couple of kings, and apparently we're still on the road. When I'm in another time, I never know if I'm going to lose a few hours or a few days.

I let the packhorses pass and fall into step beside Guaire. I'm too tired to push myself.

"You're limping." Guaire pays attention.

"Didn't mean to." I adjust, taking my weight evenly.

"Let me try again." Guaire's easy smile flickers. "Rian of Kilkirk, honored leader, *why* are you limping?"

"Beam fell on it," I answer. "Large-ish beam, if you want to be precise."

"Hm." Guaire pretends to be satisfied, but I know what he's up to. Just planning his next attack. The little bugger isn't going to leave me alone, so I give in.

"Uprisings in 1918," I tell him. "Insurgents set fires in Kilkenny town. I was there about a week, and yes, I stopped by the hospital for antibiotics before I came home."

"And pain meds?" He uses the English words, which he ferreted out of me half a dozen trips ago.

I grunt in agreement. "But I'll need you to..."

He gives me a sharp look. "What?"

It doesn't matter. He figured out about the armlet already. "There's something hurting." I pat my bicep, the armlet hidden under layers of clothes. "Not bad enough to bother the nurses about, but it's on the back of my arm. I just can't see it, so if you..." I shrug.

"You know I will. We'll be home soon, and I'll do it then."

"Home?" I pause, searching the trees and shapes of the hills. How did I not see it? I flush with unaccustomed anger, but come on—if Fionn and the fianna were an hour from home, why didn't the magic just put me down in the castle? It wants so much of me, can't I ever get—

I shake my head, stopping the useless train of thought. I'm not a sorcerer, I just do what I'm supposed to do.

"It was children, wasn't it?"

"Hm? What?" I stop, staring at Guaire.

He puts a hand on my shoulder. "Children. That you were sent to rescue this time."

I grunt and keep walking.

He keeps his hand in place. "You always have a haunted look to you, when you have to rescue children."

I'm not answering that. "Speaking of children, is Liath Luacra here with the boys yet? Have I missed Solstice?"

"You haven't missed Solstice. But..."

"But what?" Not that I care. This time of year, I don't care about anything but my visit with my son, River.

Guaire shrugs, throwing out his hands with an extravagant gesture. "I'm not sure. We were visiting in Leinster, you know, and there were rumors."

"There's always rumors."

"Something about the king of Uí Néill visiting in the area."

"All the way down south? But I don't care about—"

"If he's visiting Liath Luacra, then it'll make her late to come visit us, then she doesn't bring River. So you do care."

"Then I'll go visit them."

Guaire shrugs again. "Wait a few days. Let your foot heal, and—"

"I don't care about my foot!"

Guaire raises his eyebrows. "*And* make sure the rumors are true, so you don't miss them on the road."

He's right. I'm not usually impatient. "Fine," I agree. "And this thing"—I pat my arm—"had better not want anything to do with me for a few weeks."

Guaire glances me over again. "You need some rest," he says, his teasing tone belying his tense expression. "Enjoy a good book, drink some fine wine. Take your pills and get some sleep."

"Bossy," I grumble, although he's right. I'm not as young as I used to be, and I can tell my body's on the edge.

He elbows me, grinning. "I learned from the best."

"Ai-yi-yiii—"

The cartier yells, and Guaire and I leap forward as the cart totters in a slow arc down the slope. The next hour is nothing but the familiar grunt-work of winter travel, but despite cargo falling in puddles and a downed tree, the men are in a good mood. We're almost home, and they'll be a feast, bards, Solstice merriment. Fionn got married a few months ago, and now the castle is full of women.

Guaire catches my expression and raises an eyebrow.

"They need to win a few more battles before they go making plans like that," I explain. "The ladies are here to make a good match. Y'all need some more rewards first."

"So you're the only one among us who's ready to take a noble wife."

I snort. "I don't care about a wife."

Guaire takes the other end of a thick branch, and on the count of three we heave together.

"More children?" He brushes off his gloves, chunks of bark sticking to the wet leather. "You're a good father."

I push the branch with my foot and turn back to the path. "River and I are enough."

Who am I fooling. My fianna might not care if I'm dragged off to emergencies on any side of time, but a wife would notice. A wife would want my attention. She wouldn't want me doing work that I'm not paid for.

Not that it matters. It's been a couple of years since I've even had the energy for the casual, playful affairs that I used to enjoy. Flirtation is nothing more than another tool in my arsenal; another way to solve the problems that I'm assigned. I'm good at it, but I'm good at killing monsters, too.

"Heave-ho!" I call, and brace my shoulder on the down-slope side of the cart as the cartier calls to the horses.

And getting cargo through a muddy road. I'm great at that. A man of many talents, that's me.

I rub my aching arm, trudging after my men. If I can't see River today, that hot fire and good book sounds pretty tempting right now.

CHAPTER TWO

By the time we get to the castle, my entire arm is burning and it takes all my energy not to limp. And I'm tired of being wet. And there's bark dust down my sleeves, and it prickles, and that is just one thing too much.

And it's getting harder to hold back my foul mood. When I thought I'd be seeing my son today, I could push aside my body's complaints. Based on Guaire's gossip, at the very least, he won't be here today or tomorrow, and at the worst, I might have to wait for another self-important king to be done with his pompous visits.

I'd like to go down to my library and do nothing but eat sweet biscuits and read in front of the fire for—oh, for days—but I need Guaire to look at my arm, and he's got to finish in the stables first. So I head to my regular room, the one upstairs, that everyone knows about.

Good heavens. The Great Hall is full of activity, Queen Saba standing in the middle directing everything. I'm too tired for conversation, so I keep my head down, zigzagging through the tables to avoid getting in the servants' way. Someone thumps a load, startling a dog—right under my feet, damn! I swing my arms, only managing to catch myself on—

More crashing. A feminine gasp.

The dog lays back its ears and flees. I grit my teeth, suck in my breath, and prepare to confront my mistakes.

A woman was sorting out fancy tableware, which I knocked all over the ground. Spoons with inlaid handles are scattered across the table and at my feet; gold-twisted candlesticks have fallen helter-skelter; the queen's wedding goblets lay like a deer after the hunt. And if this is the settings for the high table, then this is no servant but...

Yup. The woman who emerges from beneath the table is dressed in fine linen, her dark hair tucked up into—

No.

No.

I have a sense that I know her, but my logical brain informs me that I've never seen her before in my life. That's a sure sign of someone who just came through the Veil. I narrow my eyes, and indeed, her clothes might be an illusion, which means she *just* arrived, and—

"I'm sorry," the woman says.

She oughtn't be. I'm the one who knocked everything over.

"Nonsense." My voice comes out gruff. I should have been the one to apologize.

She's holding two parts of something, looking dazed.

"Here, let's put that back." I don't want to be rude, but I also don't want to deal with a dazed, brand new lady-in-waiting from the wrong time. I start stacking things, fast and efficient. Upright, all in a row—

"No, not like that." The woman, now apparently recovered from her shock, plonks her own items on the table, reaching for my nice stack, batting my hand.

Another goblet crashes to the ground.

The lady disappears under the table after it, and I need to get a grip on myself. I don't know what she is here for or why the armlet brought her to me, but clearly this fool girl got herself tangled up with the Good People and some bargain she didn't understand, and now I'm left to deal with it.

She reappears, rubbing the edge of the goblet with her flowing sleeve. Her face is lowered, and she at least she's not screaming. Or sobbing.

"I didn't mean to." I sound defensive, and if River tried to apologize like that I'd give him another think. "I'm sure it's fine. Here, let me help put them—"

"I think it would be better if you just leave." She still doesn't look at me, but her tone is surprisingly calm. Especially given that she just arrived in Heroic Ireland from heaven-knows-when.

"I made the mess, it's the least I can do..."

She takes the candlestick out of my hand and finally meets my eyes. Her smile is tight and guarded. "You are going to get mud on the dishes I just polished. Please just go."

I step back. "Fine."

"Besides"—her eyes dart up and down me, as sharp as Guaire's—"you're limping, and it looks like you've hurt your left shoulder. You should go take a hot bath and then put your feet up until dinner."

Bossy little thing. "I wasn't limping."

She smiles, something sparkling behind her tense expression. "Not much, but you should still get it looked at."

Is she laughing at me? I bow, my arm searing with the movement. "If you don't desire my assistance, my lady, then I obey your command."

She raises her eyebrows.

"Take care of your shoulder, then. That's my command." Her mouth goes tight as she picks up a rag and starts polishing.

Guess that didn't come out as courteous as I thought. I'm all too eager to step away. I'm tired of damsels in distress, and my arm hurts like hell.

But as I am scanning for the best escape route, I overhear something that sounds an awful lot like "I'll clean up after you. Just like I always do."

Given that I've never seen her before, she's got to mean the general "you," not specifically myself. But I prefer to think of myself as a different kind of man, not the one who is always leaving messes and ignoring the women who fix them. I am a fixer.

I thought. I stride out of the Great Hall, not sure if I am more annoyed with the new lady or my own fool self.

***

By the time Guaire arrives at my room, I'm clean and dry and still all worked up with righteous indignation.

"Want to show me your arm?" Guaire pushes his damp hair off his forehead, eyes shadowed with exhaustion.

I finish tying off the fresh wrapping on my ankle. "I'll have you know, I asked you to come before that *new* lady said anything whatsoever."

That was my own grumping, but Guaire answers as smoothly as if it made sense.

"Maura of Kilkenny?" Guaire's face brightens as he makes his own calculations. "Odd, I thought I knew her, but I don't. That means she just came through the Veil, doesn't it?"

I grunt in agreement, pulling off my tunica.

"Like that pair of brothers who arrived last summer. And the monk who was being pursued by—"

"That means," I growl, "that she's in some sort of trouble. And I've got to get her back home again."

"Why does it have to be you?"

Why me—don't I wish I knew. "Like calls to like." I tap my armlet, the easy answer, now visible against my bare skin. "Besides, this thing is burning. It always pulls at me when it has a rescue it expects me to manage."

I turn my back, and Guaire comes over to examine the sore spot behind my arm.

"Seven hells, Rian." Guaire lifts my elbow. "Your *thing* is burning you because it's digging into a burn. A regular old human burn, right here on your regular human skin."

"Good. Because I don't think I can manage to rescue anyone tonight." My joke falls flat.

Guaire dips a rag in water, and I feel the cool cloth and his steady hands on my back as he cleans my arm. He's not a healer, but all of us develop basic skills out in the field. I don't want to have to explain to a real healer why I wear my best jewelry under my clothes, or how it molds to my skin like a spiral tattoo, snaking gold and jewels around my arm.

"It just needs a salve and a bandage," Guaire says. "Can you...can you take the armlet off?"

"In ordinary circumstances, of course." I glance back, but can't see him. "How do you think I bathe and dress? But right now, it doesn't feel right."

"I told you, it's stuck on the burn. I can get it off, but it's gonna hurt."

This after-battle part is always worse than the fight itself. One of these days, my armlet is going to get me killed, and I need to finish raising River first. He's getting to a tricky age, and needs a father's steady hand. Resigned, I brace my hands on the table, and nod for so Guaire to get to work.

Fifteen excruciating minutes later, my left bicep is wrapped in clean bandages, I'm wearing a fresh tunica and drinking willow-bark tea, and Guaire is washing my armlet in the basin.

"Have you ever considered just leaving it off? Give yourself a few days when you know you'll be in the same place..."

I sigh. I guess he hadn't gotten through all his questions. "Eventually, my arm starts to tingle. Like...a string tied too tightly. Or brushing a nettle."

"And then?" He drops into the chair across from me, propping his feet on the hearth next to mine.

"It burns. It hurts." I bark a laugh. "You'd think I could deal with that, right? But I used to test it. Give myself a breather, like you said." When I was younger, some of the rescues were really rough. Thrilling when I was in the middle of it, using my fists and sword and quick-thinking, but then I'd get home and it would all hit me. These girls who would fall in love with me because no one had ever been kind to them. Delivering kids to families who would keep them safe in body, but nothing more. The cruelty of the world. I wanted a break, some times.

"It hurts worse than a battle? I can give it back…"

"Not yet, don't worry." I chuckle. "Eventually. Slowly. If I left it off for hours, it—I don't know how bad it got, because apparently once I'd pass out, I'd put it back on again." In some kind of weird unconscious blur, which bothered me even more than the pain. I don't like doing things when I'm not awake to know what they are.

Guaire doesn't answer for a long moment, and then his voice is bitter. "I'd always imagined I would hate being controlled by that *thing*. You seem to accept it. Just do what the fates have decreed that you must. I never knew that…you felt that way too."

"I don't mind it, most of the time." But as I say it, I wonder if that's true. "I'm honored to help people. I'm glad to see a little more of the world. When I have my last battle and face the judgement call, I will be able to say with confidence that I have helped the innocent and fought on the side of good."

I don't know if that's an explanation for Guaire, or simply the argument that I've used on myself. The only way that I can get through the years. Look death in the face, over and over again.

"Don't you want anything more?" Guaire passes me the armlet. "Your own family?"

"I have River." My voice is sharp.

There's a long pause. "Fine."

I shouldn't have been short with him. I can't expect Guaire to understand how powerful a father's love really is. So I ask about the trip that I just missed, get him telling stories. Warmth soaks into our legs, the willow-bark tisane dulling the pain.

I slide the armlet over the smooth skin of my right arm. I'm more aware of it on the wrong side, but it works fine. Molds into my muscles, sparkling in the firelight like an old friend. Maybe a friend I wouldn't have chosen, but my fate could have been worse. At least I can sleep in my own bed before I'm off to manage another damsel in distress.

CHAPTER THREE

By the time the feast begins, I have dressed in my finery and regained my equilibrium. I was churlish and childish this afternoon, and I am determined to make it up to Maura of Kilkenny. She's new and unsettled; I'll be charming and complimentary, and find ways to tell her all about our traditions while making it seem like she's been here all along. Then she can have a nice quick disaster, I'll vanquish her enemy, and send her back to her family in time for the holidays. Actually, it's good timing that the king of Ui Neill is keeping Liath Luacra busy. By the time she brings River here, I'll be done with Maura.

So—fine. I'll do the hero thing until River arrives.

I join the throng in the anteroom, nodding at the salutes of the younger men. I double check that my cloak is draped so the silk lining shows, the brooch positioned just right. Although the new lady probably won't even know what's fashionable, since she has the air of being from a long time away. Those one are always the most difficult, all shocked and feeling sorry for themselves.

When I reach my queen, I am not surprised to find the new lady-in-waiting hovering behind her. Fionn is just slipping away, but that's fine, I just needed his wife right now. I bow over both ladies' hands. At least Maura's old enough to flirt with, a good ten years older than Saba herself. I refuse point-blank to flirt with girls young enough to be my daughter, even when they fall for me. It's their trauma response, nothing personal.

"May I escort you to a table, my lady?" I take Maura's hand and sweep a bow, a little too low, flipping my cloak and tossing her my best grin. I don't want to mention what happened this afternoon in front of Saba, lest Maura be blamed for any dents in the silver.

Maura smiles slightly. She accepts my arm, but I can't read her expression.

Saba catches my sleeve with a charming grin of her own. "She is seated by me, Commander Rian. So bring her to the high table, if you will."

I bow my acquiescence. I prefer not to sit where everyone is watching me, and only join the high table to give Fionn honor when we have important guests. This is my punishment for getting mixed up with the new queen's new favorite lady, I guess.

I escort Maura through the crowd, pull out her chair, pour her wine, peppering her with compliments all the while. She ought to notice all my attention sooner or later, but she's busy looking around the Great Hall, gathering the skirts of her léine as she sinks into the chair I'm holding. The polite little smile she gave me is melting into something bright and joyful, her blue eyes wide and sparkling.

"The music!" Maura clasps her hands, her expression so amazed that I can't help but smile.

"Our players of the buinne and guthbuinne are some of the best in the land, are they not?" I reply courteously, and then roll into describing other things around the hall. I make it sound as though I am merely bragging about Fionn's castle, while ensuring that I add in the context and history that she wouldn't know. It's risky to start talking about moving through the Veil when you don't know someone, and might attract Fae attention besides.

"Do you always have jugglers, or just for the Solstice?" Maura asks. "I mean—do we have jugglers. How thrilling to be part of this castle, now." She smiles and ducks her head, just as smooth as though she arrived the regular way, in a grand procession on the muddy roads, with a proper contract between her father and Saba.

The king and queen arrive at their seats, and I pause to allow Fionn my respectful attention. He likes to have a fuss made over him in public—but I'm being petty. We haven't spoken since the fianna got back this afternoon, and it's only reasonable for him to check in with me.

Instead, Fionn throws his arm around Saba, laughing at a joke that I can't hear. He holds up his goblet and makes a short speech, but it is simply announcing that he is glad to be home and praising his wife for preparing this feast.

Saba takes the seat next to mine, radiating joy. "You are enjoying your dinner companion?"

"Of course, my lady." I smile courteously.

Saba grins mischievously, but someone else calls her name before she can tell me more.

A servant arrives with bowls of stewed meat, and I serve Maura and then myself. I glance her over, looking for something I can flatter gracefully. She's quite pretty, actually; not in a flashy way like Saba herself, but she has a sweet face and holds herself with calm reserve. Her combination of dark hair and fair skin is almost unknown in our time, but I've traveled enough to know that it becomes common in Ireland later. Her eyes striking, bright with dark lashes and brows. I can make those into compliments. Her cheeks go round every time she smiles, and her skin looks like it would be soft—now *that* is not a decent compliment. That is my imagination running away with me.

"Do you know what the figures represent?" Maura lifts her goblet, turning it in the candlelight before she takes a sip. "What birds are these?"

I have to examine the etchings to remember which they are, my fingers brushing hers. "Cranes. These must have been a wedding present for Saba, with their representation of the triple goddess, encouraging her to reach inside herself for her own innate wisdom."

"Beautiful." Maura smiles, more beautiful than any royal goblet. "What is your favorite crane legend?"

I don't mind sharing stories with her, but the feast is loud and only getting louder. By the time I am half-shouting and we are still misunderstanding every other sentence, she shrugs and laughs, and I turn my palms up and sigh, and we are both smiling as we give up on complex communication for the evening.

On my other side, Saba leans forward to call to the steward, and I recall my duty. Raising an apologetic finger to Maura, I try to catch Fionn's attention.

"What?" He glances at me, then leans towards his wife again.

She's still talking to the steward, and nothing else requires his attention.

"Just reporting back," I say. "Were the carts unloaded smoothly?"

Fionn scowls. "How would I know? I'm the king. I don't unload the carts."

I'm taken aback. "Of course not. But the cartier would report to you." Unless something went wrong.

Fionn flaps his hand at me and turns to the warrior on the other side.

Now I'm worried. "My lord? If he hasn't reported to you yet—"

Donnchad catches my expression and leans closer to our boss, clearly trying to get Fionn to respond to me. Fionn scowls at both of us.

Those carts were certainly hauling gifts from the other kings, fine tapestries and more goldwork for Saba's table. I don't know what it was, because I missed the actual visits, which is another problem, but we can't afford to incur our neighbors' displeasure by losing their gifts.

"Pardon me," I say to Maura, and walk carefully around Saba's chair so that Fionn can hear me...

...but there is nothing underfoot. Where are Bran and Sceólang, Fionn's hounds? He is never apart from them, and since his marriage they are equally loyal to Saba.

Fionn finally swings towards me, so I don't have time to contemplate.

"If the cartier hasn't reported to you, I can find him," I half-yell, making sure he can hear me.

"Why would you worry about the cartier?" Fionn asks. "He isn't anyone important."

What an odd thing to say.

"Did he report, darling?" Saba interjects. "That's all that Rian needs to know."

Fionn scowls again. "He came to the room, but I was—busy. I sent him away."

Then perhaps the luggage is fine, but something else is wrong. "My lord? What occupied you?"

"How dare you question me!" Fionn bursts to his feet, forcing me backwards. "I can be busy if I wish!"

"Of course. Of course." I move towards the wall, placating even though inside, I'm fuming.

Fionn's shoulders relax, and he turns back towards the room. "Go sit down. Enjoy the food. Drink up, drink up!" He bursts into laughter, and I'm not sure if that last injunction was for me or the crowd.

I shake my head. Fionn can be moody, but this is ridiculous.

Donnchad grabs my sleeve before I can return to my seat. "You'll check in with him later?"

"Aye." That's the downside of my position; I'm the only one who can hold Fionn accountable.

Donnchad leans closer. "He's a little giddy tonight."

Behind us, Fionn explodes into laughter again, Saba's silver joy trilling along.

"He's probably just glad to get home to her." I jerk my head towards the newlyweds. "It must be nice, after all these years."

"True." Donnchad's smile spreads. "Can't wait until it's my turn, and hey—I might forget a couple of my direct reports if I had something so pretty in my room, too."

I grin in agreement and return to Maura, but I'm not so confident in my own explanation. When Fionn said he was busy and I questioned him, Saba looked curious, like she wanted to know as well. If they had been occupied as Donnchad imagines, I think Saba would blush and appear mischievous. Although she is very capable at managing the castle and its ladies, she shows no talent for hiding her emotions. And Saba has lots of emotions.

Maura smiles gently as I return to her side, and I notice she has placed a bun neatly in the middle of my plate. Here and *I* was supposed to be fussing over *her* tonight; I'm falling down on my job. I grin in the way that plenty of women have called dazzling, deliver my prepared compliment about her eyes like bright guiding stars, and refill her wine.

She merely smiles and asks about the embroidery on my inar. Only after I've explained the significance of several designs do I realize that she is using specific words correctly. Going through the Veil gives someone the language they need, as well as the clothes and the awareness of basic tasks, but it doesn't teach you about holiday traditions and the correct terminology for metalwork and embroidery. Who is this woman, that she knows these things?

Hands and teeth don't lie. She has all her teeth, white and in the right places, and—I catch her hand as I pass the stewed plums—smooth without being pampered. That says either extreme youth, which doesn't fit, or living in a time with advanced hygiene and medicine.

"Who made it for you?" Maura touches the designs on my cuff, unaware of my twisting throughs. "Was it a special woman in your life?"

Is she asking if I am married?

"Your mother?" she suggests, and I relax.

"Sadly, no." I try to smile in a carefree manner, not think of my mother in her faraway village, far too exhausted for fine needlework. "I merely commission what I like. I buy it in the town."

"Oh!" Her face lights up. "Would you—I mean, I have barely had a chance..."

"I would be delighted to escort you to the town," I answer. She is not unpleasant company, to be honest. My armlet will drive me to keep tabs on her until whatever her disaster is actually happens, so I might as well take her to the village.

The trumpeter makes the call for silence and Fionn stands to make a speech, every movement deliberate and ponderous. Maura turns to listen politely, and I put a smile on my face and let my hearing go fuzzy and my thoughts wander.

River isn't here yet, but I'll see him soon! We had a few days after harvest time, but we always get a good long visit at midwinter. Last year, he still curled up in my lap when we stayed up late listening to stories, but I wonder if he'll feel like he is too big this year. If the weather is agreeable, I'll take him to the ruined temple at Ennisleague. We can watch the sun go down, and I'll talk to him about being an honorable man. Those lessons are always best served in small doses, hidden within intriguing stories, especially ones where one's own father makes foolish mistakes. I smile to myself, bubbles fizzing through my veins.

Thoughts of my son makes me reckless and tender both. I glance down, looking for an outlet, wanting someone to smile at me. Maura's hand is resting on the table, lightly touching the stem of her goblet. I run my fingers across the edge of the bowl of nuts. Drum them on the table. Rub a spot on the embroidered tablecloth...inching ever closer to hers.

She was watching Fionn, but she glances down as our hands brush. Without looking at me, she smiles that little smile, and returns her attention to the speech. I follow her gaze back up, and realize I was wrong. She is watching Saba, not the king. Interesting. Women usually can't take their eyes off Fionn.

"My beautiful wife!" Fionn declares. "More refreshing than a summer rain, and lovely even as a deer."

Beside me, Saba shifts uncomfortably.

"Of course," Fionn continues, "she never need take her deer form again, given that she is safe from any enchantment as long as she is under my protection."

The men cheer, and add the phrase that I expected—"Within these walls! The fortress you built for her!"

Of course, Fionn started this castle years before he met Saba. But that's the way he tells the story, and he's good at nudging the truth into the form that suits himself. People believe what they expect; they believe the stories that make sense.

Saba shakes herself, then cheers and ululates back at the men who are praising her, and they cheer more. In the happy chaos, I let the back of my hand rest against the side of Maura's.

She doesn't move away.

Fionn talks and talks. I slide my pinky finger up the back of Maura's knuckles, one step at a time, like climbing a ladder into the dark.

I haven't gotten either a no or a yes from her all night. Of course, I'm just pretending to flirt with her. Rian the commander, obedient to Saba's hints, doing honor to her newest lady-in-waiting. I'm just raising her status with my attention, but my heart is pounding a little harder than is reasonable.

I hook my pinky over the top of her hand.

It would be so easy for her to turn her hand over, palm up, and then her hand would be in mine. Then I would know that she forgives me for the debacle I made this afternoon, and I could forget my lurking shame.

Or, it would also be so easy for her to raise her goblet to her lips, pulling away from me entirely.

She does neither. She's smiling that tiny smile, which I hope is for me and not Fionn's ridiculous speech. I like her face. It's expressive and gentle, laugh lines at the corners of her oh-so-starry eyes.

I slide my ring finger into her palm, and she turns her gaze to me, and I remember suddenly that we're at the damned high table, and half the room is probably bored with Fionn's pontificating and looking for gossip. It's one thing to do her honor by flirting in the usual way, but I don't want to engage her emotions.

I quirk a grin of my own and slide my hand forward, up the stem of her goblet. I bring it to my lips, my eyes on hers the entire time, and she bursts out laughing.

"Pardon me, was this yours?" I tease, and she laughs more, shaking her head as though I'm absurd. If we were alone I would hold the cup for her to drink, but even though I'm fairly sure she'd take it, it would give the wrong idea to whoever is watching. I settle for passing it to her, our hands brushing.

Fionn concludes his speech, and we have to join in the applause. Then the servers are coming round, Saba asks me a question, and Maura is distracted by the jugglers. By the time I can get Fionn to respond to a simple question, the moment is over and Maura is not paying me the slightest attention.

I am more annoyed with Fionn than ever. I liked this moment.

***

I usually retire as soon as I can, but tonight I stay at the feast as long as Saba and her ladies—trying to catch one more smile, one more hint from this Maura of Kilkenny. I get plenty of smiles, little ones and soft ones and laugh-out-loud ones, which keeps me in my seat past midnight.

I stand to help escort the ladies out, joined by several of the other knights although Fionn stays sprawled at the high table. As soon as we are out of the noisy hall, Saba sags, her face drooping with exhaustion. Ailbe is immediately at her side, their arms around each other in the comfort of their life-long friendship.

Maura turns to me with a little smile.

"Please"—I bow over her hand—"lighten my heart by admitting that you have forgiven my terrible misstep this afternoon."

When Maura pauses, I realize my courteous words were true. I do care if she thinks well of me.

"I was not only clumsy," I add quickly, "I also didn't even apologize properly. I'm sorry for adding to your work."

"Oh no, oh no." Maura shakes her head, dropping her eyes. "I wasn't upset. I was just worried about you."

"There is nothing..." I trail off, confused. "I'm fine."

"So you claim." She turns her starry gaze to me, her hand still in mind. "Still, I want you to get good rest tonight. Drink your healing tisane, and sleep late in the morning, do you hear?"

No one has told me such things in years. That's my job, reminding my men to take care of their bodies so they're strong enough to fight another day. Bemused and confused, I simply bow again.

"Goodnight," Ailbe says clearly. "It is time for the women to retire."

The other knights, like me, step away, and the servants bring rushlights. We murmur our farewells, and a couple of the men return to the gathering but I am relieved for the excuse to leave.

I don't bother to hide my limp as I trudge down the stairs to my library, sighing in anticipation as I open the door. Mm. Finally, I'm home. The fire is crackling merrily, the rugs soft and inviting, lamps glowing. Books, beautiful books, line two walls. I have to check out the volumes laid out for me on the shelf; the library always picks something it thinks will fit my mood. *Gaudy Night*, by Dorothy Sayers. Haven't read her before. I flip the book over to read the back, but the words blur with every blink. I'm too tired to read, and that's really damn tired.

Now that I've traveled around a bit—well, quite a bit—my guess is that Herself pulled this entire room from some manor house in the late Victorian. I don't say her name, even in my head, the same way I don't speak of any of the Good People. She told me once that she was in trouble, banished from her land and assigned a human to keep her busy. That would be me. She stayed very busy indeed, fetching this library and putting it chock-full of enchantments. Chief among them seems to be that it pulls an ever-changing rotation of books from any time period; it always has the fire going and a basket of baked goods when I arrive, and it makes its books readable to anyone who truly desires to understand them, which is quite a feat given that written language doesn't exist in Ireland just yet. There are dozens more, though. Herself took her job seriously. Just before this last rescue mission I discovered a pillowcase, that if you turn it inside out, becomes a different color. Not just once, but infinitely, one after another after another. Is there a point? Probably not, but she made my library with dozens of tiny enchantments like that.

I peel off my clothes to wash up in the basin, but pause as I fold my léine. I touch the coil on my bicep. Funny, I didn't notice it pulling at me, even though I spent the whole evening with Maura. Well, the Great Hall was loud, and I had it on the wrong arm. Guaire was right, and the burning was from the metal irritating my actual burn. I test the pain through the bandage and decide it's going to heal quickly now that the armlet is off. After all, I spent a week recovering in a hospital, even if I didn't show them that exact spot.

I don't want to think about what happened before that. The uprising, shops set on fire to make a point. Or maybe it was in retaliation; I don't really catch all the details of these things. In every time, it's the same. Someone wants to be more powerful, someone fights back. Meanwhile, who ends up hurt? The children, the grandmothers. The people who are a little different, living alone at the edge of the village. The women who speak out. I am so tired of it, so tired.

And Guaire was right, this time I was sent to rescue children. I don't want to think about that. I don't.

I turn out the lights and climb between the nice smooth sheets, breathing in the scent of dried herbs and sunshine, savoring the softness beneath my aching shoulders. I'll think about River...but then something catches the edge of my mind. I heard something about the king of Uí Néill, but I can't remember what it was. It reminded me of...no, I really can't remember. There is so much gossip about the kings, it probably isn't true anyways.

Tonight. A woman so confident that when she lands in another time, she is curious and joyful instead of sorry for herself. So clever that she conversed for hours without yielding to any of my gambits to hint at her true identity. I am half into slumber, her face as vivid as if she were here. Blue eyes. Soft cheeks. That enigmatic smile, and I still can't figure out what she expects.

I guess my armlet will show me. I might as well get some rest before her story ensnares us both.

CHAPTER FOUR

"There ain't no rest for the wicked, and the righteous don't need none." That was in some books that I read last winter, Jan Karon if I remember aright, and now it runs through my head whenever I don't want to get out of bed. I don't know if I'm righteous or wicked, but I certainly don't get much rest.

I wash and dress and drag myself up to the kitchens, where I eat my porridge in the corner with my eyes half-closed, enjoying the congenial warmth and hubbub. Besides, all the news goes through the kitchen. Cook isn't expecting Liath Luacra and her foster sons any time soon, and despite Guaire's warning, my heart sinks all over again. Then the women chat about the hunters heading out to get game for another feast tonight, for Queen Saba has declared a festival with a display of combat at noon...which means Fionn wants to show off. Damn. I flex my left foot, which is pretending to be made out of granite. I'll take another paracetamol before my bout, and still have a dose left for tonight.

I suppose I'm supposed to show off for this Maura of Kilkenny. With my foot aching, and grumpy after two pieces of bad news in a row, I can't remember why I found her appealing last night. I have strict rules for my romantic liaisons. Never during a job, never someone I have to work with, never someone who's expecting a long-term partner. Fine then. She's smart and has a nice smile, so I'll do my best to enjoy the time with her while I'm waiting for River, then send her off home.

It's more important to figure out about seeing River. If Liath Luacra doesn't come here, I'll go and visit them in January. She won't be excited to see me, but I'm a highly respected warrior and she won't kick me out, either. I'll give lessons to all the fosterlings, that's what I'll do, and spend some extra time with River.

Feeling much better about the state of the world, I bring my empty bowl back to the scullery, stooping to kiss Cook on the cheek as I pass.

"Cocky young thing!" She shakes her ladle at me, chuckling so her shoulders bounce.

"I missed you and your fine food, that's all, good auntie!" I tease.

She shakes her gray head, smiling. "Just as well you're such a fine looking fellow."

"He can kiss me any time," declares the head server, whisking at me with a dishcloth.

So I do, earning another thwap and a round of laughter from the entire kitchen. They're both old enough to be my mother, confident enough to tease back. The playful camaraderie energizes me, gives me a place in the world.

I just have to go up to my bedroom to check over my weapons before heading down to the training yard. At my age, it helps to do some stretches, and at this rate I'll have time to fix a few other things. Even though only a few days passed here, I was in the future for almost a month, and I'm discombobulated.

I'm trotting up the stairs, warming up my muscles, when I hear a funny noise down towards the ladies' wing. I don't want to get involved where it's not my business, but I'll just check. I turn the corner, where I can see into the solar. There's a small blond figure with her back to me, stomping her feet and building her sobs up to hysteria.

Gráinne, the littlest lady-in-waiting. She's properly too young to be fostered out, but her father sent her early, probably as irritated with her histrionics as half our castle is now. I'm about to shake my head and move on, but my gaze is snagged by a second figure kneeling by the distraught girl. Maura of Kilkenny is so calm that she draws my eye, but I don't understand why she is here. She doesn't have any reason to spend time with Saba's problem child. She won't be around long enough to expect a reward from Gráinne's father.

I lean back against the doorframe, crossing my arms, into the shadows.

Gráinne is upset about having lost something, and also something about hurting her elbow, and *also* someone hurt her feelings. It makes my elbow hurt just to listen to her, but I can't stop watching Maura. She steadies Gráinne's flailing hands and convinces her to explain one thing at a time, until Gráinne's gasping sobs settle into the cadence of functional speech. Then she examines Gráinne's skinny arm, unbuttoning the sleeve and running her hand up her skin, cupping her elbow gently. I shiver, watching her. Holding the contact between them, Maura asks slow questions about where Gráinne might have lost the whatever-it-was, taking a pin out of her own hair to help fix the girl's headpiece. Gráinne is finally settled, and only now Maura stands, buttoning the girl's sleeve and brushing out her clothes. From this angle, I can see Maura's face clearly, and this smile is easy to read.

Kindness. Comfort. Praise.

Gráinne laughs at something Maura said in that low voice of hers, and they walk together out the far side of the room, Gráinne tilted slightly towards the older woman. That was masterful, and I whistle under my breath as I turn towards the stairs. It was like the senior workers of the stables or dog-yard, who can soothe an injured beast with their gaze and their soft hands. Except Maura used her power for the good of a child.

I wonder if I have done as well for River. After I pulled the children through the building as it burned around us, did I spend any energy comforting them? I always tell myself that I'm not around long enough for it to matter, but I spent days in their town. Maura made a difference to Gráinne in just a few minutes.

Then my mind wanders back to my own time as a new fosterling. I never would have dared to pitch a fit like Gráinne does, but how much it would have helped to have one person calmly listen to me. Focus on me. How much one hairpin would have showed that I mattered to the world.

It's not the way people act around here.

It's not the way people act through most of time, and I should know.

***

Before I head out to the training yard, I go by the kitchens and toast some buns and cheese. I want something of the fianna, so I bring them food. While we adjust our breastplates and check our weapons, I distribute warm bread and nudge for gossip.

Their reports are odd. Fionn just got back from a job up north, but a couple of the guys are still missing, and no one mentions them. Odder still, no one seems to have seen Bran and Sceólang. Fionn is never without his hounds. If either men or dogs had fallen in battle, we'd already have songs for them and the others would be beating their breasts, but everyone seems to assume they're just around the corner somewhere. This is what magic does; it distracts, draws attention away. As soon as one stops to focus, the truth is as clear as gas-lamps in the Victorian fog, but most people never stop to focus.

But if I tried to unravel Fionn's mysteries, I'd spend the rest of my life tangled in it, and my armlet has apparently assigned me another task. I need to find out more about *her*.

I take my staff and join the first set of eight men, working through the training sequence as the master beats his drum. Starting slow. I settle into my feet, reaching for the earth beneath me, listening to each muscle and ligament. It's time to clear the clutter in my head. The training master calls the sequence, but I swing a little slower or reach a little farther, warming up the way my body needs the best. Just stay with the drum, with the beat, with the earth.

By the time we go faster, I'm ready for it. The familiar lunge and swing, feint and parry. There's always a thrill when I return from a job and come back to this work; this dance I have spent so much of life inside. We run the field, switch partners, down the line, duck and leap. Finally the master beats the signal for "rest," and we drop into formation to walk around the outside perimeter of the yard.

"So… tell me about the new lady." I ask Guaire, wiping my brow as we fall into step. The next group comes forward, the drum slow once again.

"You seemed to get to know her well enough last night." He quirks his eyebrow.

"It was too loud to hear anything sensible. And I couldn't ask her things I'm supposed to know already."

"The men at my table were full of comments, although I can't promise they're sensible." Guaire loves gossip, and he warms to his theme. "They say she arrived while we were on our trip north. But have you heard? She's not a fosterling—she's actually been married before."

I stand straighter too. "But why she didn't go to her husband's family after he passed?"

Guaire nudges me, his eyes bright. "She *divorced* him!"

"Divorced, hm?" More and more curious. In our time, a woman is permitted to divorce her husband for a variety of reasons and all the shame goes to him. But once Christianity comes to Ireland, women are bound to their marriage contracts with increasing severity, all the way into the late 20th century. That means that if Maura is divorced, she is from very close in time or very far away, and her hands and teeth told me the answer to that.

Guaire clucks his tongue. "Can you imagine mistreating someone like her? Pretty girl, and elegant."

I have a visceral reaction to another man calling Maura pretty, and I note my feeling. It could get in the way of whatever I'm supposed to do while she's here. I touch the armlet again, still awkwardly on my right arm, although I wouldn't expect it to guide me when I can't see her.

"He must be a scoundrel," I agree.

"They had children together, too," Guaire adds.

Now a fierce tongue of flame surges through my chest. Once a man has children, it is his rock-bottom, bare-minimum duty to treat their mother with honor. Every day. Every year. After that brief moment this morning, I am positive that Maura is a good mother. Her first husband should have treasured her!

I growl.

"Knew you'd feel that way," Guaire says. "Me too."

The training master yells a command and races the beat, and the men slam forward into a rhythm of attack and parry. I adjust the grip on my staff, knowing we'll be called back in soon.

"This afternoon." Guaire darts me a grin. "Think you could go a little easy on me? I want to impress Maeve..."

I'm watching the training, eyes half closed, sensing where I would dive in, the right gesture to knock each man down.

"Rian...?"

My armlet hasn't twitched, so probably nothing's happening today. The new girl isn't in danger yet.

But a sweet smile like hers, and one husband who's already treated her wrong? I think she deserves a man to fuss over her a little bit—and I like the idea of being the man to do it.

"Naw." I grin back at Guaire, giving him a playful swipe. "This time, I've got a lady to impress, too."

Chapter Five

I rock back and forth on my feet, letting my arms move loosely in the shoulder joints. While I watch the first match, I work out what I would explain to River. Feel the earth beneath your shoes. Cool or hot, dusty or clingy; it all makes a difference. If I spent the month with Liath Luacra, I would teach all the boys how to slow down. See how the warrior in yellow is rushing into combat. Look at his elbow, he's coming for an overhand blow—there it is. Ah, his opponent is a good swordsman, but he didn't need to attack back. Let them come to you, boys. Block them, wait. Let your opponent expend their energy while you are drawing strength from the earth beneath your feet.

"Your lady is looking for you."

Guaire speaks so suddenly that I jump. That won't do; I need to teach River and the boys about being aware of their surroundings, and—

"Wave, Rian," Guaire says.

Yes. That's really what's going on at today's display of combat. The ladies, and I have a lady from another time that I've got to deal with before I see River. A lady who didn't even flirt back last night.

I'm trying to adjust my angle so I can see the audience, when the training master passes behind us and taps my shoulder. "You're up next, Rian. Against Donnchad."

He names the flashiest of the young warriors, and Guaire rolls his eyes. "Oh, that'll be a hard match. The betting's going wild, isn't it?"

The training master gives us his veiled smile. "I've got to put Rian earlier in the lists so the numbers work out by the end. Besides, Donnchad thinks he's invincible lately, and that's when warriors die."

In other words, he's got to rig the pairings so I never end up facing off against Fionn, because Fionn wants to win. Fionn doesn't even spar against me.

"So do I knock him out fast," I ask, "or draw it out until he's wheezing?"

Guaire cackles. "Oh, make him wheeze. I want to see it."

The training master gives that ghost of a smile. "It's a display, Rian. Draw it out."

"And Rian's got a girl in the stands," Guaire adds.

I should never have made that joke to him. Never.

"'Bout time you had a woman to warm you," the training master tells me. "You're not getting any younger. I'd be glad to see you hand-fasted. Now—go."

I jog out around the perimeter obediently, raising my hand while the trumpets play and the ladies cheer. The men have unsettled me, or maybe Maura unsettled me, or maybe I have unsettled myself. I don't have the energy to smile and make merry. Donnchad jogs the other direction, pumping his fist and blowing kisses. He is tall and blond and has no trouble with energy.

Still, I glance across the stands, searching for one face.

She stops me in my tracks, for her eyes are fastened on me, that soft little smile on her lips. But before I can become frustrated what it means, she laughs and applauds. For me. She is not even glancing at Donnchad. I touch my heart, a smile pulling at my cheeks.

Maura glances at the ladies on either side of her, uncertain about something. Maeve laughs and makes a go-ahead gesture, Saba claps, and even Ailbe smiles. Maura puts one hand over her mouth and beckons me with the other. As I come closer, the women are all laughing and Maura's eyes are dancing, like a girl. She's out here having fun, and I like that.

I touch my heart again and bow, just for her. She fumbles with something under the edge of her cloak, blushing pinker than the cold weather requires. She finds a little while cloth, but she's in the bench with the best view, which is not close enough to the fence for me to see what she's holding. Now others are laughing too, passing the thing from hand to hand, calling out to me. A token from a lady to a knight is not yet a practice in our time, but we like everything with emotion and story. The ladies squeal at me and I laugh back, predicting that King Fionn's ladies will have a new tradition. I reach up as someone passes it over the fence.

"Rian of Kilkirk, your mother was a dog!" Donnchad shouts. "Nay, a dog's behind!"

So, he wants to start this way. Insults remind me of real battles, when the attack means that men will die. But the audience cheers, and this is all about Queen Saba and her ladies today. So I shove the scrap of cloth under my leather armor and turn to face Donnchad.

He roars, swinging his head to make his hair-beads clatter and wave the horns on his helmet.

But hey—Maura is definitely flirting with me now. I don't mind putting on a show for her when it isn't all on my side, so I raise my shield and beat my sword against it, grinning when the ladies ululate. I spare one glance to catch Maura's sweet smile—this time, I'm pretty sure I know what it means, and that puts a spring in my step. Which is just as well, because I'm under orders from my training master to drag this match out...and when I end it, I want to make it clear that I could have done so at any time.

This is getting interesting. I bare my teeth and let Donnchad come at me.

***

By the time I come out from washing off the battle sweat and mud, the servants have built a bonfire, and the beat of the bodhran tumbles across the courtyard. I grin and skip into the dance, my blood still zinging from the exertion—oh fine, I admit it. I'm chuffed because those were excellent matches, and everyone who knows sword-work is impressed with me. I went up against two of the young knights who are making quite the flash, and I proved that I still have it.

"Have some ale with us, Rian?" calls the master of the kennels.

I hold up my hand and shake my head.

"Fionn's men are still on duty," one of the guards teases. "Better for us, get to enjoy the queen's bounty."

"Ho, Rian!" calls the drummer, and breaks into a wild beat. Several of the others clap and sing, and I laugh and let my feet go free, stamping and skipping to victory song. A pretty woman today, and seeing my son soon. I ignore the pain in my foot and just dance.

"Rian!" Fionn calls from the far side of the meadow. "We're waiting on you!"

I throw a salute to the group around the bonfire, and half-walk, half-dance over to where Fionn is waiting with the fianna and the ladies. Queen Saba is holding on to Fionn's arm, gazing at him with stars in her eyes; several of the men salute or thump my shoulder as I grow close; several of the ladies are swaying to the drumbeat.

My eyes seek out Maura of Kilkenny. She smiles at me.

"Come now!" Fionn claps his hands, ignoring his wife. "We're taking the ladies up the ridge, and we need to leave in time to see the sunset! Only three more days until the Sun Stop of Winter. Let's go, let's go!"

"I'm ready, my dear," Saba says, Fionn bows to her with a flourish, and they vanish down the path.

There's a shuffle of competition for who gets to walk with Maeve, but most of the men and ladies walk in one large bumbling, laughing group. Ladies are contracted to a queen in order to make an advantageous marriage, and Fionn's men are mostly too young to please the ladies' fathers.

Besides, what lady wants to walk with a warrior who was just trounced like the two I fought? I'm unable to hide my smile when I bow to Maura.

"Well, weren't you just the clever one on the field today?" She smiles back, linking her arm through mine.

"It was your handkerchief that did it," I tell her. "Usually I'm a complete doofus. Trip over my own feet. Get my sword stuck in the mud."

She laughs, and my heart thrums.

"Shall we take this path?" I attempt to turn us, but she is looking after Saba. "I wish to show you the view, and perhaps the birds will be out."

"Will we be far from Sa—the others?"

I wonder if she is worried about Saba's safety or her own. "We are near to the castle, my lady. We are all going in the same direction."

"Then I would *very* much love to see the landscape," she answers, letting me move her forward.

She's solemn again, and I can't have that.

"There!" I gesture to the dense undergrowth around us. "Isn't the view magnificent?"

"Well...the trees are lovely."

"I meant my view." I turn to her, making sure she catches my teasing smile. "I am looking upon the loveliest lady in all the Kingdom of Osraige."

She shakes her head, just one corner of her lips tilted up. "Now that is nothing but a specious compliment, sir."

I thump my chest. "I am stricken, my lady!"

She raises an eyebrow. "I am so bundled up you can barely see anything of me, let alone decide if I'm any more or less pretty than anyone else."

There's an edge of tension in her voice, and I want to keep her smiling.

"I can see your nose," I reply, instead of admitting that her expressions are captivating and her cheeks are kissable.

She shakes her head, almost smiling. "I suppose you can. But it's just a nose!"

"It's the loveliest nose in Osraige." I brush my thumb against the tip of said nose, and earn her beautiful laughter. I let my knuckles brush her cheek.

She smiles into my eyes and steps backwards in the same gesture. Another yes-and-no.

"And your eyes…" I let my words trail off, holding her gaze. If she smiles again, I'll finish the compliment.

"What birds are out here?" Maura starts back up the path, away from me.

"Red kites."

She holds out her hand as she walks, and I take it. Yes and no. Taking what she is willing to give, I tell her about birds, her breath puffing as we climb.

"Oh!" She pauses and glances back through the clearing. "Now, there's something beautiful!"

I run my thumb across her fingertips, oddly frustrated. "It's just a castle," I say. "A pile of wood and stone. It is nothing compared to looking at your face."

"Ah, so you prefer human life to architecture?"

As it so happens, I just raced children out of a burning building with never a thought for the walls and furniture. But I don't like the way she deflects from herself.

"I prefer you," I say bluntly. "The expressions that run across your face. Your ideas. Your curiosity."

"I'm curious about the castle," she interrupts. "That side isn't finished." She points. "Were you here when it was started? Do you know about it?"

Her hand is still warm in mine. If she wanted to discourage my attention, she would have pulled that one away to point, but she remains close, her cloak brushing my legs.

"I have been living here while Fionn builds the castle." My throat is tight so I speak slowly, careful of keeping my tone light. "Let us walk while I tell you the stories."

"Where are the stones from? Who designed the Great Hall?" She almost gives a skip as she falls into step with me.

"I don't know those things. I just do simple work, give a hand here and there when the fianna does not have another assignment." I walk slowly, adjusting my step to hers as we loop around the ridge. I tell her some stories, suspecting that she has some connection to the castle in her own time. There are scholars who say that time is anchored by place, not by sequence. I do not care, particularly—I just go where I am pulled—except that I am intrigued to imagine Maura in a different role, perhaps the confident mistress whisking up and down the staircases, making decisions. I wonder if the castle was her husband's, and she had to leave after she divorced him. I wish I could ask her, but I cannot afford to draw any attention to myself. I need both the Fae and the Fates to ignore me until I have my visit with my son. That's more important than anything.

Or after he divorced her. When I am in my own time, it slips my mind how misogynistic the world becomes. Besides, I cannot imagine why any man would leave a wife like this, clever and pretty and thoughtful.

But if she has been divorced, it would explain why she is so jumpy with me. I have never really thought about what abandonment would feel like—I have lost friendships as we move on in life, had to leave my family and my foster family, but that was because we grew into the next stage. The point of marriage is to grow through life together. If Maura's husband betrayed her trust, she might find it difficult to take any man seriously.

We have lapsed into comfortable silence. Reaching the top of a little rise, Maura pauses, breathing hard, leaning on me just a little bit more. I smile down at her headscarf, little dark curls against her fair forehead. I like taking her weight, feeling her trust. I like the softness of her.

Aw, seven hells and a bucket of dung. I wasn't going to get emotionally involved with this rescue. It was just supposed to be fun and quick and send her home.

I wonder what it would feel like to kiss her. Right now, her skin cool, her heart beating fast. If I went slowly enough, tenderly enough, if she would go along with it. Rian of Kilkirk, this is definitely emotionally involved. Stop it.

Maura laughs an embarrassed apology and starts walking, and I shake my head. Hard, as though I could shake my thoughts away like water droplets.

"You are a mother," I say, not quite a question. "Tell me about your children."

She perks up. "Oh, I have—" And deflates again.

I want to keep her talking. "Four, I believe Guaire said? How many boys and girls?"

"Boy, girl, boy, girl," she answers. "But I don't wish to bore you."

"I like children." I'm frustrated by the way she pulls away from what she likes. "I would love to hear about your family."

Hesitantly, she begins to tell me stories, breaking off to give me opportunities to change the subject. Instead, I ask her questions. I'm listening beyond her words, to the parts when her voice is animated or her face goes tender, trying to reach into those moments.

Besides, I actually do like children. I act mostly on instinct, and I'm intrigued by the way Maura thinks. From her stories, she spends more energy observing her children than jumping in to change them. It sounds like her older daughter—maybe Gráinne's age—is prickly and difficult, but Maura never uses phrases like "girls are so catty" or "I'll teach her to mind" or "after all I've done for her."

"She's had some difficult times," Maura says instead, immediately pivoting into a story about how the girl made a special pudding for her siblings.

I listen carefully, because sometimes my armlet calls me to help girls of this age, and I'm always afraid of doing something wrong. I always try to imagine my sisters, but I'm the eldest, so was fostered out before any of them reached young womanhood.

My armlet—come to think of it, why isn't it warm? Here I am, touching the person who is lost from her own time, the one the armlet clearly pulled over to me, but now it is telling me...nothing. No heat, no buzz, no images fluttering through the edge of my subconscious.

"Do you have children, Rian?" Maura asks.

I am startled into answering honestly. "I have a son. He's ten."

"Mm..."

Before Maura can even form a sentence, arguments tumble at me—the ones that people always make.

"He's fostered out," I add. "It's better for him that way, with a mother and siblings. They can give him more than I ever can, while he's young."

"Is your wife—"

"I haven't got a wife. Never have." Usually people assume I'm a widower, but I don't want to fake anything. Not with her. My heart is pounding, my throat tight. "River is not—he isn't"—the right words don't exist in this language, this culture—"I am not his parent by blood. His mother was my friend, but another man's wife."

"But clearly you love him."

Maura is perfectly calm, as though I am not dropping bombshells, ripping apart our conversation and leaving my heart torn and bloody.

"I do." I still feel the need to prove something. "I was—there—when he was born. His mother told me to—to take him." I don't think Nessa had the slightest idea what she was asking. River had not even properly woken up yet, by the time she said goodbye, and neither of us knew about babies back then. "I spent months with him, just him and I." I swallow, my voice growing stronger. "I was the one to rock him when he cried, to sing him the songs and show him the trees. He smiled for me and..." I remember the sensation of his little hands on my face, bumping my cheek, gripping my hair in his little fists. I blew on him and he giggled.

I can't say that, even now, as though turning it into words makes my memories less precious.

Maura is listening, her head cocked. We seem to have stopped walking.

I swallow again. "That was a long time ago, of course. I used to see him a lot, when he was a wee lad. Now he is training most of the year, and I have to work." And I'm pulled away by my armlet—more years have passed for me than for River. "But I still am the one he goes to. I answer his questions. I show him what matters. I..."

"You are his father," Maura finishes.

"Yes." My shoulders slump, and I begin walking again. I am not quite sure why I have said all these things; usually I hide the details of River's and my relationship. Fatherhood is an odd thing, defined differently in the different ages. I don't have words for what it means, just this raw burning throbbing passion.

"There are different ways of being a parent," Maura says, as though she is following my thoughts. "You are doing what matters—what fits you and your child."

"I suppose it is easier for a mother," I say. "You give birth and hold the baby, and you know it's yours. The love is obvious." Even Nessa loved her baby. I saw it in her eyes, in her tender fingers. She sends word occasionally, but has not yet had a safe home for a child.

Maura laughs, but there's sadness in it. "Mothers also have to find love another way. I have—I am not old enough to have birthed a son of sixteen. The older two..."

She pauses for a long time. I wonder if she is figuring out how to define something without revealing that she is from another time, or if these words are painful to her. I wonder if she loves the older two less, and find myself resentful on River's behalf, which makes no sense.

"My children all share a father," she concludes, and I understand immediately.

"Does their father live with them?" I ask. "Does he take care of them?"

"No-ooo..." She walks around a puddle, choosing her words as carefully as her steps. "He lives far away from us, and only sees the children...occasionally. But of course he loves them. He loves them very much."

I ought to be empathetic to a father who cannot live with his children, but that "occasionally" strikes me wrong. "A father who loves his children cares for them in a practical way," I say firmly. "He finds a way to see what they need. He most certainly supports his children's caregiver at *every* opportunity."

Maura flashes me an uncertain smile.

"A father honors his children's mother," I conclude firmly.

Maura lowers her head, leaving me with only the top of her headscarf. She does not drop my arm, but she pulls forward, away from me.

"There—is that the view? Are there cottages in the valley? The sky is so pretty!"

So Maura doesn't want to talk about her children's father, otherwise known as her ex-husband. Very well, it was a little close for comfort for me, too. After all, I'm not getting emotional about her.

I point out the distant blacksmith with his big courtyard, but encourage her to come a little farther. We fall back into easy conversation; the birdsong, the village, the swordplay this afternoon.

We're at the crest of the hill as the winter's sun begins to bleed rose and violet into the horizon. I point out the moon through the scrim of silver clouds, and Maura leans ever-so-slightly into my shoulder. I dip my head, smelling the over-bright sweetness of her shampoo—we don't have scents like that now—and the sugar-bun smell of her skin. I brush my fingers across her arm and down her back, and she leans in. She gasps and turns as a flock of red kites wheel out, weaving around each other on their way to their roost. As beautiful as the birds are, I've seen them on many winter evenings and I watch her expressions instead.

Sensing my gaze, she turns, looks up at me; flushed and merry.

"What?" She touches her own cheek, eyes fastened on mine. I want to put my hand over hers, touching her.

"How fair is your face!" My smile is easy. "Your cheeks bloom like roses, and your eyes are full of sparkling joy and color."

She stiffens and drops her gaze, then glances back up at me. "Are you sure that your lord didn't tell you to say that? Flatter the new lady, he says." She's teasing, but only half-way.

"I'll tell you who tells me to flatter the new lady." I thump my breast, aiming for that smile. "My own manly heart tells me to catch her eye."

Maura cascades a beautiful waterfall of laughter, her eyes still on mine, as sweet as a caress. This is it, then. I close the slight distance between us, brush the back of her cloak, and lean down—

She ducks her chin and steps forward. "The birds, what did you say they were they? Harrier hawk? Kites? And so many of them!" She's already moving down the path, pulling her cloak with one hand and pointing with the other. "Look! He's back! And another!"

"Red kites," I answer automatically, my mind wheeling through what happened. I didn't actually hold her, so she didn't pull away from me; I would never pin a woman into an embrace. But she was close to me, she was smiling right into my eyes—she must have known. She must have understood what I wanted; how beautiful I find her. She just doesn't want me. Fine, that makes it easier.

"They're so beautiful against the lavender sky." She sighs, and turns back to me with a wistful smile.

"Yes..." To me, that smile feels tender. It pulls me in.

I step closer. Next to her.

"But lonely." She pulls her cloak tighter and shifts, ending up closer to me. Her skirts brush my legs again; I can smell her hair. "Why is it that the sight should fill me with that loneliness, when they are all together? And we..." She trails off and shivers.

And then leans against me. Lightly, not her full weight, but seeking me. Hesitantly, I lift my arm. Slowly, across her back, giving her time to move away, but as my arms settles over her shoulders she rests against me. Her face is still turned to the kites and the sunset, but she has definitely softened in to me.

Definitely...so maybe she did not intend to avoid my kiss? I assumed she must have known what I meant, but assumptions are dangerous.

But I just *told* her that I find her beautiful; I just told her that she touches my heart as a man. I said those words, and I have been acting on them all day. How confusing can that be? Does she want to be kissed or does she not?

"And we are the ones who are lonely," Maura says softly. I am not sure if she meant it for me at all.

"Something so beautiful always makes the heart ache, doesn't it?" I say, grasping for conversation. "Perhaps not in summertime. Or perhaps it does, when it is lovely enough."

You are beautiful and make my heart ache—I push the thought away.

"Yes," she answers. "Yes, you understand."

My heart thrills as though I have won another prize, and I can't help but squeeze her shoulders.

"I'm sorry, am I bothering you?" She pulls away enough look up at me.

"Of course not—"

"I'm too weak. I should climb hills more often. I'm sorry, you must be tired after all that sword work, I shouldn't—"

"You're fine. It's fine."

She blinks at me, her mouth pressing together for just a moment, as though she needs to hold something back. And I realize I was wrong, she didn't hear anything I said about her being beautiful or the way she makes me feel. She said I was joking because that was what she believed.

No, she said that Fionn made me say these things. Frustration prickles and bubbles inside my chest. Fionn deserves no credit; I don't want even the thought of him near my feelings for Maura.

"There is still time to get home before dark...?" She reaches out her hand, tentative.

"Plenty of time. Dusk is long." I crook my arm and tuck her close, the gesture coming instinctively.

I want to. I want to comfort this woman. I want to convince her how I feel—even if this is only a short-lived flirtation, I want her to believe it. I want her to know that a man can be drawn to her, desire her.

"You can lean on me," I add. "I am strong."

"You are," she agrees, which feels surprisingly good.

Her boot skitters on some wet sticks and she half-falls against my chest. I brace her easily, pausing for her to secure herself. She leans into me even after her feet are back under her. Then she glances up, tentative, as though I might scold her.

"Are you all right?" I ask. "Do you want to rest a moment?"

"No, thank you. It will only get darker."

We pick our way more carefully, the path a tunnel in front of us.

"Thank you for taking such good care of me." Maura squeezes my arm. "You guessed just what I would love to see. I am so grateful that you are the one who is walking with me today."

Her words are easy, casual compliments that she throws around as easily as I throw jokes. But they pierce right through to the real me, the Rian that no one sees behind the jokes and the muscles.

I hold every sensation so I can remember this moment for years: the rhythm of her words, the smell of decaying leaves, the warmth of her arm against mine. You are the one, I am so grateful that *you* are the one—my heart soars like the red kites, swooping broad spirals through the darkening lavender sky.

Chapter Six

By the time I've settled Maura and changed my boots, three separate people have come to tell me there's a messenger to talk with me. Out here in the countryside, visitors are always exciting. Since they have made clear that his comfort has been cared for, I pause to warm myself by the fire in the Great Hall. I want a moment to think over the conversation with Maura before rushing off, and realize that my armlet is still not pulling at me. I wonder what it wants with her.

"Rian?" Saba's head lady-in-waiting is beside me, quiet as a breeze. "I will walk you to your audience."

Ailbe is the most sensible of Saba's bevy of young women. If she offers to walk with me, it is because she has something important to say, and concern seeps into me. I bow to accept her offer, brushing off my léine and running my hands through my hair. Perhaps this meeting is more important than I had guessed.

Ailbe is silent as we pass through the main floor. Fionn's castle is large only because so many people live here, every room used for work and socializing, tables and bedrolls coming out where the servants or herdsman eat and sleep. There are only a few rooms set aside for private use, and Ailbe must be taking me to Fionn's outer chambers.

Ailbe lights an oil lamp before we leave the main wing. The temperature drops, and Ailbe pauses, head bowed diffidently.

"What did you wish to say?" I ask.

"I mean no disrespect..."

"None taken."

Ailbe jerks her head at the curtain beyond us, and we duck through to the far side of the room—just in time, as two servants bustle by with platters of food and tea.

I don't know her well, but I have always figured that Ailbe is a little like myself. We are both Fir Bolg—although our people are still common now, I know from my rescue missions that our race will virtually disappear in favor of the pale-skinned Celts and later, Normans. But more than that, Ailbe has no more noble blood than I do; we were both given one opportunity in our childhoods and have catapulted far beyond anything our families could have dreamed. I was selected for military training; Ailbe was born the same day as Princess Saba to a servant-woman in her father's castle. I have not the slightest doubt that Ailbe worked just as hard as I did, and held her tongue just as often, in order to retain her position as Saba's second-in-command.

When Saba brought her ladies to the castle, there were several who thought I might court Ailbe, so I have given her a wide berth. I will certainly not marry Ailbe. First of all, she is too young for me. Second of all, I would never, ever bind myself to Fionn by marrying his wife's best friend. I will owe Fionn no more than our agreements within the fianna, nothing.

"I have two things you might wish to know, if I can be so bold as to advise you." Despite the formality of her words, Ailbe is not shy or self-deprecating.

"I welcome your observations."

"Yonder messenger"—she leans her head towards the visiting chambers—"knew you by name, and that you are River's guardian."

She pauses, but this could mean anything so far.

"He is from Nessa mac Euchaid. You know that she married last summer and is now the Queen of Uí Néill."

That was it! The rumor I heard and dismissed. I slow my breath, taking in this news. "I have heard of her marriage more than once, such that I do not trust whether this report is more true than the others."

Ailbe glances up at me. Her eyes are large, dark, and sharply slanted, reminding me of my second-youngest sister. "Queen Saba has her sources. Trust me, this one is true."

"And the king of Uí Néill is visiting in the south? Is his wife with him?"

Ailbe lifts her hands. "I have not heard that. I cannot answer. But this messenger wears the Red Hand on his brooch and shield."

"So he is from Uí Néill and knows my name." My heart slows, pulsing heavy against my ribs. Nessa always said she would care for her child when she was able.

"Most people assume that Fionn is River's guardian, not you," Ailbe adds.

I nod, unable to find polite words. Usually the king takes responsibility for all the young warriors associated with his castle, which in Fionn's case train with Liath Luacra; only a few would know that I maintained responsibility for River.

A few—like the child's mother and only biological parent.

"There is not much I can do if Queen Nessa makes requests regarding the child." I try to keep my voice even. Furthermore, I have lied to Fionn and pretended that Nessa has no connection to the child. He would not have agreed to foster a rival—another reason that I have never released fosterage to him.

"I know." Ailbe touches my sleeve. "I wanted you to be prepared before you walked in. That's all."

I take another slow breath. So she suspects more than I have ever said. "Very well. What was your second item?"

Ailbe turns away from me, the shadows of her face flickering with the lamp. "It seems that you are interested in our newest lady-in-waiting."

This is not what I expected. "And if I am? Do you know something bad about her?"

Ailbe shakes her head. "Personally, she seems both kind and willing to take on her fair share of work, which is more than I can say of many of the ladies. But..."

Usually I live at the edge of castle life, friendly to everyone and doing my duty. Having not just one personal drama—but two—is too much. I shift my weight, barely able to resist snapping at Ailbe to say what she means.

"She arrived very quickly." Ailbe meets my eyes again. "*Very* quickly."

So she noticed too? I am not entirely shocked that Ailbe is one of the ones who is not fooled.

Ailbe steps closer, dropping her voice even more. "Peculiar things happen around my lady. Guard your heart and keep your eyes open, that's all."

With that, she spins and hurries through the castle, the lamp flickering behind her cupped hand.

I follow, shaking my head to clear it. Ailbe doesn't know about my armlet, and thinks it is *Saba* who brought Maura to this place?

I don't have time to think about Maura right now—not to mention, she doesn't have anything to do with my heart. My son is the only one who has my heart, and it's time to focus on the conversation ahead.

***

Hywel has made himself at home, with his feet propped up by Fionn's fire and a tankard of ale beside him. He has grizzled stubble, narrowed eyes, and the sort of prideful defensiveness that I immediately recognize as the kind of man that Nessa likes to use. He glares at Ailbe, but after making introductions she stands at the edge of the room, eyes cast down. Hywel clearly decides she is only there to add to my consequence and promptly ignores her.

He inspects me, suspicious eyes raking me up and down. I lower myself into the chair beside him, not reacting to his disrespect. Despite his age, I am his social superior, and I will not make this conversation easy for him.

"First of all…" Hywel reaches into his pocket and holds up a pale rock, swinging on a chain. "Take this."

It flares with light and heat as my hand closes over the stone, but I expected something like that. Years ago, Nessa bought enchanted moonstones and used them to connect her fianna. I glance down at the familiar shape—I suspect this was my own. It led me to her, and she took it back when she released me from her service. It would be easy for her to enchant the charm to find me again; or perhaps she never released the connection and has kept track of me all this time.

Or at least, kept track when I am in this world.

"Does she intend to call me back, then?" I ask Hywel.

He waves his hand, dismissive. "No, no—my lady knows you are bound by other oaths. She sent this to prove you are who you say…and to prove to you that I am her messenger." He says the last grumpily, as though he does not want to give me even this much. "You keep it now." Definitely grumpy.

I loop the chain over my head, sliding the stone under my clothes.

"Ten years ago, you undertook a favor to my lady, now Queen Nessa of Uí Néill." Hywel settles into the story he is charged to recite. "She bore a child when she was young and powerless, and for the benefit of her son, she sent him to foster away. All these years, she has loved him from afar, striving to secure a position wherein she can nurture and honor him as he has always deserved." He pauses.

This is where I am supposed to praise Nessa's motherly feelings, but I merely sit back and wait. I have no illusions about my old friend. Caring for a child would have been a burden, whether her plans were making war or seduction, and they almost certainly involved both. Nessa does not like burdens.

"But now, Queen Nessa has a grand palace, and a doting husband with young brothers and foster sons of his own. She thanks you for your service, and is prepared to bring River home again."

As though River's home is a place in the north that he has never seen!

I raise my eyebrows, as calm as I always am when I am facing an important battle. "I am glad to hear that River's mother is now secure. When he is finished with his training, I will send him to Uí Néill."

Hywel frowns. "He is supposed to go now."

"Surely, Nessa would prefer some time with her new husband. I can arrange that River will visit them in the summer, when travel is easier."

"The king has sworn fatherhood to the child. You are relieved of your duties."

I do not betray any of my feelings. "I tell you, he is not yet prepared. He cannot go."

"But..."

"He will go when he passes his tests."

"Which tests?"

"Tell Queen Nessa that she might choose—she can overtake his training when he becomes a squire, or wait until he is knighted." Choice is always powerful, and either option will give him longer with me.

Hywel glowers into the fire. "That doesn't work."

"I am responsible for the lad's training."

"This is an order! Do as you are told!" Hywel glares at me, baring his teeth.

I remain as calm and expressionless as I was on the field this afternoon, letting Donnchad come at me again and again. "You may be Queen Nessa's servant, but I am not—and I never have been."

I let those words sink into the room.

"Fine." Hywel leans forward, elbows on his knees. "I'll tell you everything. But I'll warn you, you're not going to like it."

"Ailbe." I lift my hand. "Refreshments, please."

Without turning my head, I can feel her swishing through the room. I suspect this is exactly what she planned. Dressed as she is, her obedience proves that I am powerful, and meanwhile it is an excuse for her to come closer. I am not sure why I trust her, but I rely on my instincts and I do.

"Go on," I tell Hywel, while Ailbe fusses with boiling water and herbs at my side.

Hywel's eyes flick from side to side and he licks his lips. "My lady has already made a bargain with her husband the king. She came to the castle with her own trusted advisors, you see. Her own guard."

"Of course."

"The king..." Hywel pauses, picking at his léine.

I notice this is not 'my lord king.' So Hywel is Nessa's man and does not even pretend loyalty to her spouse.

"...has a bit of difficulty in terms of military strength," Hywel hisses.

"Thus making a warrior queen an attractive partner?" I suggest.

"Hm. Mhmm." Hywel gulps from his tankard.

I consider what Hywel does not dare say, even though the moonstone has proven my loyalty to Nessa and he considers Ailbe unimportant. Regardless, he is the guest of a king who could at any minute be a rival to Uí Néill, and should not spill its secrets. I will not expect him to tell me about his king.

Through all the years that I knew her, Nessa was bent on revenging her twelve foster fathers, who were brutally murdered in a raid. She accomplished that by killing her first husband, River's father, and then—as far as I can tell—has turned her considerable strength to amassing her own power. I don't blame her; I understand the yearning to get back at everyone who ruined her youth through pillaging and rape. Nessa is loyal and intelligent, but I hold no illusions that Nessa is kind.

A woman can best solidify her own power through a man, so it seems to me that Nessa will be happy with her king. Especially a weak king. Come to think of it, Nessa must be strongly motivated to keep him on the throne, while maintaining his debt to her. And what male can Nessa manipulate even more easily than a husband?

"So what about River?" I ask, my tone harsh. "What is the bargain?"

Hywel shrugs and opens his hands, licking his lips again. "It sounds strange, but I can only say what I know. My lady made the wedding contracts that her son will be named the king of Uí Néill for one year only. Then the kingship will revert to her husband, the rightful king. This way, she says, her son's children will be able to say they are the children of a king, giving them great honor. The king has agreed, but insisted that this year takes place while River is still a child. Therefore, my lady Nessa needs her son before he becomes a squire or his voice deepens. If you refuse to break the contracts, you can send *me* home, but I suspect my lady will send someone else to retrieve him."

Several someones, I have no doubt, with large swords and no morals.

A plan drops full-grown in front of my eyes: I will tell Guaire to trap Hywel and ask Ailbe to disguise this meeting, and with their assistance I will escape in the night. I will fetch River and run away with him. Because of the lies I told to protect Nessa and her child, no one here knows that River is her son. I am the only one named in all the fosterage agreements. I can take him. We can flee to Scotland—even to France.

A father honors his child's mother.

The words are my own. I spoke them to Maura not two hours ago, and I have been alight with righteous anger for the truth of them all day. If I take River against Nessa's wishes, than I am worse than her ex-husband, and I *hate* Maura's ex-husband. Rage rises in me, flaring against my ribs and throat. I hate that man who has made her doubt herself, who has leaves her with four of her children and no respect for herself. I hate him, I hate him—and I will not become him.

"I never wished to argue with Nessa," I say out loud, smoothly. "We have always been loyal to each other."

"Ah. Good." Hywel deflates, and I wonder if he saw the same vision that I did, complete with himself tied up in the cellars.

"I will order that River may be released into Nessa's care," I continue, thinking quickly. "But it must be to Nessa herself. The lad is in a precarious position, you must see. I have guarded him for all these years, and whether or not you carry a token, I cannot release him to just anyone. I will send word to Liath Luacra that he may be released to Queen Nessa herself."

It's all true, but furthermore that will buy me some time. I will go to my son, and damn this armlet—I will not let it pull me away.

Hywel nods. "My lady approves of such caution. And it shall be no difficulty—the king has brought her to visit his allies here to the south. She is only a short distance away, and will be at Liath Luacra as soon as your messenger arrives to release the child."

Short distance—will be—for a moment, my vision goes blank. Fionn's castle is much closer to Liath Luacra than the kingdom of Uí Néill, but still several days' journey. My hands cannot feel the arms of the chair. My ears roar like a thousand monsters are laughing at me.

"Thank you, good Hywel," Ailbe says. "My lord Rian will prepare the message that he has promised. You are dismissed."

And with that, Ailbe gives me the one gift in anyone's power.....she leaves me to my misery, alone.

***

I am a warrior.

I have the strength to make it through bloody battles, rescue children from burning buildings, and with the same unthinking, gritty fortitude I do what needs to be done tonight.

I commission one of the messengers from our own ranks. I teach him the message he must recite to Liath Luacra, releasing my son (my child, my beloved, my innocent) to Queen Nessa of Uí Néill. I give the messenger the code words that Liath Luacra will know, and send him with a personal token of my own. Never have I wished more bitterly that my time understood writing, that all I must do is scrawl a note and sign in. Instead, I have to say the words. Look people in the eyes. Make promises.

All the while, holding tight to my feelings. Letting nothing show in my face.

River, River, oh my beautiful child. There is so much that I haven't yet told you. You are so eager and hopeful, you believe so much in your own strength.

When Nessa was his age, her passions were moderated by the calmer, wiser, voices around her. I have moderated River's as best I can; warned him when he takes risks, punished him when he was disrespectful. He is eager to please and malleable to my will because I have earned his respect.

Now he will be malleable to Nessa's will. She is his mother; she is my friend.

But she is handing him a kingship. His morals are not yet sturdy enough to withstand such strain. It will not be good for him, and neither for his subjects.

As I arrange the logistics, hearing the preparations for the feast in the rooms beyond, I consider whether I could forgo the messenger and go myself. I only stay with Fionn because of River; I could rejoin Nessa's fianna instead.

If it were only my heart involved, I would swallow my pride to stay at River's side, although it is hard to even contemplate living near him but being forbidden to parent him. I could not give him guidance nor affection beyond that of a loyal servant.

I do not know what Nessa has done recently, or what she plans to do soon, but I am certain my heart would not agree. Our moral paths divided years ago. She dismissed me out of respect, rather than ask me to witness what she planned. But if it were for River, I could push away my moral code. It would be for his good. The chance to guide him just a little longer would make up for anything, wouldn't it?

But it is not only my heart. I would have to formally sever my contract with Fionn, which will take weeks of negotiation, and he would be in his rights to forbid me to go to Uí Néill if he is not currently friendly with their king. I must admit, I have not kept track of the ever-shifting alliances. I am the most senior general here, and Fionn will not make it easy for me to leave.

But in the end, my armlet leaves me no choice. I cannot go to Nessa.

Because although I might sever my contract with Fionn, there is no option to sever my obedience to the armlet. It will continue to pull me through time, sending me back and forth willy-nilly. All these years, Fionn has never paid attention to anything that does not directly affect himself, and my coming and going does not matter.

But the magic only obscures, it does not hide. Nessa is clear-sighted and sharp-eyed, and she would figure out all my secrets...except they are not mine. And Nessa would find some way to take this power, the need and desperation that calls me through time to save the innocent, and use it for her own gain.

So in the end, this is the truth. I cannot exchange the vague possibility that I might help River, that I might love him from a distance—not for the lives of all the children and grandmothers and yes, even the silly maidens.

I cannot give that power to Nessa.

So today, I lose my child.

CHAPTER SEVEN

I get to the Great Hall after the party has already started. The flutes and drums cast their eerie, pulsing net through the room, Fionn and Saba sparkling in the torchlight as they move through the crowd, lesser bodies ebbing in their wakes. There's music and stories tonight, not a formal dinner, so at least I don't have to sit next to anyone. I turn my shoulder forward and push through, collecting bread and meat from the trestle tables. I have donned my embroidered inar, my best jewels, and my casual smile. I am supposed to attend Saba's party and keep an eye on Maura, and I will do exactly that. No more.

A juggler takes the center of the room. My eyes skim past his flying balls and scarves—there she is. With several other women. And there's Fionn, ignoring the performance while he talks to the knot of men around him. Nice and far away from Maura, that's all I care about.

Not that I care about Maura. I am losing my son and my heart has turned to coal, burning and crumbling within me. But she is my responsibility and I might as well do my duty, since there is no other purpose to my life.

My duty...I remember Ailbe's words. *Peculiar things happen around my lady.* Like calls to like, and I know that my armlet has pulled in other people who are slipping through time. But since Fionn's marriage, I am no longer the only person at this castle with a magical pull. Saba herself is magical; one of the White People who has an animal form. Unbidden, my eyes find her in the crowd, where she is laughing and clapping for the juggler, wreathed in mirth. That is how I see her—on the cusp of womanhood, in the throes of her first love, well trained in household management. I know all about princesses, and they're exhausting.

Last spring, when Fionn brought her home, I was on border duty when we had unexpected action from the south. Forced to evacuate two villages. Our whole troop arrived home too grumpy to want to hear much about the wedding celebrations that we had missed while battling foe and fire. But Ailbe knows more about Saba than I do, and I should take her warning seriously.

As though my thought conjures her, the quiet woman is at my elbow.

"Did you hear about Fionn's trip?" she asks.

"*What?* By the gods' blades, haven't I had enough to manage?"

"You have, I know. I'm sorry."

I take a slow drink of ale to calm myself. "No, it is I who am sorry. I had no call to lash out at you."

A wistful smile flickers across her face. "You are quite something, Rian of Kilkirk, if you call that lashing out. Men say worse every day."

She doesn't deserve that. "Please. Tell me about this trip."

"Fionn has decided to take Saba to an Cnoc Rúa for the solstice."

I am stunned. "But—that's only a couple of days away. Men could make the journey well enough, but Saba will need..." I don't even know what a queen needs for a cross-land journey, but it's a great deal. Tents and attendants, several ladies and all their servants—

"He is only allowing Saba to bring one lady."

"*What?*"

"I know. It's not very respectful, but it is his choice. So please, sir, will you keep an eye on Maura? That she might keep an eye on Saba?"

"Maura is going? Why not yourself?" This is more and more peculiar.

Ailbe shakes her head. "Maura is—sir, she is a grown woman and a mother, herself. She knows things that I do not."

I furrow my brow, concerned for all three women. This is essentially a confession that Saba is with child, which is all the more reason that Fionn should not take her anywhere, especially not in winter, especially not at the speed we will need to travel. Fionn is selfish and blustering, but he is not a fool, nor is he cruel to his own people. Something suspicious curls inside me.

"Besides"—Ailbe looks up at me, her eyes huge in the flickering light—"remember what I told you? Something strange...I do not know what it is, but I do not want to separate them. Saba and Maura. I believe this is better for—"

I hold up a finger. I can't have anyone speaking of the Fae near me.

She shakes her head. "I know better than to say *that*. I was just speaking of my lady." Her voice cracks, so filled with emotion. "Watch over them, all right? Since I cannot?"

"I cannot do anything for your lady with her husband present."

"I know. That's what I mean—watch Maura. Take care of her. Do—all the sweet things you do, so she is alert and thoughtful."

"All the sweet things." My voice has gone bitter.

Ailbe lays her hand on my arm. "I know you are hurting. I know I am asking too much, but I love Saba as you love River. *I love her.* Please, Rian."

It turns out, my heart is not coal. I cannot resist Ailbe's love, knowing it thrills and pains her as much as what I bear for my son. My son, who was never really my son.

"Ailbe, I will watch out for her." I flick her the salute due to a commanding officer.

With a sad smile, she touches my hand and melts into the crowd.

***

In this mood, another man might pick a fight, or drink too much. I gird myself with a foolish grin and take the stage to sing a comic song. While people are distracted by laughter, no one sees my raw and throbbing soul.

Almost no one. Guaire watches me steadily. As I step down from the dais he offers me the chair he has been using. I thank him, but when he starts to ask me a question I hold up my hand, tense. For once, he subsides.

Three years past, the story was told up and down the kingdom when King Fionn hired Guaire and his identical twin, brilliant new knights both. Fionn placed them under my command. The night before our first battle, the twin was killed—a silent arrow in the dark, his life draining out before his fellows even knew what had happened. It was not only death, it was ignominious death—no glory, no praise, no song. Even knowing men as I do, I had not expected the depth of Guaire's despair; I had never before held a warrior in my arms, using all my strength to restrain him as he fought to kill himself. I convinced him to stay only because we were outnumbered and could not afford to lose another swordsman, but when the campaign was over he was in no shape to return. I made excuses to Fionn; spent weeks in the wilderness with Guaire. I do not claim to have brought him back a whole man, but I brought back a functional one.

Since then, he watches me. He sees.

Tonight, he relinquishes his comfortable chair, punches my shoulder lightly, and goes away. No longer just the professional bards and jesters, the men and women of the castle take their turns to sing and spin stories, and everyone clumps tight to listen—serving maid and warrior, dog-boy and farrier. I half-close my eyes, ready to let the performance carry me away.

Until Maura's voice snaps me out of my reverie.

What is she doing? I lean forward, bracing my elbows on my knees, glaring at the figure on the dais. Bright léine, dark hair. It's her all right, and a flush of anger races through me. She doesn't know anything about us and our time and our values. This isn't a stage for showing off.

But my frustration dissolves as I listen to her, or maybe I simply haven't enough energy left for any emotion. Despite myself, I am pulled into her story. Storytelling is an art of its own, and for some reason, it is an art that Maura has done the work to acquire. She speaks simply, her stance easy, her hands only sketching the occasional point. But she has the balance right, her voice pitched to carry easily, adjusting the plot based on the audience reaction.

I wonder what on God's green earth she is in her time. I wish that I could see her in her own world—and that surprises me, because I have never wished to leave the life in front of me, at least for anything short of antibiotics.

"You don't care about her, Rian," I mumble under the noise of the room. "You don't have space for anyone else."

But she tells another story, and story can seep through that chink in my armor—the one that Ailbe chipped with her plea.

Maura finishes her second story—there's a Winter Queen who turned soft at the end; I like it—and the crowd calls for more. I tense, because she's going to say yes and that won't be appropriate—but Maura smiles and shakes her head, declining in the most graceful way. She steps off the dais and is consumed by the crowd. I'm impressed with her, as pleased as if she were my own student.

A few moments later, Maura reappears, jostled towards me. Her confidence has vanished, and she's holding her arms close to her torso, eyes casting around too quickly for a seat. One of the warriors presses against her as he moves past, and she shrinks into herself.

Without thinking, I catch her eyes and pat my knees.

Damn. No. Wrong for her, wrong for me.

But she jostles closer and casts me a little smile, tentative, as though she expects me to change my mind and be disgusted by her. I hate that insecurity, I *hate* whatever man undercut her this way.

Good heavens. I am not usually this angry, and I don't like it.

A new song is ringing out, the crowd shifts, Maura pressed against my knees. I put my hands on her hips, worried as soon as I do it that it's too much for her, but she lets me pull her onto my lap.

I can't help noticing she has nice hips. Nice curves. Nice smell.

But she holds herself carefully upright, which is highly uncomfortable on my thighs. She glances anxiously at me. I already have my hands on her and she doesn't seem to mind, so I take a wild guess that she's worried about what I'm thinking. I slide my arm around her waist and pull her across my lap and against my chest, so she's settled nice and solid and comfortable. I'm surprised that as soon as I have her close, she melts against me.

As though she always knew how we would fit together.

As she watches the performance, I can feel her alert curiosity through her limbs. Her hands rest light in her lap, not touching me. But she snuggles under my arm, against my chest, even her head relaxing into me. This woman is nothing but a study in contradictions, and I can't help but wonder if she's doing it on purpose. Playing games with me, knowing how to draw a man's curiosity.

Even in my current frame of mine, I can't believe it for more than a few seconds. I'd bet my best jewels that this woman has practiced story-telling and seduction in exact inverse proportion—and that thought amuses me so much that I smile against her hair, another piece of my internal armor cracked right through.

The singer trills to a climax, and as her song spins higher and higher she bursts into her bird form. The audience cheers as the lark ascends into the dark above us, other human voices taking up the chant below. This is another of the ladies-in-waiting; I suppose Ailbe is right, and odd things happen around her mistress. In the hot press of noisy people, I can't tell if my armlet is tugging at me—or if Saba's magic pulled Maura here, and I have nothing to do with it.

Nothing to do with it. No obligation to Maura whatsoever.

The thought is so alien that I cannot even parse it. I'm *always* expected to deal with things. My armlet expects it me to rescue people willy-nilly; Fionn makes grand schemes and expects me to work out the logistics; even Nessa expected that she could just hand me her newborn baby and I would manage everything and return it to her as a full and healthy human. And I've done—

I can't complete the thought. I've lost too many. The girl I carried through the building won't survive her burns; Guaire's twin bleeding out; so many others. River is lively and healthy but leaving me. My arm tightens involuntarily, and Maura runs her fingertips across my hand, resting her own hand on my wrist.

I don't deserve her comfort.

The bird-woman is done and now they are chanting for—oh no. Saba.

Our queen is a gifted performer, just like she is a gifted herb-woman, and basically much more competent than her husband deserves. Which is why, whenever she takes the stage, I slip out the door. Because like the twin and the burned girl, Saba is one of the people I've failed. Fate put her in Fionn's orbit, not mine, and I can't do anything to help—so it's better not to like her too much.

Seven hells. I'm in the middle of the thrice-damned room, and there is nothing for it but to listen to Saba's story, and then I'll pity her and want to defend her even though I can't help her—and damn and damn again. Because if Maura is Saba's magic and not mine, I probably can't help Maura either. Probably should leave her alone.

It's a good idea in theory, but the woman is currently on my lap. Clearly I'm not leaving.

Furthermore, she's got that whole anxious-thing about men. I want to make her smile and feel attractive again. Damn this magic net; I just want—

I focus on the stage and don't let myself complete that thought.

Ailbe follows the queen, strumming the harp and echoing phrases as Saba tells the story, half-song. She is a princess, and the Dark Man follows her and her women searching for herbs. Fionn hasn't entered the story yet, and I know he's supposed to be the happy ending. Ailbe watches her mistress as they perform, and her love shines out and pins me to my chair. Yet again. I was better off when we were just warriors; before Fionn brought all these women home.

A shift in my arms pulls my attention out of that mire of self-pity. Maura stiffens, transfixed. She gasps and shivers as the Dark Man enchants the attendants and chases story-Saba into the dark forest. The story-Dark Man raises his knife, and real-Maura winces. Saba isn't casting a spell—she's not a sorceress—but she is an intrinsically magical being, and stories are intrinsically magical as well. It's catching Maura like a fish on a line, gasping and twitching as she is reeled towards danger.

I unclasp my brooch and shake her gently, breaking her odd twitchy stillness.

"Don't let it get to you," I whisper. "The music is strong tonight. Here, look at this while she is playing."

Our fingers brush while I pass her the knot of silver. She runs her fingers across it, following the patterns. I shiver, imagining those fingers brushing across my skin.

Not helpful, Rian. Not helpful at all.

I'm caught between Saba and Maura. I need to leave Saba, but I have to stay with Maura. By the time the next player takes the stage, I've ended up hearing more of the queen's story than I want—how the Dark Man kept her in her deer form as he pursued her, and only Fionn's love could save her, only within the walls of Fionn's castle could she maintain her human form—and *also* Maura is wiggling and sighing and she told a really good story, and I'm getting some masculine feelings that I don't welcome at all. I'm a mess. Either way, the women have foiled my plan to withdraw from humanity into a deep pit of depression.

I still can feel it—the aching longing for my son, the knot of fears pulling tight, my angry desire to snatch him and run—but it isn't everything.

There's also the sugar-cookie scent of Maura's skin. Song, thrilling and skittering across my skin. My over-sensitive awareness of Maura's every movement, the precise weight of her legs and her head and her hand on mine. Curiosity...about who she really is, and...

I turn her hand over and run my thumb across her palm, and tonight she does not pull away. My skin is dark against hers, my fingers work-roughened against her softness. But not too soft—I have the sense that Maura has fought some battles of her own.

And I wonder what might come next. Never mind Fionn's bumbling, and Nessa's plotting, and my armlet and all its tricks.

If it were just Maura and just me...what we could be together.

CHAPTER EIGHT

I roll out of bed, my chest tight and my eyes gritty as though I haven't slept at all.

Nessa. Coming for my son.

Fionn. Taking his wife and my Maura.

Not mine—I mean my armlet. She's tangled up in my magic, so it's not like I have a choice. I have to go.

Damn. Hells. Damn. I throw things at my rucksack, aiming a curse with each toss. My job with Fionn involves constant travel, so it doesn't take me long to pack.

Well, my job with the armlet involves constant trips too, but I don't have the chance to pack for those.

Lastly, I unfold the worn bag printed with purple daisies. Over the years, I've sewn it into a leather satchel to preserve it, because it goes everywhere with me in this world. I tuck a couple of books inside, plus a packet of black tea and a jar of my favorite hand lotion. That's enough to represent my library. If I reach into the purple-daisy bag without looking, it will produce books it thinks I should read and other useful items from its shelves. The library follows me through time—I always find bookshelves somewhere—but the purple-daisy bag seems to help it in the physical world. It's like a dog, always striving to be close to me.

I pause, staring at the worn cotton, inspired. Could I give this to River? Imagine how that would help him! The magic of my library means that anyone who holds its books can read them, and it could give him all kinds of great things. Stories of benevolent leaders, stories to remind him of proper morals—

The purple and yellow seems to fade before my eyes, and I sigh. Just like I couldn't expect a trained and bonded hound to work for my son, I can't—

Bran and Sceólang. If they are not back with their master today, it is proof that Fionn is lying. The problem is, I don't know what the deception would be about.

Time to find out...something. River isn't coming, so I might as well work on the problems in front of me. I tuck my library bag into the big one, swing the whole kit over my shoulder with a grunt, and trot through the dark castle. When I get to the room behind the kitchen, men of the fianna are milling in the lantern-light while one of the kitchen maids passes around a tray of rye buns and cheese.

I drop my bag and crouch by the tarp, getting bundles ready for the cart. Good gods, I wish coffee had been discovered.

Guaire hands me a parcel, leaning a little too close. "What are you doing here?"

I'm startled. "Where else would I be?"

"In bed. Warm. Dry."

"I thought we were going to an Cnoc Rúa!"

"*We* were." Guaire drops his voice. "Fionn didn't assign you to this patrol."

Just then, a bustle near the door means that the king himself is swooping in. He's talking, but interrupts himself to glower at me. "Rian! What are you doing here?"

For just one second, I'm tempted. I'm absolutely exhausted, I still have burns from my excursion to the Troubles, and this is going to be a wet and miserable trip with no particular purpose. But then anger rolls in, hot and flat and steady.

I brace my hands on my thighs and push myself to my feet, my eyes still locked on Fionn's. I'm glad that Guaire gave me an extra second to prepare.

"I heard you're taking the ladies to an Cnoc Rúa." I don't bother arguing about his orders.

"*My* wife." Fionn crosses his arms.

"And her lady."

Fionn smirks. "You heard that Maura was coming, and you can't miss the chance to get in her skirts?"

My hand flies into the air and there's a hiss as the men suck in their breath. I am a warrior, and rage makes me clear-sighted and fearless. For years, I've swallowed my thoughts about Fionn because I want to live at his castle to see my son. Today—I don't give a damn.

"You may not speak that way of a lady—*any* lady—in front of me."

Fionn startles, his head snapping back as though I had touched him. His eyes dart to my raised fist and back to my face. "You challenging me, Rian of Kilkirk?"

I don't say anything. I am rooted to the stone, waiting for him to come at me.

Or not. Fionn glances around the room, but his men won't meet his eyes. He went too far, and they all know it.

Fionn tosses his head, turning away from me.

I lower my hand. He's backing down, and I'm not going to demand an apology. I don't actually *want* to fight the man.

"Donnchad." I toss my bag to him. "Put mine in the second cart. I'll start out on point."

Donnchad stows my bag, but really I was pressing my advantage with Fionn. I'm going.

For a moment, I think I've won. After all, why would this even matter to him? But then he saunters towards me, jaw set.

"Go back to your bed, Rian of Kilkirk. Stop ordering my men around." He crosses his arms. "I'll bring the men I want to bring, and assign the lieutenants I want to work with. And you're not either."

I step closer, eye to eye. "I'm going on this trip. I'm taking the role I always take."

"I'm your king and you'll do as I say!"

"Do you know how much you owe me?"

Doubt flickers across his broad face, and in that moment I know I have him. But why would he be surprised? Whatever he's hiding, it also involves his missing hounds. Fionn is lying about something, and I don't have the power to stop him from doing what he chooses but I do have enough power to stick to him like a burr. He'll make another mistake, and I'll figure it out.

"I'll call in a favor," I add. "If that's what it takes."

"You just requested two things," Fionn snaps.

I laugh, unamused. "Two favors, then. You owe me more than I could possibly use on this entire trip."

Fionn glances around the room. Donnchad's brow is puckering, and the other men look wary—no one wants to work for a someone who picks fights with his own generals.

"Fine!" Fionn throws up his hands and spins away. "Give me that cup, girl! Hand me my coat! And *you*—I couldn't care less if you want to drag your sorry ass to the next kingdom! In the rain! Enjoy yourself, and enjoy your *courtship!*"

"This isn't about courtship," I snap. "It's about doing my job. The right way."

The words aren't for Fionn any more. It's a warning for the men. I don't know them well enough to speak clearly, but please the gods, maybe some of them will start looking carefully, before he pulls us all down into a story that we never wanted to be part of.

And Maura—and the magic—her being pulled here.

I can't do anything for Saba, I'm not allowed to do any more for River, so this—I'm going to take care of Maura if it's the last thing I do.

CHAPTER NINE

Anger is hot, and our journey is damp and frigid. My ire cannot survive slogging through this much mud.

As the heat of my righteousness fades, so does my conviction that I'm doing the right thing. Maybe I *should* be back in bed. Or running away with River. Or ignoring Maura entirely.

I stay on point guard the whole day; looking out for enemy bands, finding the best path for the cart, scouting out clean water. It gives me space to grumble to myself, talk it all through out loud. I don't want to be here. I don't want to be tangled up with Maura, who is tangled up with Saba, both of whom are way too complicated for a guy like me. Most of all, I grumble about River and how much Nessa ought to appreciate me.

It's all absurd and I know it. The only thing in life that I can control is whether I act with honor, and no matter how much my heart is breaking I'm not going to go back on a lifetime's worth of choices. River needs Nessa, too; I know he has an ache inside of missing his mother, not understanding how she could let him go. She promised she would raise him when she had the resources, and she is fulfilling her promises. But I still don't like it.

Apparently, back in the cart, Saba and Maura are talking about their husbands and families. All the warriors and carters keep their eyes averted, giving the women their privacy, but everyone is fascinated. Every time we stop to water the horses or clear the road, the men share their gossip. Anyone new is fascinating, but Maura's circumstances are especially so.

"Can you imagine—her husband set up a new household! The husband!"

"He must have been rich."

"He must have been foolish!"

"Where was her father in all this?"

"I dunno. She hasn't mentioned her parents yet."

"Listen closer, Donnchad!" The men laugh.

Donnchad shrugs, defensive. "Maybe Queen Saba knows already. Be patient. It's not like I can just ask."

They cast me glances but I keep working, laying one branch beside another so the cart can cross the mud. I set each one carefully, not looking up.

But I'm listening. I'm curious too, and I fill in more holes in my mind; knowing she is from a different times, knowing the stories she has told me.

At the next stop, the men report that the ladies talked about children. They confirm the hints that Maura dropped with me; that the older two are from her husband's first marriage. The other men all assume that his first wife died, but knowing that her time has a great deal less illness and more divorce, I have my suspicions. They report that it's difficult for Maura to make decisions, since the children's father apparently gets some say.

"Her father should call the magistrate and revoke the ex-husband's privileges," Donnchad declares, irritated. "The situation is highly irregular."

"Does she have a foster agreement?" asks the farrier.

The others scold him. She needs no such thing, they say. She is their mother—or even, some admit, if she is not exactly their mother, she is as good as their mother.

"No one should argue with a child's mother," our rear guard says. The others chorus their agreement; the mother is always right.

Guaire glances at me. He, too, has been quiet. I wonder what he heard about Nessa.

I haven't been to Maura's time enough to understand how their legal system works, but I know it is more nuanced than ours. Society gets more complicated, laws change. The father still retains rights even though he left their mother; they have words like "step-mother" and "adoption" and "custody."

In our time, fosterage is about training, not about parenting. In our time, if Nessa takes a new husband and he accepts her children, he is the father. I am neither. I am nothing.

The men talk about the arguments that might take place—this is all gossip and speculation now—with the father demanding something different from the mother (poor Maura has earned everyone's sympathy)—and I try to convince myself that it wouldn't be worth it. Trying to co-parent with Nessa would be a disaster, especially since she would always win.

Still...I want River. My anger is suffocated under the mud, but the pain only increases, my back howling with all the bending and lifting, wet boots chafing with each step.

***

That night, I finish changing and arrive at the big tent as Donnchad approaches from the stream-side. Owls hoot, branches drip, the servants clatter at the crackling fire. I nod and pull aside the tent flap.

In front of me, Donnchad freezes. I push inside next to him, the flap falling behind us, and he grips my elbow, too tight.

"This is bigger on the inside than the outside." Donnchad's voice is thick with fear.

"Hm." I examine the space, carpets laid out, fine pillows, golden goblets in the ladies' hands. We only took two carts, and one is full of Maura and Saba.

So this is Fionn's next mistake, and he's not even hiding it. As though we are all trapped with him, and now he doesn't care what we figure out.

"Is Fionn a sorcerer?" Donnchad's voice is barely the echo of a whisper.

"I think you know the answer to that," I reply.

"Am I dreaming?"

I sigh. "I think you know the answer to that, too." I put my hand over the young man's, pressing his fingers, hoping he understands that it's not a good idea to answer. It's not a good idea to ask.

Donnchad looks back and forth, eyes wide. Fionn is reclined at the far side of the tent, throwing his head back and laughing. Where Fionn is gleeful, Saba is delighted, and when Saba is joyful no one else can resist.

"Is it because *she* is a sorcerer?" Donnchad asks.

I just sigh. If it's easier, he can believe that. As for myself, I think if Saba had any magic other than changing into a deer, she would use it for something more useful than a fancy-looking tent.

Like getting her own damn self out of here. I shake the useless thoughts out of my head. Saba is in charge of Saba, and she's in charge of Maura. At least Maura in this world, not sure about the magic. I touch my armlet as I move into the tent, accepting a goblet of my own. No buzz, no pull. I'm nothing but a warrior, well trained but getting to the age when his body starts to get in his way. Nothing but strong arms and quick reflexes. That's it.

Even as just a man, my duty to Maura is clear tonight. There's almost a dozen men here and only the two women. The others would take advantage of my absence, and she doesn't deserve that.

So it's only respectful to stand close, let her lay her hand on my arm.

It's only decent to fetch her pillows, refill her wine, and chuckle at her jokes, which are clever and observant.

It's only proper to dance with her, sashaying up and down the tent as she laughs.

Then of course, there's the issue of what her ex-husband did to her confidence, her image of herself as desirable. I've got to stay mindful of that, so it's only reasonable to glance up and down her (quickly now), and smile my approval into her eyes. She laughs again, holding herself a little taller. And I can't help enjoying that, just like I can't help enjoying her soft curves and bright face.

I'm only being a gentleman. The least I can do.

***

I pause for just a moment, rain dripping down my hood, my hand on the corner post for the women's tent. I've got to listen to the forest. Any dangers. Despite myself, my head sags, spine drooping.

I don't let myself hear their words, but Saba's voice is upturned, sparkling. Maura is laughing, happy, but even so her tone is low and soothing. It warms me. Despite myself, a vision leaps into my head—coming home at the end of the day, tired like this, Maura rolling over in my bed. Saying my name. Her gentle voice rising and falling, telling me about her day. Myself making her laugh.

It would be easier to cut myself off from the temptation of the vision, but I grit my teeth and hold onto it instead. It'll help for what I've planned next. I slip through the bracken back to our tent, holding the memory of her smell, her voice, the texture of her hand. I kneel down to crawl through the tent flap, feeling Guaire's presence in the dark as I unlace my boots and tuck them away. I'd rather test this out on my own, but at least it's just the two of us. He thinks the armlet means I'm some sort of magical chosen one.

I think I'm just tired.

I undress my outer layers, heavy cape and belted inar, pull the léine over my head. Even in the huddled dark, the armlet glints as I slide it down my arm.

Cast it away across the bedrolls.

"Is your arm hurting?" Guaire asks.

I grunt. I'm concentrating on Maura, staring at the sparkle of jewels.

After a long minute, I pick it up, weigh it in my hand. Tip it back and forth, like the scales of justice.

Nothing. No pull to the tent only a few yards away. Maura laughs, and still nothing.

I drop the armlet, turn away, breathing hard.

Fine then. There is no connection between us. I imagined there was, but she's in someone else's magic. I have nothing to do with her.

"May I try it?" Guaire is subdued now.

"Go ahead." I unroll my bag, searching for something clean and dry.

Behind me, I can hear Guaire fiddling with the armlet; after a moment, the sound of metal sliding across a sleeve. Despite myself, I'm curious. No one else has ever put it on.

"Does it fit?" I wonder if it burns. If it pulls him.

"Are you trying to get me to admit that your muscles are bigger?" Guaire teases. "Because I'd have to admit they are." More shushing noises. "But it doesn't do what it does for you. The edges poke into my upper arm and it's loose on my lower arm. Like metal usually does on skin, right?"

I slide into my bedroll, propping myself on my elbow so I can watch Guaire, or at least the shadow of him in the dark.

"It just feels like jewelry," Guaire says. "Nothing more."

It has never felt like jewelry to me. It feels like part of myself, as essential as my throat or arm.

"Can you feel anything?" Guaire asks me.

"It wants me back." The pressure is building, faster than it ever does when I simply let it sit on my bed.

"I wish it could let you go." Guaire slides the armlet down. "I don't like this bargain it made."

"I like it fine, and I'm the one who has to live it." I've said that for years, and I'm too tired to excavate the truth.

"It demands so much from you." Guaire drops the armlet on the blankets between us. "Don't you want anything else?"

"I have River." But my voice breaks. I roll over, my face to the canvas.

"Love is all that tethers us to the world, isn't it. I know that too, my friend."

I have no answers. The armlet is calling to me, pressing like a thirst, but I don't touch it.

Finally, Guaire slides into his bedroll. We usually sleep back to back, but tonight the metal spiral is between us, his weight pressing it into my spine.

We are battle companions. I do not need to hide from him that I am crying, but I need to bury it from myself. There could be brigands or wolves in the forest, we are probably the only ones who are sober, and the king we are following is an imposter. I don't have time for misery.

Guaire rustles in the blankets, pulling out the armlet. He reaches over my shoulder to put it in my hands, and I feel that familiar comfort when I slide it into place. Like sliding a bolt into the door, locking it firmly.

"When I lost my brother, do you remember what you asked me?"

I don't want to hear my own questions. I don't want to think about loss.

"What else do you want, Rian? What makes your life—"

"I know."

"—worth living? Where is your own heart, Rian?"

I grunt and curl my arm over my head, and Guaire chuckles.

I want to be able to rescue my lover with tenderness instead of violence. I want a soft voice and peaceful hands. I want someone who notices—

I was going to say "the little people, the ones in the shadows, who aren't rich or important." Those were the words in my head. The argument I make for myself.

Instead I just hear "me." It's painfully selfish, but I want someone to notice me. Me, me, me.

But my armlet didn't pull Maura here, and there's no connection between us. It was all in my imagination, and it's time to let her go.

CHAPTER TEN

W e've got to get Fionn and the ladies to an Cnoc Rúa, and my feelings don't come into it. So I help break down camp, load the carts, clean the camp. I keep my eyes and hands on each task, my mind controlled. Shoulder my pack, lace my boots, check the path. Keep everyone safe, move us forward. I focus on sounds in the woods, scat on the trail, woodsmoke on the breeze. Just do.

But the more I try to withdraw into minutiae, the more the other men want me. Fionn has gone too far; maybe now that he has us out in the woods, out of the castle, alone, he doesn't care what we think. He throws tantrums about our pace, and when the wood smolders to heat our lunch, he sends the bonfire blazing with a curse.

In ones and twos, the men crowd up to me. Some speak low, some daren't speak at all, but they all want to know the same thing: what do we do next, Rian.

I haven't the foggiest idea in seven hells. We just need to get over this hill, ford this stream, make a crossing for the cart.

Listen.

I don't know if it's Fionn or an imposter.

I don't know how he could become a sorcerer, let alone in the span of a few days. Is it possible? Probably.

I don't know why we're going to the biggest Solstice festival in southern Ireland.

There's druids? Well, I don't know what Fionn wants with druids, either.

No, I don't think we can send a messenger to Saba's father. Yes, I think Fionn would notice. No, I don't know why he cares.

All day, these are the things I try to say, without drawing the interest of any of the Fae or the magic in the air, which is another thing I don't know how it works. I don't know anything, but they come to me in ones and twos. Looking for reassurance. Answers.

Well, one thing I do know. We're not going to fight, or run, or call attention to the Fionn-who-is-not-quite. This I tell them: All of those actions would hurt the ladies, and our first duty is to the ladies.

At this, every man—from the cartier's boy to the most well-born warrior—nods his head and subsides. We all know our duty, and as their ranking officer, my duty is to remind them.

As their ranking officer, my job is to get them all home safe, and I wrack my brains to figure out how. I can't see a strategy when I don't understand the enemy.

And that's when I realize...I can't make a plan until Fionn makes his next move.

So I just have to pray he is more than one step away from destroying the ladies.

***

I avoid the women all day. I don't want to invade their privacy, and Maura is not mine and never was. They are my responsibility and I respect them, nothing more, nothing less.

Today, we travel on the more-established lamráite, but the weather is dense and every furlong is slow. The packhorses struggle in mud up to their hocks, so the ladies get out and walk. Guaire leads them into the woods, circling around the worst mud-holes. I remember how Maura's breath puffed and her feet slipped when we climbed the paths near the castle, and—no, it is not my place to worry. I just take that into my calculations for pace.

Fionn has no calculations; nothing will sway him from the evening stop he has fixed in his mind. We must be close enough to arrive tomorrow. By the time we lurch into the campsite, one of the horses is lame and another is winded, one of the front guard has a bad scrape that is not bound properly, and half the crew never received their lunch rations.

Can we—

Will we—

The men make excuses to brush by me, anger and fear hot in their voices. I growl back a warning, lips pressed together, no words. Celts are known for being hot-headed, but there are times when you just have to *wait*.

Dusk is gathering too quickly, given everything we have to do. The men fill a cauldron over the bonfire, where Saba presides. She tends the injuries, then throws herbs in the water to brew a tisane, singing lilts as good smells rise on the steam. Maura has unpacked the mugs and trudges back and forth around the camp, bringing each man a steaming cup. I'm busy with my jobs and not paying any attention at all, but her gentle laughter floats across the clearing. She asks each man a question, waits for his answer as he drinks.

There. I've done my tasks, and everything urgent is under control. I survey the camp, checking each activity. I've done my duty, and I'll do better tonight if I step away now.

I follow the path to the stream. No one's fetching water right now, but just to be safe I go a little farther. There, I'm surrounded by leaves, the noises from camp far enough that they fade into a blur. I sit on a downed log.

My library isn't great with non-fiction, but I've read novels about emotional struggles and there's some useful ideas in there. Five things that you smell, four things you touch—they're all damp—three things you...smell? Aw, to hell with it. I lean forward, my elbows on my knees and my head braced on my fingertips.

There's a sound in the bracken and I jerk upright. It's a person, probably Guaire, or someone to ask me—

It's Maura. She comes around the bend slowly, focused on carrying something small, at chest-height. I'm so intent on checking her health that she startles me completely when she holds out a mug, a sweet hopeful smile turned up to me.

I turn away. I can't keep this up any more.

"Take the tea," she says. "It will help you feel better."

I grunt. Still don't look at her.

"At least, it's burning my fingers, so will you please take the cup now?"

I may be rude, but I'm not that rude. I accept the mug, and since I'm holding it I might as well take a sip. It's spicy, burning a path that fizzles with energy and heat. Saba is a good mná feasa, and this will be good for the men.

"May I...sit?"

Maura has nothing to do with me; my armlet makes no promises that I can save her. I don't want to sit close to her, not in the mood I'm in. But I move over, finding the smoothest place on the log for her, spreading my cloak so she doesn't get as wet. The log is full of branches and knots, so she ends up right next to me. A stick presses into my calf and her sleeve settles on my arm. I can smell her sugar-bun skin, shiver with her warmth.

Every fiber of me wants to just make a joke, drop a compliment, make her happy. For once, I don't. I don't owe her anything, and I'm worn out with owing.

"The men respect you."

I almost slosh my tea, and have to sip it instead. That's the absolute last comment I expected.

"I've noticed that, watching you." Maura adjusts herself on the log, neat and upright.

I warm with pleasure at her compliment, her attention, but then the weight of her words sinks onto my shoulders. The men I'm responsible for, this trip to nowhere that I haven't figured out.

"You should have some too," I say, passing back the mug. "You're cold."

She sips, obedient, then glances at me side-long. "You're worried about River."

I should stop being surprised by anything this woman says. But really, I should stop having intimate conversations with her. Emotional thoughts. Anything.

"Is he sick?" she asks. "Upset? Maybe I could help."

"It's nothing, really." Focused on keeping my tone light, I realize she has put the mug back in my hands and I've drank half of it. "He's going to live with his mother. It's good for children to be with their mothers. Right? Right."

Maura furrows her brow, watching me intently. "When was he with her, last?"

I shrug. "Well...she carried him. All those months. He probably...recognizes her voice from the womb. And... Mothers are always best for children, wouldn't you say?"

Instead of agreeing, Maura sighs. "I think motherhood can be complicated, just like fatherhood."

I gulp the rest of the tisane, then berate myself because I meant to give it to her. "I'm not his father any more. Nessa has married, and the—the man has claimed River. It's *best* for him!" Maura's a thoughtful, loving mother, and it's oddly important to me that she agrees. I want to hear it—her saying that I've made the right decision, even though I haven't any other choices.

She turns towards me, her knee pressing mine. "Maybe it is, maybe it isn't. River isn't here and I can't see what he thinks."

"If—" I cut myself off, looking away. What she thinks doesn't matter; she's with Saba.

"But *you* are! Rian…"

When I still don't look at her, she touches my forearm. At first the pressure is so light I'm not even sure it's her, but she lets her hand settle. Pulls me, very very gently.

I turn to her. The dark has gathered around us, making this is my entire world: the stream at our feet, the rustle of leaves, Maura's blue eyes and solemn mouth. I want to kiss her. Instead, I lift my hand. Adjust her hood. When she doesn't draw away, I run my thumb across her cheek. Her skin is cool, rounded, velvet.

"I am talking with you," Maura continues softly, now that she has my attention. "And it is only reasonable that you are upset about River leaving. Those are valid feelings. We can acknowledge, right here, together—"

She breaks off, catches her breath, glances down and away…as though she is as overwhelmed as I am. Right here. Together. Maura and I.

"That you miss River," she mumbles. "That this change is going to be hard for you. That…that's real too."

Her head is bowed, and I think she's done. But her fingers scrabble across the fabric spread between us and find my hand. She squeezes quickly, but I tighten my hand around hers. We stay like that, one breath, then another, our joined hands clasped firmly, resting on my mud-splattered thigh.

"Thank you," I say, because I have to diffuse the tension and bring her back to camp.

"I'm sorry to be another burden on you," she answers, which doesn't diffuse anything at all.

"You aren't! You—"

"I am. I'm the slowest and weakest, and you're the one who has to figure everything out."

I sigh, rubbing her knuckles with my thumb. She's too smart for platitudes. "Very well, it does take work to keep you and Saba safe. What I meant was...that is not a burden."

She looks up at me, her face pale and unreadable in the dark.

I think she needs to hear this again.

"You are not a burden to me," I tell her.

I catch the flicker of a smile and squeeze her hand. "Now, I need to get you back to camp."

"Are there dangerous things in the woods?" Her voice is curious, not afraid.

"Not really." I lever myself to my feet, not allowing myself to grimace at the aches, and offer her my hands. "But we need to be there for whatever my lord and lady have planned tonight."

She stands, slowly. "I...can't really see the path. Is it...?"

I think this is Maura's version of asking for help. I loop the mug onto my belt so I have both hands for her; she's tentative, double and triple checking each step. I can feel through her hands that she is terrified of falling, but she doesn't complain.

"You were brave, coming out here alone," I say, just to keep her spirits up.

"You didn't have your cup of tea." She is surprised. "I needed to bring it to you, that's all."

But that's not a little thing—to be remembered.

I bring her back to camp, past the bonfire with trout grilling and the horses munching their oats. She is tired and leaning on me, and despite everything I know in my head, that feels good. I like being strong for Maura, even if it only lasts for tonight.

CHAPTER ELEVEN

Last night, Fionn was carelessly cruel to his wife, and whatever delicate thing Maura and I have going apparently cannot survive that. Faced with Fionn's callous disregard, Maura has curled tightly into herself and her friendship with Saba. Today, neither of them speak to any of us with more than polite words and a tight smile. They slip into the woods together, staying far longer than their excuse of relieving themselves, and return with their shoulders together and not meeting our eyes.

That's fine. It's just as well. I have my hands full with making sure Fionn doesn't cause actual injury with his demands. He threatens to have me whipped, while I'm standing on a small rise overseeing our equipment portaged across a stream. Properly. There is not one single person in Fionn's employ who would would attempt to whip me, and if the Fionn-imposter doesn't know it, the other men do. I'm glad, though, that Donnchad has escorted the ladies upstream to a bridge, so they don't have to hear this.

We get to the area around an Cnoc Rúa in the mid-afternoon, still time to set up and rest before the Solstice festivities begin this evening. The men know their jobs, so I set off for mine—checking the other camps, making sure I know who is around and that we all remember our settlements. I've been working in this area for ages, so it goes smoothly. Most of the others know me, and the ones who don't know my reputation. No one makes me wait before their leader comes to greet me, and a boy always runs over with a sharing cup. One campfire to another, I pass it back and forth with the head men, mead and tisanes and spiced cider, whatever that camp has prepared for their own men. I am a little surprised to taste stimulants among the herbs, glad I'm only having a sip.

We all need our luck for the coming year, eh, Commander Rian.

I've brought a cow. Asking for visions about who to name as my heir, getting older, don't we all.

What did King Fionn bring for the sacrifice?

I don't know the answer to that one, and I don't like it, either.

I hear you have a lady. This isn't the festival for weddings...

I agree, not sure what my flash of heat means—that I wish I were marrying Maura, that I'm afraid for her, relief that the druids won't expect us to leap the fire tonight.

By the time I return to our own fire, I am deep in a layer of mystery. Why are we here? My best guess is that Fionn wants a prophecy for the child that Saba carries, which explains his sudden manic desire to bring her here, but not his flashes of sorcery. Unless—

The tent flap closes behind the ladies and everyone converges on me.

Fionn has—

Saba asked—

What if—

I wave them off. "Wait. Wait! I hear you, I get it. No, don't tell me the details. Wait!"

So there's another crisis, another argument between Fionn and Saba, another reason they can't trust the leader of our fianna. Another thing for me to solve.

I consider it, kneeling in our little tent changing into my best clothes. Guaire keeps glancing at me as we both shake out our best embroidered inars and careful rolled cases with necklaces and brooches. I'm increasingly irritated with his silence, and the tension crackles around us like a lightning storm in the distance.

By the time Fionn takes the women down to the festival, I have some plans ready. The men huddle around me, and after the lookout announces that Fionn has truly vanished into the crowd, everyone's concerns spill out. Fionn threatened this, Saba was gathering herbs, what if he leaves, what if he comes back, what if, what if. I try to get them to slow down and draw a map in the dirt. Here's how we'll get home. We'll bring the ladies to Saba's father's castle until Fionn's strangeness blows over. I count the supplies, calculate how we can divide them out if we need to separate, how many days' travel we have left.

There's a thump in the trees. Guaire swears, then calls out. "Rian! I need you."

I pause, frustrated.

Guaire appears at the edge of the clearing, his expression rueful and playful. "Sorry, men, but I need to talk to Rian. It's about time to go down the celebration anyhow."

"We can finish tomorrow, while Fionn sleeps it off." Donnchad rises, brushing off his hands.

"Do we have guards assigned?" I run through the jobs, moving towards Guaire. He ranks everyone else; he has the right to call me.

The others salute as I give them assignments, dispersing to the fire and into the big tent to change.

Guaire pulls me into a scrim of trees, halfway to the next camp. His cheerful expression melts into a scowl. "What the seven hells do you think you're doing, Rian of Kilkirk?"

"What's your problem? Why'd you pull me—"

"You! You're the prob—" Guaire shoves my shoulder.

I punch his ribs, and he doubles with a grunt. I'm angry.

"I'm making a plan for my troop to get home safe. Like I always do." I cross my arms, glaring down at Guaire, who is still leaning over and gasping. "Like I've done for you. Aren't you glad I didn't leave *you* in the woods with a madman?"

"I am." Guaire straightens up, and he is angry too. "So I don't repay you by asking you to do it again and again, for forever, at any cost."

"What cost?" I fling my hand back towards camp. "This is my job! These are—"

"Why?" Guaire demands.

I gape at him.

"Why are you going back with Fionn? Why are you protecting his men?"

"Because they need me! Because—"

"They don't need you."

"They do! Didn't you hear—"

"Of course I did." Guaire steps closer, grips my arm. "You're good at this, you're confident, you're one of the best warriors in Ireland. Of course they want you."

"What about you?" It's hurting in a way I didn't expect, Guaire arguing with me.

"I love you." Guaire shakes my arm. "I'd lay down my life for you, no question. That's why"—his voice cracks—"I want you to think twice right now. I want you to..."

I stare as tears well in his eyes. He's not saying this. Not Guaire. Not my one friend.

"I want you to go, Rian." He runs his other sleeves across his face. "You stayed with at Fionn's castle because of River. Not because of me. Not because of them."

"Go where? I can't..." I'm stunned. I don't know what I can or can't do.

"Fionn has broken his vows to you, and if this isn't the true Fionn, then it's his problem for another day." Guaire attempts his usual insouciant smile. "River is going to Uí Néill. The men can take care of themselves." He smiles again, and it works a little better. "Go with Maura, Commander. Follow her."

"But I don't..." I fling my arm to the side, out of his grasp and away from my cloak. Tonight I've worn my armlet over my clothes, like most men do with their best jewelry. I tap it. "It's not about her. We're not connected."

"Not connected? What kind of horse-shit is that?" Guaire shakes his head. "I've known you for years, and I see the way you look at her. I see the way she leans on you. What do you think connection is, if it isn't what you have?"

I close my hand over my armlet. "But it will pull me away. But I'm not meant for..." I don't know what I'm meant for.

Guaire pulls my hand down, straightens my cloak, his smile odd and wistful. "For all these years, you've loved River with the biggest heart I've ever known. Despite everything Fionn asks, plus this ridiculous magic you're tangled up in, you've always put him first. Don't tell me you don't have room for loving Maura."

"But... Maura is Saba's lady-in-waiting. And we'll be going back..."

Guaire shrugs. "You and I both know she arrived out of nowhere and no one else noticed."

"So she might go back to our castle. Saba might—"

He clasps my shoulders. "But following Maura is different from following Fionn, isn't it?"

It is. And it's different from following my armlet. I can't meet Guaire's eyes, my breath coming too fast, my eyes searching through the branches to the dusky, glowing, setting sun.

I am not bound to Maura, which means I can choose.

I can choose.

I turn back to Guaire, my heart beating faster. "And the men? And the Fionn-who-is-not Fionn?"

His hands are calm and firm. "They are grown adults. You don't owe them your life."

My voices shakes. "And you?"

He smiles, and this time it is genuine but his face crumples at the same time. "Go with your heart, Rian of Kilkirk."

I bow my head, and Guaire touches my forehead in blessing, and then he kisses both cheeks. There is nothing more to say. I will see him later tonight, or I will not.

I push through the trees until I can see the festivities below, search through the colorful cloaks and dancers until I find what I need. Fionn has made a circle around himself, golden-haired Saba by his side. And behind her, a dark head, and a smile that I want for myself. We don't know each other yet, but I've decided—she is worth it. I don't know where she belongs or if I'm the right partner for her, but I'm not going to give up until we both have a chance to decide.

I start down the hill, and before I know it, my feet are pounding the ground. Running. I choose Maura, and I choose tenderness and understanding.

Chapter Twelve

T he sun is fading, the bonfires are leaping. From above, I could see the standing stones themselves; a circle our ancestors placed hundreds upon hundreds of years ago, where the light shines through only on the moment of winter solstice. Obviously, they have no use at night, so I head towards the meadows where crowds are gathering. Fionn was in the larger one, and by the time I reach it the musicians are in full thrall while dancers gallop up and down. I wait at the edge, scanning the crowd. There are not many women here tonight, and I'm even more concerned about Maura and Saba.

I catch sight of Maura's colorful léine as a red-haired warrior swings her down the lines. I step forward and she must say something to him, because he laughs and she absolutely flies into my arms. I step back with the impact, closing her safe in my embrace. For just a moment, she rests there, her face in my shoulder, unmoving except for her heaving chest.

When she looks up, she is smiling.

"All right?" I brush her hair out of her face.

There is something sad and strange in her expression. "Saba will be occupied tonight."

"I'll stay with you."

"Did Fionn ask you to? Did Saba?"

She's anxious. I don't answer, just tucking her arm into mine and leading her towards the lower meadow. I'm not sure if she wants them to be taking care of her, or making sure they are not, but it doesn't matter now. Saba is holding Fionn's arm and laughing into his face, besotted and giddy and tumbling towards whatever fate he has planned. I'm with Maura.

I buy us both skewers of goat meat from one fire, and roasted nuts from the next. Maura is thirsty, but I shake my head.

"You don't think I can hold my drink?" She smiles, playful and brittle.

I don't, actually, come to think of it, but I was thinking about the herbs I tasted earlier. I don't know what's simmering in these kettles, and I don't trust anyone here. I find some honey-cakes, and then an entrepreneurial old woman who is selling birchbark cups and access to the stream. The spring is coming straight from the good earth, and I stand over Maura, hands on my hips, as she crouches on the bank and drinks her fill.

She stands, lips wet, and offers me a tentative smile. "Do you like to dance?"

"I love to dance."

So I take her back to the big meadow, pulsing with drumbeats and the smell of sweat. She's twitchy tonight, unsure of herself. She snaps away if I pull her too close, but at another moment she presses against my side, sheltering under my arm.

I can be patient with her. She's in a strange world, pulled away from her home and children, and this festival is even stranger. I study her; something has changed between yesterday and today, so Fionn might have done something worse yet. I want to talk with her, but everything is too loud and too dark.

She moves away from me to look at a puppet, a skeletal human figure on some kind of stilts. Still watching her, I pat my hand across my robes and jewelry, thinking about what I could use to charm the Veil. On Solstice night, it should be easy to find a doorway. When the armlet doesn't pull me, I use symbols to persuade the magic where I belong. Like calls to like. It's easiest to come home, and the bare oak and holly brought me out before Solstice, but what do I have to take me away... My fingers find several jewels from Fionn and other kings here, Nessa's moonstone, and the embroidered belt that Ailbe wove for me. None of those will help us escape this world.

"Do you know what it is?" Maura comes back, warm against my side.

I shake my head. "I usually celebrate Solstice at home, burning the oak log and telling stories all night."

"Home?"

We have to half-shout, the drumming pulling our words away.

"Most of us do," I reply, but she shakes her head, meaning she can't understand.

Maybe I can use something on Maura for the charm. In my experience, if the magic decided to bring her here it won't bring her home until it's done with her, but maybe she has something we could use to trick it to get us somewhere else. Oh—in my rucksack. I have a shaving set, of all things. It worked so much better I brought it home, but I could use that to get us back to...I think it was Victorian times.

Several men, loud and drunk, lurch past us. Maura sinks against my chest, and I pull my cloak around her, looking over her head, over the field.

Damn. The druids are forming their lines, starting to snake out of the forest.

"Are you done?" I lean close. "I could take you back to camp."

She jumps away, shoving hard against my chest. "No. *No.* No, thank you. Where's Saba? No."

Well, that's an unreasonable amount of terror. If she thinks I'm propositioning her, it's going to be hard to get her away from the crowds to find a doorway.

Hells, if she thinks we're bringing Saba with us, it's going to be impossible to get her away. Saba is wound up in Fionn's magic, and—

Where *is* Saba?

The druids enter the meadow, chanting and dancing, all the pipes and drums bending to their rhythm. As the crowd scuttles back to give them space, suddenly there are druids right in front of us.

Maura lurches forward, and I catch her. She reaches out but I keep my arm as a strong bar. I understand she is upset tonight, but she can *not* go to the druids. She subsides abruptly, back against my side.

A man throws himself writhing on the ground. Women ululate, and one of the druids puts his foot on the man's head. Maura pulls close to me, shaking. I don't know if the man is a supplicant or a slave, if he will die tonight or have his fondest wish granted, but I want to get her out of here.

Now a man leads a calf into the clearing, the animal bracing its knobby knees and swinging its head in the torchlight. Maura presses her face into my chest and I bend my head. My heart is pounding, and I'm angry at every man who ever frightened her, at the imposter who has taken Fionn's place, at Fionn himself for being so selfish that it takes days for anyone to notice that he has an evil imposter. There's the swoosh of a knife drawn from its scabbard, Maura whimpers, and I kiss her hair.

Wait.

The smell is wrong. I know by now the scent of her skin, the fading modern shampoo in her hair, the smell of her fear and her breath. This is...

Maura turns, watching the ceremony in growing horror. I can't be debating things; it's time to move.

"We do not need to stay." I enunciate every word.

"Let's go! Now!"

Relieved, I plow our way through the edges of the crowd. We're on the wrong side of the meadow, farthest from our own camp. It's all right, I can guide us through the woods, even in the dark. It's just longer, and all uphill, and I know Maura is not strong.

The sounds and light falls away as soon as we are a few steps into the forest. Maura rushes down the path, and it's not the right direction but I let her lead. Anything to keep her momentum going. We'll get away from the meadow and I'll turn us around.

She stumbles and scrabbles for my arm. I'm positioned to catch her, but instead of pulling herself up she sinks against my chest. She whimpers and her arms go around my waist, under my cloak, her hands pressed against my back. Her mantle slides off her shoulder and I go to fix it, but my fingers brush the bare skin through her decoratively split sleeve. She's cold, and I run my palm along her arm. She shivers close to me, and I brush my lips against her hair again.

And I figure it out. Deer. She smells of Saba's magic, of musk and pelt and leaves.

But Maura raises her face to mine, and I don't have time to figure out anything. Her lips are parted and her hands are warm on my waist. I'm suffused with want, but I hesitate—I know how fear and mortality turns into sexual tension, and I don't want that to be the way we come together. I adjust my hands, but that sends another shiver through her, which thrills me, and her soft face is against my cheek, and—

She shoves again, lurching back, gasping in fear.

Do I capture her, try to explain, or—it's too late; she's darting through the forest, one tree to the next, splashing into a puddle. Now I'd have to chase her down, grab her—and I realize the deer-magic is driving her forward, making her believe that safety is running, running.

"Maura!" I call. "I am not trying to harm you."

I have to chase her, but that drives her more desperately. Her furs fall away, she is sobbing, limping.

"Stop, please! This is no place for a woman alone. Maura!"

I know she's afraid of me, but if I let her escape then someone worse will catch her. I push down my hurt feelings; this is time to be the warrior, not the gentleman. Focus on keeping her safe, not trying to make her happy. I head through the trees, keeping my gaze trained on her, my senses alert to danger.

So I know she's running towards the solstice stones. I know there's a light when no one should be there. I don't call out because she won't stop anyways, and I don't want to tell whoever is out there that we are coming. I pause for the merest instant to slide one knife into my belt and the other into my hand. It is uncouth to bring one's sword to a festival, but a warrior is never unarmed.

Maura tumbles into the silent clearing. I blink in the torch-light, getting my bearings. I test the earth beneath my feet, pull air deep into my lungs, balance the hilt in my palm.

Maura limps slowly towards the opening in the stone circle. I can't see what is inside, and she can't fully either. I stay parallel with her, hidden in the trees. Why wouldn't she run away?

There is one thing—one person only—that Maura would walk towards tonight. So I am not surprised when Saba is suddenly before of us, outlined against the stones, white robes and golden hair blowing.

Maura is close enough to touch her, but instead, she cringes away. I catch a glimpse of Saba's face, the queer fluidity of transformation, but I have already shifted to the side, raising my knife arm and staring into the tunnel of stones. He rears up above both women, long knife raised for the sacrificial blow.

It's the shape of Fionn mac Cumhaill, the familiar form flickering away just as Saba flickers into her deer shape.

"Run, Maura!" she cries, with the last of her human voice. "Runnnn..."

Fionn's imposter is pale, with a beaked nose and a cloak made of white feathers. It's suicide to attack him while he is protected by stones on all sides, and the women are between us as well. I change my hold on the knife as deer-Saba surges forward in an enormous leap.

Saba knocks Maura to the ground and the sorcerer's knife crashes through the place where the women had been standing a moment before. Saba's deer-feet thump the grass in front of me, but her big eyes see me in the dark. She zigs wildly and I wince away as her hooves whoosh by my head, and she crashes into the brush beyond.

In the split second that it takes for me to refocus on the scene in front of me, the sorcerer has seized Maura's legs. He must not see me, because he's laughing. "At least I have this one!"

Maura is thrashing and kicking, making him unable to hold her and his knife both. I narrow my eyes, choosing my moment.

Maura is on her belly, but her head raises up, her eyes huge and dark.

The smell of deer magic. Saba's instructions. I understand.

Barely a heartbeat has passed; the sorcerer is still laughing, Maura's belly is on the stones, and he reaches for his knife.

I throw mine.

The sorcerer gasps, both hands to his shoulder. Maura's wriggling momentum takes her away from him, but then she pauses, head swinging back and forth. I don't think she knows. I don't think she realizes she is now a deer.

Her eyes latch onto me.

"Run, Maura," I tell her, although it breaks my heart. "Run."

She's tangled in Saba's story, and it is Saba's magic that will save her tonight. Maura scrabbles to her feet, finding her balance. Behind her, the sorcerer changes again, melting, darkening.

Maura leaps forward, great bounds into the dark forest. Safe, but lost to me.

My second knife is in my hand as the wolf lunges. He thinks he is one leap behind the deer, but I strike as he passes. My blow glances off fur and bone and he snarls as he whips to attack, as I knew he would.

There's no hope; I'm just trying to delay him so the women can get a little farther. He's a sorcerer and a shapeshifter, and I'm just a warrior. My armlet will not protect me tonight.

Pain sears my thigh but my fist connects with ribs. He snarls. I grunt. One day, we all face our final battle.

I block his exit and fight to my death.

Chapter Thirteen

Sunlight on my eyelids. Dull throbbing pain everywhere, the cold sweat of a broken fever. Heavy blankets, smell of stone walls and herbs.

I guess I'm not dead.

With a heroic effort, I manage to tilt my face towards the light. Open, eyes. I've done this so many times before. Forced myself to wake up after battle injuries. The pain is always blinding. Every time.

But something is different...there's a hollowness where victory should live.

Doesn't matter. Still have to open my eyes.

And I blink, sure I'm still dreaming. In front of me stands a tall blond woman straight out of my youth, hand on her sword hilt, smile on one side of her mouth.

"See, nurse? I told you my potions would work, sooner or later. He's waking up."

The nurse shuffles and murmurs beside me. She tucks a pillow under my shoulders and presses something wet to my mouth. I swallow it, grateful, and try to make my eyes focus.

"He'll be just fine now." Nessa tosses her head. "My remedy always works. That's why I use it so rarely."

Now that I look at her, I can tell she's not the same. There are lines around her mouth and eyes, silver strands among her gold, and her face has that pinched look that never goes away after years of deprivation. She's wearing a fine gown, signifying the revenge and power she wanted, but she's paid a price.

I've paid a price too, and not just the pain in my body.

River.

Maura.

That was this hollowness. I am nothing but hollowness. I close my eyes again.

Nessa's léine whishes, her boots tapping across the stone. Lays a cool hand on my head.

I don't want Nessa. I want warmth and tenderness.

"Rian," she whispers. "*Rian*."

I give in and look at her.

She holds up a tiny crystal vial so it catches the light, slowly tilts it back and forth. There's only a few drops inside.

"I have River now," she says. "Liath Luacra told me everything you have done for him, all these long years. They could not have raised him so well without you. She said that every time he visited you, he came back calmer. More ready to accept his duty. A better friend."

This pain is worse than whatever the sorcerer-wolf did to me.

"Thank you," Nessa says, taps the vial, and slides it into her pocket.

So she traded me her son for my life. I'm not sure it's worth it, but I didn't have a choice in the matter.

I think she is going to leave, but instead Nessa sits beside me, spreading her skirts around her.

"Why..." My voice is a croak, and the nurse lets me drink again. "Why...here. Where...?"

Nessa names the owner of this castle, whom I recognize as a relative of one of the local kings. I am not far from an Cnoc Rúa, but I am a world away from where I was that night. Everything has slipped away.

"You are lucky," Nessa continues, although I don't agree. "Your heart's-blood was bleeding onto your moonstone pendant. Do you remember, all those years ago—that was the one that I had enchanted to you."

I turn my face away. I don't care about her tricks and stratagems.

"Enchanted to you," Nessa adds, more softly, "when you were the person I loved most in the world."

That pulls my eyes open. "Your...love..." I subside, too exhausted to explain.

Nessa sighs. "I know I couldn't love you like other women do. Even then, I knew I could never love you like you needed. That's why I never..." She shrugs, her mouth upturned in a bitter smile. "I never asked for more."

She asked for a great deal, back when I was young and vulnerable. She took my youth, and then she gave me River, and he needed my young manhood. But I suppose she did not try to become my lover or demand that I marry her. I would have, but neither of us could have made the other happy.

Nessa shrugs again. "I don't know how to love the way other women do, but it's real, and it brought me to you the other night. My moonstone woke me, searing pain in the darkest hour of the night. I woke my husband's guard, and the pendant led us over hill and dale. We rode all night and I found you in the first light of dawn. Half-buried in the bracken. Cold." She smiles that half-turned, melancholy way. The Nessa of my youth smiled with her whole mouth.

"Days?" I ask.

"Not dead, apparently," she adds. "You're a tough one. Yes, it was almost two weeks ago."

I grunt. It's all I can manage, my thoughts hovering just out of reach.

Nessa sits back, setting her jaw. "I loved you then, and I will love River now. It's not the way other women do it, but it's real. Look. It worked."

"Good," I grumble. "Love him. Take...care."

"I will give him more than he ever imagines," Nessa muses, looking beyond me. "In him, my fate will be complete. My son will fulfill what my fathers have lost."

I don't think that being given more than one can imagine is healthy for children, but I am glad Nessa will love him. And if she's thinking of her foster fathers, she will be thinking of accomplishments. Learning. Wisdom. Discipline. That's all to the good. My thoughts drift, trying to remember about Nessa's fathers, imagining River as he grows.

Nessa gives me another drink and takes my hand—not like a lover, like she's determined to keep me awake even if she needs to stick pins in me.

"So." She smiles again, mischievous. "Who was the girl?"

"No girl," I mutter.

She raises her eyebrow, disbelieving.

This is important. "Woman," I rasp.

"Ah." She sits back. "So you were in love."

Was it love? I'm too tired, in too much pain to argue. "Where? Now? ...Maura."

I'm filled with a jumble of emotion, scattered memory. A woman who trusted me, soft smile, kind hands. It couldn't have been true. I've spent years in the background, fixing things, making jokes. She couldn't have wanted me.

Nessa taps the back of my hand, pulling me back to her.

"We're not really sure," she says, crisp. "I've sent my messengers everywhere, and I wasn't positive she existed until you looked at me like that."

"She...is!"

Nessa raises her eyebrows. "She is something more than she appears. I think you know, but I'm not going to expect you to share your secrets. You never do."

I wait.

"Saba escaped to the Peaceful Valley, but she apparently can't come back home. The real Fionn returned, but his castle is an awful mess. Ailbe, the head of the ladies-in-waiting, has disappeared, along with that little pretty one. Gráinne."

That's strange, but I'm quite sure that Gráinne is not my story. "Maura," I gasp.

Nessa gives me a drink. "I'm getting to that. You see, no one was quite sure if she had been there or not. I think Ailbe would have known the truth, but she was gone and the others were confused—but just enough confused that I guessed something was missing."

A fish, I try to say. Slipping in and out of time. Never unexpected. Never missed.

But I miss her. Me, me, me.

"My messengers couldn't figure it out," Nessa continues, "but finally, Guaire came here and told me. He is going north to search for a new fianna, and brought your belongings. Said you would want them, especially the bag with purple flowers, whatever that is. But once I heard his story, I could figure out the missing pieces. The memories that people didn't quite have. The feeling that someone had been there."

I open my eyes and look straight at her. Nessa, my oldest friend, who saved my life when we were kids with a pig and saved it again now. Who lies and murders and takes my son away, because he belongs to her and she needs him.

"Where...Maura...now?"

"She made it back to Fionn's castle and rejoined the ladies-in-waiting. I wish Ailbe could tell me what happened, but she is just gone—and one day, Maura was just gone, too." Nessa snaps her fingers.

So, I suppose that is the end of our story? But no...I shift on the bed, testing my shoulder. I am still wearing my armlet.

So my days of being a hero might not be over. And my tricks for getting through the Veil, to whatever time I need, aren't gone either. And if Guaire brought my rucksack, then I have my magical library, and my medicine bottle to get back to the hospital in 1971, and—something else comes to me, and I smile, my lips dry and cracked.

The day of the tournament. Maura gave me a handkerchief, which she had embroidered herself. It smelled of her. That's enough of a charm for the Veil, enough to send me in her direction, if I ever have the chance to leave...

"So, first you have to finish getting better." Nessa grins, eyes narrowed. It's her scheming face. "Rian. Go and find your Maura. Go and love her, the way you always needed to love. Go."

Oh yes, Guaire told me that too, and I will never see him again. I am floating free, untethered to the responsibilities I have spent all these years building.

I stare past Nessa's head at the window, the glow of the January sun, but my mind is soaring far away.

To a woman who was kind but strong. A woman who felt just right in my arms. A woman whose smile was so beautiful that it made me want to be a good man so I could earn it. She's out there, and Maura deserves love that is fierce and passionate and loyal, just like she is herself. *My* Maura.

"Thank you," I rasp to Nessa. "I think I will."

Just as soon as I recover, I'm headed out. Me and my magical armlet. There's nothing keeping me here, and there's something very, very important out there.

I'm going to find her.

* * *

After years of traveling the Veil and vanquishing enemies, Rian has the skills and determination to search for his beloved.

But Maura is back home and doesn't know how to leave her ordinary world. Until her youngest daughter brings home a swan and Saba tries to fix their money troubles—and in an ever-building chaos of enchantment, the entire Robinson family tumbles into another fairy tale.

Order "Oona & the Swan" from your favorite retailer at https://buy.bookfunnel.com/seftexhg6d and then follow the author on Amazon, BookBub, or her newsletter https://sendfox.com/ChristyMatheson, to follow Rian, Maura, and all of their children as they journey through stories into togetherness.

About the Author

Characters you connect with. Adventure. Love. Family. And endings that are more than a sugar rush.

When Christy Matheson is not throwing ordinary characters into fairy tales, she is busy raising five children. (Very busy.) She writes character-driven historical fiction with and without fantasy elements, and her "fresh, smart, and totally charming" stories have won multiple awards.

Christy is also an embroidery artist, classically trained pianist, and sews all of her own clothes. She lives in Oregon, on a country property that fondly reminds her of a Regency estate (except with a swing set instead of faux Greek ruins), with her husband, five children, three Shelties, one bunny, and an improbable quantity of art supplies.

Please join Christy in conversation about books and determined women throughout history.

Join her newsletter to get free stories, art giveaways, & puppy pictures. https://sendfox.com/ChristyMatheson

And you can always find her at: www.christymatheson.com